Praise for Ga
Crouch's Da

'Gabby is **one of the funnies_ _____ _ know**.' Sarah Millican

'Very funny. **If you like Terry Pratchett, or think gothic fairytales should have more LOLs, 'tis the book for ye**.' Greg Jenner

'I have read this and it is great. **Pratchetty fun for all the family**.' Lucy Porter

'**Magical, surprising and funny**.' Jan Ravens

What readers are saying about the Darkwood series:

'**Clever and funny and so very very entertaining.** I would encourage everyone of every age to go ahead and read *Darkwood*.'

'Completely **fabulous, can't wait for the rest of the series**.'

'A **fun, exciting, action-packed** story that once I started reading I couldn't put down.'

'I **loved the mix of humour and fantasy**, the tongue in cheek style of writing and the **quirky characters**.'

'I could go on and on about how much **I love this book** and why.'

'A delightful new mashup of old familiar fairy tale characters and themes, with loads of originality and memorable characters. … I think this **may well turn into one of my all-time favourites**.'

'…incredible! It **made me laugh out loud in several places**, but also managed to pull off some intricate themes around power and bigotry – **I adored the characters and the fun, genre-savvy writing**.'

Wish You Weren't Here

THE ROOKS
BOOK ONE

GABBY
HUTCHINSON CROUCH

Farrago

This edition published in 2021 by Farrago,
an imprint of Duckworth Books Ltd
1 Golden Court, Richmond, TW9 1EU, United Kingdom

www.farragobooks.com

Print ISBN: 9781788423793
Ebook ISBN: 9781788423809

For Nathan

Contents

CHAPTER ONE

Soft Dove

Think about death. Hate to hit you with a downer right at the start of a story, but death is kind of an integral part of this tale. To tell the truth, it's kind of an integral part of every tale. Even yours. Death is lingering in the narrative of every single thing that lives in this world. The plot twist that everybody knows is inevitable and yet, somehow, still doesn't usually see coming. You push it to the back of your mind, a horrible detail too big and too scary to do anything about right now, like the warming of the tundra, the rising of the sea. Yes, you'll have to deal with it sooner or later, but that's a problem for Future You to have to cope with. And then, all at once, there it is, and it's not Future You who is faced with it, it's Present You, and that sucks, because Present You is You-You, the fleeting you of now, and the time is just so short and death is just too big, and it gobbles you up.

It's the plot twist in every story. But not necessarily the end of every story. It's only the end if you're lucky.

Does this story end with death? I'm not going to tell you that — what's the point of telling you the ending now, right at the start?

That would make me a pretty terrible narrator, and I don't want that, since narrating's pretty much all I can do.

What I can tell you, here at the start, is that the story begins with death. It's the kind of death that doesn't bring an end, but a sea change to even more turmoil. The kind of death that brings no peace – only rage, confusion and fear.

The fear sought comfort.

Comfort came in the form of an email address.

The email address summoned the Rooks.

It was November, and the British countryside had clearly had enough of autumn and just wanted it out of the way so that it could get cracking with winter as soon as possible. In populated areas there was the mild novelty of occasionally spotting homes that hadn't bothered taking down their Halloween decorations yet. There were other homes that had already put up a Christmas tree, in the vain hope of cheering things up and ushering through the tail end of the year. But, along the country road, there hadn't been so much as a desolate farmhouse in over a mile. The sky was the sort of colour that a paint company would call something like 'Soft Dove' or 'Mountain Mist', and the hazy, cool damp of it extended all the way to the ground, in something that wasn't quite dramatic enough to be called a fog. The deciduous trees lining the road had already lost their leaves, and the constant moisture of the 'Soft Dove' coloured air had turned the resulting carpet of orange and red into a deep brown mulch. Sheep huddled together in wet fields and glared at the occasional passing cars.

One such car was a fairly innocuous-seeming Ford Focus, driving at just under the speed limit, side lights on as a precaution, coloured a pale silver-grey that seemed to whisper 'Please don't look at me, I'm just doing my job'. It had a parcel shelf at a slight angle, betraying that perhaps the boot was a little over-filled. The only really odd thing about it was that it had five adults crammed into it, which you don't usually see unless it's a bunch of students. The passengers were not students. They were the Rook family. They were on their way to work and they were playing a car game that they had played since the kids were small.

In the front passenger seat, Brenda Rook spotted something, leaned around to the back seat and flicked her son on the top of the head. Darryl Rook – once a gangly and awkward boy now fully blossomed into a gangly and awkward thirty-five year old man – responded more with annoyance than with pain.

'Ow! Mum! That's not fair!'

'Of course it's fair,' replied his mother, sitting comfortably back into her seat. 'If you see one first, you get to flick me.'

'When do I ever get to be the one to flick you?'

'Why would you *want* to flick your own mother?'

'Because that's the game, Mum! You made up the rules!' Darryl folded his arms and leaned against the back window, glaring out at the 'Soft Dove' of it all. 'And you know it's not fair because you can see them better than I can.'

'Maybe if you practiced more,' retorted Brenda, quietly.

'Maybe if I were allowed to sit in the front once in a while,' snapped Darryl.

Brenda turned again, and gave her son a hard stare over her shoulder. 'I happen to enjoy sitting next to my husband on car journeys, don't you?'

'You and Dad could both sit in the back,' argued Darryl, 'I could drive and Janusz could ride shotgun—'

'Shotgun…?' asked Janusz from the middle of the back seat, a crease of worry furrowing his exceptionally symmetrical face.

'Figure of speech, love,' replied both Darryl and Brenda at the same time.

'OK.' Janusz nodded serenely and got back to his laptop.

'Your mother doesn't ride well in the back,' Richard Rook reminded his son. 'And you're very expensive to insure after you drove the Cinquecento into that bin.'

'That was fifteen years ago, Dad! I was literally learning to drive, and one of *them* had jumped out at me!'

'Oh,' snorted Brenda, 'so *that* time, you could see them.'

Darryl sighed, defeated. Only once the argument was effectively over did his father reassert the car rules.

'Sorry, guys, grown-ups in front, kids in back, that's just the way.'

'"Kids"?' huffed Charity, squashed against the right back door. 'I've got grey hairs.'

'Princess,' replied her mother, 'you mustn't upset yourself with little cosmetic imperfections. All this Instagram lark is just the internet's funny little way of trying to sell you military grade laxatives.'

'It's not an imperfection, Mum.' Charity twirled one of her prematurely silver locks around her fingers, gazing at it with pride. 'I look like one of the X-Men.'

'Another one,' cried Brenda, suddenly, before flicking her son again.

'Ow!' Darryl shouted. 'Dad! Tell her! It isn't fair, I can't see!'

'Dear,' sighed Richard, 'you should probably stop your game with Darryl. He isn't very good at it.'

Charity snorted a little-sister-laugh. Darryl tried to reach across Janusz to nudge her, but Janusz raised his laptop to block him. 'No hitting!'

'You don't stop Mum flicking me.'

'Brenda is not my husband.'

'Brenda is nobody's husband,' added Brenda. 'Another—'

'I see them,' said Darryl, excitedly, over her. 'Two—'

Brenda turned around and flicked him anyway.

'Ow! I said I saw them!'

'Too slow.'

They both watched out of the side windows as the car passed by the figures in the field.

'Odd to have a pair,' muttered Darryl.

'That's quite a lot, the past few miles, isn't it?' asked Richard. 'Even for a country road.'

Darryl nodded. 'I've got a bad feeling about this.'

Janusz put a hand on Darryl's knee, still not looking up from his laptop. 'You've been complaining of a bad feeling about everything since 2016.'

'Yeah, well. It's like Mum keeps saying, that's when everything started falling apart.'

Janusz finally glanced up from his computer, to give Darryl a hurt look. He pulled his hand away. 'That was the year we married!'

'Ha ha,' smirked Charity, 'Darryl's bad at being a husband.'

'Shut up, Charity! At least I've got one!'

'Oh yes. Thank you so much. That makes me feel very special,' replied Janusz. 'To be just another status symbol to show off to your sister, like the slimy skull palace for your plastic homosexual man.'

'Castle Greyskull,' said Charity. 'And He-Man wasn't gay.'

'He was in my room,' Darryl replied. He reached forward and flicked his mother lightly on the shoulder.

Brenda half turned to face him, scandalised.

'No hitting!' repeated Janusz, his voice only slightly elevated above its usual placid tones.

'That was a flick.'

'No hitting or flicking!'

Darryl pointed out of the window, by way of explanation. The bridge to Coldbay had just come into view around a corner.

'I see one on the bridge.' He squinted a little, then flicked Brenda again. 'Two actually.'

'Darryl! What did I say?' Janusz's tone was in danger of sounding ruffled.

'More than two, *actually*,' retorted Brenda. She turned again and flicked Darryl. 'Grey one,' she explained, pointing, 'over there.' She flicked her protesting son again. 'Sort of green one over there…'

Darryl squirmed away from her relentless, pointy fingers and managed to get three good flicks on her shoulder. 'Three, near those trees,' he announced, proudly.

Brenda scoffed 'Three? More like seven.'

'No…'

'Dear?' warned Richard.

But his mother was already flicking him, hard, in spite of Darryl's attempts to block her while simultaneously trying to administer retaliatory flicks.

Janusz huffed down at his laptop. 'So proud.'

'My lovelies?' said Richard, gently, 'it's getting very hard to drive with all this going on, could you both stop now please?'

'Can you two really see that many dead people on the bridge?' asked Charity, over her father.

Brenda and Darryl came to a sudden ceasefire in their flick-war. They both looked out of the car windows.

Around two dozen blurry figures stood, stock still, in the dank ditches lining the road, the fields beyond and the road bridge onto Coldbay Island. Many stood alone, little pillars of murky sadness. This was the norm for roadway ghosts – usually young people who had gone too quickly from speeding and laughing, drunk with freedom and cheap beer, to being a crushed mess of meat and metal – lost now on a strange, dark road, miles from home. There had been a time, long ago, when

Brenda would always stop and try to help stranded roadway ghosts. It had just landed her with a car full of dead teenagers, too bewildered to so much as remember their hometown. She didn't stop to pick up dead hitchhikers any more.

Some of them stood in pairs, which was certainly not unheard of, but it was odd for there to be so many on a road. The bridge was… there were so many on the bridge. Brenda had seen clusters like this, a depressing number of times. Beachy Head, Clifton Suspension Bridge, the tube… Lots of bridges had clusters like these.

'Suicide bridge?' asked Janusz, quietly.

Brenda nodded. 'Probably. And suspicious numbers on the road. Darryl's right. Bad vibes, here. Even for post 2016. Even for the East Midlands.'

Charity looked out at the dark line of the North Sea on the horizon. 'What is your beef with the East Midlands, mum?'

'It just gives me the jeebies, princess,' Brenda replied. 'Always has. And look – I was right.' She indicated towards the multitude of forlorn shadows, despite the fact that only she and Darryl could see them. 'Here we are, and it's positively crawling with ghosts.'

The family pondered this for a moment.

'Well,' said Richard after a couple of seconds, 'on the bright side, at least we know that it's not all in the client's mind, and we're not looking at another Ludlow.'

Charity snorted at the memory. 'God, Ludlow.'

'We're helping someone who definitely does need our services,' added Richard, cheerily.

'I mean, what would a dead Royal even be doing in a semi in Shropshire?' Charity continued.

'We've probably come right on time,' said Richard, with a sage nod to himself.

Janusz grunted softly, still concentrating on his laptop. 'Not *right* on time. We could have a schedule clash with the Aldwych booking. If we can get this done by Tuesday, it would make my spreadsheet more happy.'

'Oh, it's only a haunted church, Janusz,' replied Charity, still watching the sea as the car began crossing the bridge. 'We'll be done in a jiffy, I eat haunted churches for breakfast.'

'You eat Sugar Puffs for breakfast,' replied Janusz, confused.

'Figure of spe—,' began Charity, but she was cut off by her mother and brother screaming in unison, and the sensation of having weirdly angry cold spaghetti shoved down the back of her blouse. 'One just went through us,' she hissed, 'didn't it?'

In the driver's seat, her father bit down a low, guttural growl.

'Must have been furious,' noted Janusz. 'Even I felt that one.'

The car began to veer off to the right.

'Dear?' asked Brenda.

Janusz tapped Richard gently on the shoulder. 'You need me to drive?'

Richard shook himself, and got the car back on track, with a jolt. 'Sorry about that! Took me by surprise, was all.'

'It just jumped in front of us,' murmured Darryl, watching it from out of the rear window. He turned back to face Janusz, horrified. 'It went through my mouth.'

Janusz squeezed his knee. 'Poor zabko,' he murmured, gently.

Charity met eyes with her brother. 'It'll be all right.'

Darryl just looked back at her, his gaze darting off at intervals to focus on more of the ghosts collected on the bridge.

'It'll be a piece of cake,' continued Charity. 'Figure of speech, Janusz.'

'I know,' replied Janusz, sounding pleased with himself. 'In Polish, we say "roll with butter".'

'Yeah, sure. If you like. We'll be in and out in time for the Aldwych booking. Nothing we can't handle for your little spreadsheets.'

'Aww.' Janusz addressed the open spreadsheet file on his laptop. 'You guys! They love you too!'

The car drove on, past a swarm of angry, lost, distressed ghosts, smears of misery in the 'Soft Dove' mist, and alongside the 'Oolong Grey' sea. It drove past a sign that was probably once white, but was now more of a 'Pale Walnut', welcoming them to Coldbay Island, along with a sign that was still its traditional 'Municipal Brown', directing them to the beach, in case that was something they might like to do on this freezing, damp November day.

Richard hummed a little to himself, checking the satnav on his phone. 'Just another ten minutes to St Catherine's church. What's the priest's name, again, Janusz?'

Janusz pulled up the email. 'Barry.'

'Barry doesn't seem like a good priest name,' said Brenda, watching the ghosts that continued to linger in unusually high numbers around the road. 'Doesn't instil much religious authority, does it? "The power of Barry compels you to leave this place"?'

'Maybe he's one of those young trendy vicars,' added Darryl. 'Maybe Charity will hook up with him.'

'God, Darryl,' snapped Charity. 'I dated one client. One!'

'One that we know about,' muttered Darryl.

'And I never hear the end of it,' continued Charity. 'You used to date clients too!'

'Name one!'

'I was a client,' Janusz reminded him, smoothly. 'You were very unprofessional.'

'Oh, yeah.'

'Also,' added Charity, 'I'm not so desperately alone that I'd date a priest, who's probably all old and gross…'

'Don't be an ageist, sweetie,' replied Richard. 'Us crumblies still have a lot to give.'

'So you'd be happy with me dating a priest your age or older, would you?'

'Certainly not, you're my little princess.'

Charity went back to glaring out of the window at the damp island. 'Could still be a false alarm. Some potty old priest in his old church on this rubbish island, just seeing things.'

The car drove on, at a sensible speed, side lights on, always remembering to indicate.

Eight and a half minutes away, according to the satnav, Reverend Grace Barry – indeed a priest but neither particularly old nor a man – was not just imagining things in her old church on this rubbish island. Firstly, while it was true that Coldbay Island was a bit bleak, she wasn't the type to write it off as "rubbish". Secondly, she wasn't in her church right at that moment, but crouching in fear outside the church between the vestry and the Red Cross Clothes Bank, while unseen forces smashed and crashed inside. This was the second time it had happened today. The one silver lining was that she was running out of things the unseen forces could smash. She heard something that sounded suspiciously like a toilet seat being flung across the vestry into a shelf. She winced, and hoped that the specialists she'd been told to email would get there soon. She wasn't sure how much more of this she could take.

CHAPTER TWO

Delicje Szampańskie

The crashing in the vestry stopped after a couple of minutes. It wasn't a sudden stop – it never was – but a winding down, like a tantrumming child running out of steam. Grace had grown accustomed to the sound of it lately. She almost liked the half-hearted crashes that came at the end of the attacks these days, they created a Pavlovian wave of relief in her. She listened to the last, desultory bangs until even those had stopped.

She exhaled deeply. It was over. For now. Although, she reminded herself as she peered carefully out from her hiding spot, the end of this latest destructive episode meant that it was time for her to have to clean up the mess. She didn't quite groan. She'd signed up for this job exactly so that she could sort out problems, hadn't she? She just wished it could be more sorting out what was wrong with the world – making things better for everyone, in the wider community – and not quite so much sweeping broken glass up off her own floor.

The cloying damp of the air had thickened ever so slightly into a sort of drizzle. She knew she should go in and start the clean-up. And yet, she still hadn't moved from behind the bin. Maybe she could have a nice cup of tea before cleaning. Providing she'd been left with a functional kettle, this time. Or any cups. Or any tea. She was still persuading herself to get up when a silver Ford Focus drove sensibly into view and carefully parallel parked on the street outside.

Grace wondered for a moment whether the driver of the car might be lost – nobody had come to her church for a long time, and it couldn't be the specialists she'd emailed, right? Did paranormal specialists arrive in a Ford Focus? They'd have a van, right? They'd have a van, at least. Specialists arrived in vans with the company name all neatly displayed on the side. The car engine switched off, and its doors opened. *Could* it be the specialists? Surely not.

Maybe it was worshippers. St Catherine's hadn't had worshippers in… she couldn't remember how long. Whoever it was, there were a few of them and they definitely weren't lost. They were heading straight for the church, and Grace was still crouched in the wet, by a bin for used clothes. She wondered whether she might be able to sneak in through the side door of the church without being seen, smooth herself down a little bit and make at least a semi-professional introduction to these strangers. Unfortunately, as she pondered this possibility, still frozen to her spot with indecision, the five strangers strode past her and up the path to knock on the door. Now she had no possible way to creep past undetected.

Bother.

The older man of the group knocked, waited for a response – that clearly wasn't going to come because she was still by the bin – and then called 'Hello? Reverend Barry? It's Richard Rook, you emailed about the specialist cleaning service?'

Wait, it *was* the specialists? Why didn't they have a van? Grace shifted, awkwardly. She really did need to get up and greet them – she just had to work out a way of doing it that wouldn't involve her just popping up from behind a bin like a large, damp scavenger.

One of the younger men in the group was looking around anxiously and scanning the graveyard beyond the bins with the expression of someone expecting to see something terrible. He looked like someone checking their phone after a breaking news alert had gone off. His gaze caught hers, and he jumped a little. He tapped the older woman in the group on the arm.

'By the clothes bin,' he said.

Double bother. Yes, she should definitely get up and say hello.

The rest of the group turned towards the bin.

'Oh!' said the younger woman with them. 'No, that's not one of them, I can see her too.'

Triple bother. Grace pushed herself to her feet, and tried her best to look like she hadn't just spent ten minutes hiding behind a bin in the drizzle.

'Hello there! Sorry, I was just... checking something.' She patted the roof of the clothes bin. It was covered in a thin, green algae slime, and made the mournful, hollow sound of a completely empty metal container. 'Yep,' she continued, 'that's fine.'

The older woman cast a withering eye over Grace, pausing to raise a judgemental eyebrow at Grace's clerical collar. 'Reverend... Barry?'

'Reverend *Grace* Barry, yes!' Grace took a few steps towards the group, considered holding out her hand to shake, remembered it was now smeared in bin-algae, and decided just to wave at them instead. 'Just call me Grace though, it's fine.'

'It's her *surname*,' muttered the younger woman, with an air of realisation.

'Not even that old,' retorted the younger man who had spotted Grace first.

Grace got the feeling that she was now the butt of an in-joke that she couldn't, and wasn't supposed to, understand. She continued to smile blandly at the strangers. 'Shall we go in? It, er, might be a mess in there, I'm afraid.'

'Good thing you called for a cleaning then,' said the other young man, using a cheery tone. He had a strikingly handsome face and a Polish sounding accent.

'Well, quite,' Grace replied. She fumbled with the key and reflected on the many ways she'd wondered how to frame her explanations for the recent state of the vestry, without sounding completely doolally. Unseen vandals, perhaps? An angry house guest that had run riot while she was out and then mysteriously left? Both were technically true – if not the whole truth of what she believed the actual problem to be. Ultimately, the problem of not sounding doolally to visitors hadn't been a problem up until now, as she simply had not had any visitors. Even the higher-ups in her diocese hadn't shown up, they'd just sent her the email address for these 'specialist cleaners'. She reminded herself, as she fitted the key into the lock, that it was OK for her to talk about the reality of the problem with these specialists. In fact, it was probably recommended for her to talk about it with them, otherwise how would they know what they were supposed to fix? Still, it felt weird saying it out loud. She'd never actually said the words before.

She opened the vestry door. Goodness, it was a state. Smashed bookshelf. Strewn vestments. And yes indeed, there was the toilet seat, on the counter of the kitchenette.

'It's the ghost,' she said, out loud for the first time ever. 'A ghost keeps doing this.'

She went straight over to the kitchenette. The toilet seat looked obscene there, next to the toaster. She had to lift it off, straight away. Here she was with guests for the first time in forever, her little kitchen counter looking like this just wouldn't do. Grace had always hoped that someday it would be utilised for charity coffee mornings or even mid-morning refreshments at a kiddies' playgroup, but so far it had only been used for lonely caffeine and despair breaks, by herself. She checked the kettle. It was mercifully intact, this time.

'Um. Can I do you all some tea?'

The handsome Polish man strode up to her. 'I will make tea, we'll all help you clean. Won't we, zabko?'

'Mm?' muttered the other young man. The Polish man gave him a very certain look, from which Grace could only extrapolate one possible conclusion – they were married. 'Oh,' said the man, noting his husband's expression, 'Yes, of course. Here – I can fix that toilet seat.'

'Zabko's an unusual name.' Grace allowed 'Zabko' to take the toilet seat off her.

'It's a pet name.' 'Zabko' hauled the toilet seat over his shoulder. 'He swears blind it's not usually just used for girls, but I've seen things online that suggest otherwise.'

'He's had ample opportunity to learn Polish for himself.'

'I know all the swear words,' replied 'Zabko'.

'Polish swears are better.' The Polish man gave her a big, handsome smile.

'So,' she said, watching the group, 'this is a… family business?'

The oldest of the men – Richard, she seemed to remember he'd called himself – smiled warmly. 'Indeed. This is my wife, Brenda…'

Brenda, the judgemental looking, older woman nodded at Grace, and made careful work of milling about, superficially looking like she was helping but actually not lifting a finger.

'Our daughter, Charity…' Richard gestured to the younger woman, who was picking up some of the scattered books.

Charity smiled brightly at Grace. 'Adopted,' she announced.

'Nobody was going to mention that, princess,' sighed Richard, 'it's not important.'

'Course it is,' Charity told Grace, cheerfully. 'It's a whole thing. I'm adopted, I have powers, I have a secret tragic backstory, probably – I'm basically Harry Potter with a nicer room.'

Grace nodded, with a smile. 'You know, my favourite person was also raised by a man who wasn't his birth father.'

'Spider-Man?'

'No. Jesus.'

'Oh. Him.'

Richard pointed over at the handsome man, who was wiping the kitchenette counter with one hand and filling the kettle with the other. 'That's our lovely son-in-law, Janusz.'

'He's *my* husband, not Charity's!' shouted the other man from the vestry's little toilet room. 'Tell her we're husbands, Janusz!'

'The man fixing your toilet is my Darryl,' said Janusz, happily, in a raised voice that could be heard over the sound of a toilet seat getting fixed. Janusz put the kettle on. 'I think you already knew this, Father Grace.'

'Just "Grace".'

'You're not going to have an outrage with this? Sometimes people don't like two husbands.'

'Nah,' said Charity, 'Look at her, she's one of those trendy vicars. She's got a Greenpeace fridge magnet and everything.'

'And Amnesty,' added Grace, quietly. 'And Comic Relief... Bother, those must have got pulled off by the... You Know What.'

'Oh yes! There they are.' Brenda pointed to the rest of the fridge magnets which were on the floor right on the other side

16

of the vestry, and then waited for Grace to go past her and pick them up.

'Seems quite scattergun,' said Richard, conversationally, as he helped Charity put books back on the shelf. 'Bibles *and* Comic Relief magnets. Does the ghost not particularly target the religious stuff? Often with place-of-worship hauntings it's spirits angry at God, or at least angry at their idea of what God should be. You know – they devoted their life to a deity, they were promised paradise after death and then when death came they were left trapped, lost and angry. So they gravitate towards a house of worship and still nothing comes, so they start smashing up the place, like a customer who feels diddled and then the Manager won't even come and speak to them...'

'That was one time,' muttered Brenda, 'and I didn't "smash up the place". I just kicked over a sign.'

Grace put the fridge magnets back. 'Um, I don't think it targets anything sacred. It just smashes up whatever's there.'

'No crosses hung upside down?' asked Richard.

'No heads ripped off the nativity scene figures?' asked Brenda.

'No poo smeared on the bibles?' asked Charity.

'No massive penis drawn on the Jesus or the Mary?' asked Janusz.

Grace shook her head, feeling shaky again. 'Are... those things that happen?'

'At church hauntings?' replied Charity. 'All the time, mate. Obviously with your different faiths you get variations on the theme, but there's a lot of stuff upside down, stuff smeared in poo, mutilated statues and so many massive willies.'

Darryl came out of the toilet. 'Oh, are we talking about the great big willy we found in that cathedral? Ghost drew it in poo,' he added, sounding impressed. 'Now, I know what you're thinking – where do the ghosts get the poo *from?* Well—'

'I wasn't thinking that,' replied Grace, hurriedly. 'Just… is it really that common? Are there that many departed souls angry enough with the Lord to do… that?'

'Oh, yes,' said Brenda, breezily. 'Although chances are, they're taking personal issue with you, too. You sold them eternal rest and here they are – not resting. We're just the store security trying to get your dissatisfied customers to stop kicking the Oddbins sign.'

'Mum, let the Oddbins incident go,' sighed Charity, 'it was one bad bottle of wine.'

'It was a bad *crate* of wine,' replied Brenda. 'They should have had labels warning it was zero alcohol.' She gave Grace a cold smile. 'And maybe you should start putting warnings on your religion that a peaceful afterlife is not a guarantee; perhaps we'd have fewer of these cases if your lot stopped pulling the wool over people's eyes.'

Grace didn't have an answer to that. They were wrong about the heaven thing, surely. Or those angry ghosts they mentioned must have done something wrong in life – or even in death. In any case, she couldn't 'warn' her congregation about the possibility of ending up a drifting, furious spirit, resorting to venting rage by drawing poo willies in the nearest chapel, because on Coldbay she didn't have a congregation.

Richard put his arm around his wife. 'Let's be kind to clients, dear,' Grace just about heard him say.

'Well,' huffed Brenda. 'We're helping tidy up, aren't we?'

The vestry was indeed looking much better already, even though Brenda herself still hadn't picked up or straightened a thing.

'It helps to know in advance what the spirit is upset about,' Charity told Grace. 'If it's not as clear-cut as just feeling let down that their whole belief system was a sham, then we should get more details from you and try to narrow things down before we attempt a clearing.'

Grace wanted to say that it wasn't necessarily that belief systems were a sham but she didn't.

'I'll set up a trestle table,' she said instead. 'We can all have a nice chat over a cup of…'

'Tea?' Janusz turned around, muscular arms easily carrying a tray laden with a steaming teapot, cups, a sugar bowl and a mercifully unspilled carton of long life semi-skimmed. He even, miraculously, had produced a plate of Jaffa Cakes which was on one side. Grace was a woman who liked to count her blessings, and this family, whose recommendation had come to her from the Lord Himself – well… from her diocese, but it was a chain of command that was definitely headed up by the Lord – who had come to her in her hour of need to help, who had fixed the toilet and brought forth tea and Jaffa Cakes, were definitely a blessing. Yes. Belief wasn't a sham – obviously it wasn't. This was simply a test of faith and tests of faith came all the time. She had stood firm and now she was being rewarded with a handsome man bringing her snacks. She set up the trestle table, safe in the knowledge that the Lord loved her, as evidenced by the Jaffa Cakes.

'Ooh, there's biscuits!' Darryl took one off the tray. 'Where did you find those?'

'I had them in my bag,' replied Janusz, pleased with himself.

Darryl took a bite. 'Aw, yeah, the Polish ones,' he said, his mouth full.

'Delicje Szampańskie,' Janusz told Grace.

'Like I said,' added Darryl, 'the Polish ones.'

Janusz smiled at Darryl, and Grace revised her thoughts. She wasn't saying that Janusz and his snacks weren't proof that the Lord loved her, but she had to acknowledge that Janusz and his snacks showed that the Lord definitely loved Darryl, too.

CHAPTER THREE

Salt and Candles

Janusz had brought Darryl's favourite Polish Jaffa Cakes – the kind that tasted of cherry. Whether it was the cherriness of them or the general lack of orangeyness, they clearly took the reverend by surprise. She called the snacks 'interesting' – which an entire life lived with Brenda had drummed into Darryl meant 'I hate this' although then the reverend took two more, 'to make sure'. Darryl met eyes with his husband, who gave him a soft smile. That man, and his biscuits.

As she ate her third Delicje Sampang… Delicej Skamag… Polish Jaffa Cake, Grace told the family about her experiences with the hauntings in St Catherine's. Or, at least she tried to. Her accounts were infuriatingly vague for someone who shared a live-work space with a virulent poltergeist. The paranormal occurrences had been going on for… ooh, she wasn't quite sure. The way she described it, things had just sort of crept up on her without her really noticing until it was too late – as if it were a case of slow damp rot rather than a furious, violent ghost in her church. She described things feeling 'a bit off' ever since she'd arrived at St Catherine's, but that initially, she'd put it down to the general atmosphere of Coldbay Island as a whole. That piqued Darryl's interest. He tried to make meaningful eye contact with his mother. There had been far too many ghosts around that bridge, and the gnawing sensation hadn't left him since. If someone without the gift, like this priest, could sense it too, could the actual problem be much bigger than just the church ghost?

'Of course Coldbay feels bad,' his mother announced with a snort. 'It's a British seaside resort, it deserves to feel bad. Stick to the details please, Reverend, we have places to be and vodkas to drink.'

'I just thought maybe in the wider context it might be useful,' Grace said.

His mother waved a dismissive hand. 'Could you please tell us about the actual spectral phenomena we're dealing with? Anything a bit more concrete than a general sensation that "something's a bit off" – I'm afraid everyone's been feeling that lately, that's just life.'

'I'm not sure what to tell you,' replied Grace, eyeing up the few remaining Polish Jaffas. 'It doesn't happen at any particular time or anything. I always assumed these things were supposed to happen at midnight, or after dark at least, or maybe at the time the poor soul died, but there's no rhyme nor reason to it. Is that... is that normal?'

Richard nodded. 'They're always there, sometimes they prefer to cause mischief at a certain time, but they're rarely that rational. For most of them, they've been lost for so long that time has lost all meaning.'

'Sometimes it's that you're accidentally doing something that winds them up,' Charity added. 'A certain action, or word, a tune, standing too long in a certain spot, all those things can trigger a response. And Normals won't even know they're doing it.'

'"Normals"?' echoed Grace, with a frown.

'She doesn't mean it as an insult,' Janusz told her, cheerfully. 'I am also a Normal.'

'Do you think it might be something you're doing?' asked Darryl, trying to get the conversation back on track a little more diplomatically. 'Have you noticed any correlations? It could be anything – we had one ghost once that really hated the smell of cheese and onion crisps, threw glasses every time anyone opened a packet. Wouldn't have been such a big problem, but it was haunting a café.'

Grace shook her head. 'Can't think of anything. I just know it's angry about something. I mean, you know it's angry, you saw the toilet seat.'

'Hmm,' replied Darryl. It hadn't passed him by that all of Reverend Grace's cups and plates were plastic. She must have given up on crockery a while ago. People didn't tend to have tea in plastic cups out of anything but necessity – it made the tea taste weird. She must have been putting up with this for some time – surely long enough to have noticed patterns if there were any?

'I just don't know.' The priest ducked her head. 'I'm sorry. This place doesn't really function as a church, these days. Nobody comes to pray. I don't know whether it's the island, or the church, or me…'

'Or maybe it's something that happened before you came,' replied Darryl. 'What do you know about the history of the church? Maybe whatever caused the ghost to linger also frightened away the living – some sort of incident?'

'Yes, all right, Poirot,' interrupted Charity. 'Basically, Grace, do people steer clear of your church because someone topped themselves here? Or did a murder? Or both? Generally, the gorier and sadder the death, the more you can guarantee a space is going to be a ghost magnet, and er... also a magnet to the living, but the kind where you turn it around and push another magnet away instead of sticking them.'

Grace sighed. 'I had to take over in a hurry. My predecessor... something happened. My higher-ups didn't tell me much, but when I tried to update the parish blog, there was all this stuff. Strange stuff.' She got out her phone, pulled up a website and passed it to Brenda.

Brenda raised an eyebrow at it. 'Mostly this is asking people to come to a Harvest Festival.'

'Obviously the most recent ones are mine,' replied Grace, 'scroll down a bit.'

Brenda scrolled. Darryl and the rest of the family crowded around the phone screen. There were several posts about upcoming events written with a distinct air of faux jolliness tinged with desperation, clearly from Grace, but then the style abruptly changed. In one swipe, its short statements of cloying, anxious cheer became a wall of caps-lock text. This wasn't Grace's writing. This was the writing of someone who believed that punctuation marks were something that happened to people with less important things to say. Darryl squinted at the post. It was the written equivalent of someone incoherently shouting at a rubbish skip at 3 a.m. It was difficult to make out much of what the post was trying to say, but there were several mentions of 'Demons' and 'Evil Spirits', which, in the Rooks' line of work, were always a red flag.

Richard sucked through his teeth. 'Yes, I can see the problem, there. From some of this, it looks like he tried to do a clearing by himself, which we never recommend. It can go very wrong.'

Brenda barked a little laugh at that, which wasn't helpful.

'I think he was at the end of his tether at that point,' Grace told them.

Brenda continued to scroll, slower now. As they went backwards in time through undated parish blog posts, the text in them became gradually calmer, lost all of their unnecessary capital letters, and discovered the joys of commas and full stops once more. The content became much more readable, but frustratingly also became more evasive. These earlier posts were from a man who clearly had some concerns about what was going on in the parish, but was wanted to tiptoe around the matter so as not to sound like... well, like the sort of person whose final post would be an unreadable caps-lock rant. There were hints, here and there. Mentions of unexplainable disturbances, at the church and elsewhere. A lot of commiserations and well wishes to people having to shut down their businesses due to 'sudden, unforeseen circumstances'. Even more frequent were notices of funerals for a large number of surprisingly young people. Brenda kept scrolling, eventually reaching a post where the priest welcomed everyone to the blog which was replacing the old printed newsletter – what with it being 2016 and all. Even the first post wasn't what Darryl would have usually thought of as a parish newsletter. There were no mentions of summer fetes or jumble sales. There was instead a warning about the pier after another body had been found, and three funeral notices. Alongside it was a photograph of the blog's author – the previous priest of St Catherine's. An unassuming looking middle aged man in thick framed glasses smiled awkwardly against the backdrop of the very kitchen they'd just had to tidy up. Beneath his photo was the caption 'A warm welcome from Rev Duncan'.

'Poor Revduncan,' sighed Janusz.

'Was he, you know...?' Charity asked, grimly drawing a finger across her throat.

'I don't know,' Grace told them. 'I was sent here in a hurry, and… that's it. I wasn't told any of the history of the church, and I haven't heard any local gossip about it if there is any…'

'Because priests are too high and mighty to debase themselves with common gossip, all of a sudden?' asked Brenda, rolling her eyes over her plastic cup of lukewarm tea.

'Because nobody really talks to me,' replied Grace, unhappily. 'I try to be friendly, but… well, Coldbay isn't. Maybe something really bad did happen at the church, but it barely even registered with the people here. A lot of really bad things have happened in Coldbay. A lot-lot.'

Darryl thought about all those funerals, and the warning about the pier, and all the ghosts on that bridge.

'Guys?' he murmured.

His mother and sister both groaned.

'No,' said Brenda.

'I haven't even said anything yet!'

'You want to turn this into a whole thing,' Charity interjected. 'You always pull that face when you want to turn a simple house clearing into a whole thing!'

'I do not!'

'You do a bit, son,' said Richard, not unkindly.

'This is the face that made us spend two weeks in Ludlow,' added Janusz, quietly.

'This isn't Ludlow, though!'

'We could end up wasting even more time here than in Ludlow.' Charity threw her head back in exasperation, to address the ceiling rather than Darryl. Already one of nature's great slouchers, it only added to the effect of her seeming to attempt full horizontality while sitting on a hard plastic chair. Quite a feat.

Darryl turned to implore his mother instead, who was at least still mostly vertical. 'You saw the bridge too, Mum!'

'There's lots of bridges like that bridge, Darryl, we don't need to stop at all of them.'

'You never stop at any of them, Mum!'

'Of course I don't, they're covered in ghosts.'

'Ghosts?' Grace regarded them with concern. 'You think there might be ghosts on the bridge?'

'We *know* there are ghosts on the bridge,' Brenda told her. 'Lots of them.'

'Oh.' Already pretty miserable looking, the reverend crumpled some more. 'It's… the bridge is a bit of a hotspot for…'

'For people who can't take it any more,' said Darryl. 'We know.'

'I was going to say "for freak accidents", actually,' added Grace.

The entire family looked at her as if she'd just told them that her fiancé was an astrophysicist and underpants model but you couldn't meet him because he was off doing a secret project with Beyoncé in Paris.

'Did they tell you that on your first day, Vicar?' asked Brenda. 'Was that before or after they asked you to buy tartan paint?'

'Be kind, dear,' Richard reminded her.

'Well,' huffed Brenda, 'if she's going to be ridiculous about this and trot out fairy stories – although what more should we expect of a priest…?'

'You don't honestly think I didn't look into it?' asked Grace, raising her voice for the first time since the family had got there. 'As you say, I'm the priest here, this is my flock we're talking about, whether they come to church or not. Of course I noticed how many people kept dying in weird circumstances, and not just on the bridge.' She took her phone back off Brenda. 'Look!' She showed them the local paper's website, or at least what was visible of it through all the pop up ads. 'Three-car pile-up due to sudden fog. Freak wave washes the driver of a broken-down car out to sea. Seagull attack.'

'Seagull attack?'

'Mm, apparently there's been a few of those. They drive people off the promenade. Besides that, gas explosions, carbon monoxide leaks, collapsing tree branches…' she swiped through bleak story after bleak story, all partially visible under a large flash advert across the phone screen where a voluptuous cartoon pigeon in skimpy underwear advertised online bingo. 'People are miserable in Coldbay, but they're not all killing themselves. They're miserable because—'

'Because it's a Hell Hole?' interrupted Charity. 'I mean, those are the words Reverend Duncan used. Repeatedly.'

Darryl could see Grace forcing herself to rethink and reword what she wanted to say. 'I wouldn't put it that strongly,' she said, unconvincingly, after a moment. 'But people really do just have the worst luck out here.'

Darryl turned to the rest of his family again. 'You guys! Seagull attacks! Freak waves! All that stuff Duncan was raving about! Come on, that's got to be something, this is obviously bigger than just a church ghost.'

Janusz sighed. 'But my spreadsheets.'

'But his spreadsheets, Darryl,' added Charity. 'Don't you care about your own husband's spreadsheets?'

'We need to make time for the Aldwych client,' implored Janusz. 'She already paid her deposit.'

'Janusz's right,' said Richard. 'We need to put our clients above your curiosity, Darryl.'

'You wouldn't be like this if it were Mum saying it! You'd be all "we should pay careful attention to your mother's gift" if it were Mum saying it.'

'Your mother *does* have a special gift—'

'And I don't?'

His father paused just a fraction of a second too long. 'Of course you do too, son, just…'

'You know who we should ask about this?'

Richard's expression became stony. 'No. Not in front of the Pee Arr Eye Ee Ess Tee.'

Grace furrowed her brow. 'What's happening now?'

'Nothing,' replied Richard, emphatically.

'Why did you just spell out "priest"?'

'He didn't,' replied Charity.

'He did! Like you were trying to talk about the vet with a dog listening.'

Richard gave the priest a gentle smile. 'Please do excuse our little… idiosyncrasies, Reverend Grace.'

'Just Grace.'

'It was simply our way of deciding on methods and a schedule for the clearing. Due to a few other bookings, we're only going to be able to sort out your vestry for now—a'

'DAAaaAAdd,' whined Darryl, frustrated. Janusz shot his husband an apologetic glance.

'However,' continued Richard, smoothly, 'it might be useful for you to keep a diary of these unusual events and bad feelings you were talking about, and get back to us in a few months, so we can see if there's a wider issue at play.' Richard looked from Grace to Darryl. Darryl sighed. Defeated by one of his father's calm compromises, yet again.

Janusz squeezed his hand. 'For my spreadsheets?'

Defeated by his father's compromises *and* his husband's big, sad eyes. Dammit.

'If you all think that's best…?' replied Grace.

'Yeah,' conceded Darryl, 'that's best.'

So. They were dealing with a mysterious ghost, of unknown source and identity, who haunted the church vestry for reasons also unknown, had possibly driven the last priest completely off his rocker and was angry enough to fling toilet seats around the kitchen even though nobody knew why. Useful. They were just going to have to go into the house clearing blind. This wasn't ideal, but still wasn't exactly the end of the world, for two reasons. Firstly, they were pretty used to starting house clearings with very limited, or misleading, information on the ghost, if any at all. Around half of the jobs ended up being like this, and Darryl had learnt from hard experience that no information was better than lots of wrong information. It really didn't do to go into a clearing thinking they were dealing with a wailing Victorian lady and having done lots of research into three women who'd died tragically in that house in the 19th Century, only to discover that the spirit was actually the client's undiscovered murder victim from five years ago and he just hadn't fancied mentioning that for fairly obvious reasons, say. Now, *that* had been a messy case.

The second reason that going into a house clearing blind didn't bother Darryl all that much was that, once the ghost showed up, the house clearing was rarely blind for very long. After all, he had the gift... well, one of the gifts. Mostly it was the same gift as his mother's, and she rarely missed the opportunity to remind him that he had inherited it from her. It also was nowhere near as developed as his mother's – but it was getting there. It was good enough to work with at any rate, even if, in psychic terms, he was wrangling with an elderly, cheap laptop that took ten minutes to boot up and made alarming whirring sounds whenever you tried to use two different apps at the same time, while his mother had the sort of whizzy, sleek desktop that meant she could do seven jobs at once, email the kettle to tell it to put on a brew and then have a cup of tea in the time it took him to log on. Their collective gifts meant that it was difficult for a ghost to retain much of its usual air of spectral mystery, around Darryl and his mum. Mostly due to his mum, but Darryl helped and he felt that that was important, too. Probably.

The trappings of house clearances differ, not just from culture to culture and era to era, but individually, from ghost-hunter to ghost-hunter. You might wonder why, since death is so universal, since those wandering dead and lost could have been doing so for mere weeks, or for long centuries. Surely the apparatus to lure, trap and expel them should be universal too? But here's the thing. I'll let you in on a secret. Bell, book, candle, salt, holy water, prayers, flowers, herbs, ribbons, chalked outlines, anything, all of it… it's all show. Sometimes, so-called 'ghost-hunters' are total charlatans, and their equipment is simply to impress the client, but with the likes of the Rooks, it's more about impressing the prey. Rule number one of house clearances – if you can make the ghost think you know what you're doing, half of the job's done for you already. Trust me on this. I know. Or at least, I did know, before it all went wrong.

Richard lit three red candles and placed them in the vestry, at each corner of an equilateral triangle drawn in chalk on the floor by Darryl. Charity scattered salt rather half-heartedly while Brenda sat on a chair in the centre of the triangle, humming a low, continuous note. Grace sat right against the wall, next to Janusz, who half-watched the proceedings, while checking his emails.

'I'm a little bit worried,' muttered Grace, 'that this might be a little bit…' she searched for a term that wouldn't make her sound like such a hand-wringing churchy cliché, and found none, so just went with what was on her mind, '…pagan? I'd hoped there'd be more praying'

Janusz shook his head, cheerfully. 'It's fine, it's just what they find works for them. It's more like science. Trial and error.'

'Does science usually have this much chanting?'

Janusz smiled, still tapping away at his laptop. 'I was in your same situation once. I remember how ridiculous the chalk and chanting seemed.'

'You were a client?'

Janusz's smile grew. 'Turns out, getting an angry pirate to leave my apartment is very sexy to me.'

'A pirate?'

'A pirate.' Janusz glanced across at the family, who had now joined hands around the still-seated Brenda and had joined in with her hum. 'When they work, it is like a machine, every piece working just so. Every person, a cog.'

Grace looked from the strange scene in the middle of her vestry to the placid man cheerfully typing. 'And are you a cog too?'

'A very important cog,' he told her, proudly. 'I'm the cog that does the admin.'

His emails clearly dealt with to his satisfaction, Janusz closed the computer and cradled it on his lap.

The family suddenly went quiet.

And there was that sensation that always filled the vestry seconds before all Hell – pardon Grace's language – would break loose. An intense feeling of wrongness that she'd come to view as an early warning system, giving her a few precious moments to get out of the way of flying furniture and toilet seats.

There was a pause, and slowly, silently, both Brenda and Darryl turned their heads to look at the doorway from the vestry to the nave of the church. The mother and son's facial expressions went on swift journeys from a sort of blank acknowledgement, as if meeting eyes with a stranger, to surprise, to extreme concern.

'Something's wrong,' whispered Janusz.

'Oh, shi—' was all that Darryl managed, before one of the lit candles flew at his face.

CHAPTER FOUR

Duncan

It was bigger than Darryl had been expecting. It was male, or at least its shape suggested that it was the memory of someone who had been male back in life. Darryl tried to think of all ghosts as 'it' rather than 'he or she' – he found the distinction helped, considering the work he did. Beyond that, it was difficult to make out details.

Sometimes the ghosts wore easily discernible aesthetics that placed them in a certain period and class – Darryl still vividly remembered the post-war housewife, the Victorian coalman, Janusz's pirate – of course – and not to mention the Edwardian nanny who had menaced him when he was seven and left him with a lifelong aversion to Mary Poppins. Often, however, the ghosts were blurry smears of sadness and rage – vague body shapes, hollow eyes and snarling, howling mouths.

There was something about this one that was even more indistinct than usual. It was as if there was too much of it for the space it took up. As he struggled to focus his clairvoyant gift upon the ghost, the best analogy he could think of was that it looked like a sort of printing error – like when a picture in a cheaply made book would get printed twice in the same spot but with the lines ever so slightly off, creating a strange sense of vertigo. This ghost didn't just look like it had been printed twice, but five, maybe six times over. Whenever it moved, bits of it would remain in the space it had just occupied, on a miniscule time lag. Just looking at it gave him a vague headache. All that he could really make out about its messy form was that in the smear where its head should be was the shape of a pair of thick, rimmed glasses.

'Oh, shi—' he began, before he was given a far more definite and immediate headache by the ghost, as it threw a lit candle at him. He ducked out of the way so that it missed his eyes at least, but it still caught him on the forehead, leaving a painful smear of hot wax on his brow. It smelled of cranberry, not for any ghostly reason, but because Janusz had a habit of bulk buying their house clearance coloured candles from Wax Lyrical's Christmas Scents range at every Boxing Day Sale.

Brenda was already out of her chair. 'Bloody Hell, that's a big one,' she exclaimed, in the same tone most people would use if they noticed a ten centimetre house spider sprinting across the carpet. 'Richard, you may need to tell our friend to stand by.'

'You mean me?' asked Grace, but Brenda ignored her.

Richard backed away warily. Darryl knew that his father felt this wasn't his moment. Not yet. Hopefully, not at all, even though this ghost was indeed a chunky one. The family moved like a well-rehearsed troupe. Brenda and Darryl carefully, smoothly sidestepped in order to let Charity take the centre spot. They remained flanking her closely – like a full sized shoulder angel and devil, but with less ethical wrangling – in an attempt to triangulate the location of the angry spirit.

'It's coming dead on,' Darryl told his sister, but the ghost flickered and rushed away like a furious gale into one of the newly re-stacked bookshelves before Charity could focus on it. Books flew off the shelf yet again, landing in a bibliophile's nightmare heap of broken spines and crumpled pages.

'Well, now it's over there, obviously,' added Brenda.

Charity focused on the bookshelf as yet more books tumbled to the floor. 'Got it...' she muttered.

Just enough of the ghost came into focus for Darryl to be able to make out an expression of fresh outrage on it. It was aware that it was being constrained. It wriggled and struggled under the invisible bonds Charity was willing around it, its many, blurry lines swimming over one another. This was always a really dangerous part of the process, as more often than not Charity would *say* she'd got a handle on the thing on the first try, but actually...

It thrashed, suddenly released, howling with what sounded like at least four voices, and sped on too many legs over to the other side of the room. A spare chair upended and was hurled, metal legs first, at Darryl's face.

'...don't got it,' admitted Charity.

Darryl flinched, his arms shielding his head, and was dealt a painful blow by a chair leg for his trouble. Right on the funny bone, too, sending unpleasant jolts through his nerves from armpit to fingertips. He tried to shake the jangling out of his hand.

'Why's it picking on *me*?'

'Not now, Darryl,' chorused his sister and mother.

'You OK, zabko?' called Jan.

'Yeah.' Darryl continued to shake normality back into his hand. 'You guys might want to move a bit further back though, this one's a bit of a—' A tea tray hit him on the back of the head. 'Oh, come *on*.'

A teacup, mercifully a plastic one with only lukewarm tea dregs left in it, span away from the flung tea tray and hit Janusz on the ankle.

'Message received,' Janusz announced. Shielding his laptop with one arm and the small lady priest with the other, he moved himself and Grace over to stand in the nave and watch the chaos in the vestry through the doorway.

The ghost lurched this way and that, feinting out of the way every time Charity tried to get a lock on it and completely wrecking the family's earlier attempts at tidying up the mess in the process.

'Charity,' shouted Darryl, ducking out of the way of another plastic cup, 'it's heading for the toilet. I don't want to have to fix that again.'

Charity took a few, surefooted steps towards the toilet. 'Got it,' she said in exactly the same confident tone she'd used earlier when she hadn't got it. She held out a hand, and concentrated.

The ghost raged, trapped in the toilet doorway by invisible bonds. It flickered and writhed, but this time didn't quickly escape. Darryl dared a glance at his sister. Charity was struggling. Her jaw was clenched and her outstretched hand was shaking with effort. 'Strong, innit?' she managed through gritted teeth.

Standing at the side, Richard watched Charity's expression warily, and took a tentative step forward.

'It's OK, Dad,' she said.

Darryl looked back to the ghost. It might not be OK. Charity still had it contained, but its thrashing and writhing was growing more frantic. It was clearly taking all of Charity's strength just to hold it. It could still break out. Now, *this* was another dangerous part of the job, especially when ghosts were occasionally strong enough to overpower Charity. It had happened a few times lately, much to Charity's chagrin.

Richard dithered, looking from Charity to Brenda, seeking a decision on what to do.

'I said, it's OK.' Charity raised her other hand, with a grunt of effort. 'I don't need back-up.'

'It's here if you need it,' Richard told her, quietly.

Charity twisted her clenched jaw into a determined grin. 'Not today. Not here. It'll scare the preacher.'

'What?' called Grace from the nave. She turned to Janusz. 'What would scare me?'

'It's nothing,' Janusz told her with a big, fake, reassuring smile.

'On the off-chance you think this one might be open to persuasion,' said Charity with difficulty, 'now's your opportunity.'

The ghost thrashed more, the multiple outlines of it splintering and fracturing, and moving independently of one another. Darryl still couldn't make out any details of the manifestation, it looked so muddled.

'You don't live here any more,' Brenda told it. 'You know that, don't you, Duncan? You can leave by yourself, or we can make you.'

The ghost wailed at her, with what sounded like several voices.

Darryl watched his mother. Sometimes, she could make out messages that he couldn't, but not this time. This ghost really was just full of wordless rage.

'Can I help?' asked Grace from the doorway. 'Did you say it was Duncan's ghost? Maybe, one priest to another, I can—'

'I'm afraid Duncan definitely doesn't want to talk it out,' interrupted Brenda.

'Thought so. I'll just have to pop it as is.' Both of Charity's arms shook. A thin trickle of sweat ran down her neck. She planted her feet and pushed. The ghost screamed and thrashed even more.

36

'Richard?' said Brenda.

'No!' Charity shouted. 'I've nearly got it…'

She pushed again. The ghost howled, and folded in on itself.

When he was younger, Darryl had sometimes put crisp packets in the oven, watching as they crinkled, crumpled and shrank into these sad, dense little things. He was always reminded of that, whenever he watched his sister push a ghost out of the living realm, only with ghosts it happened much faster, in less than a second, and instead of being turned into keyrings like the shrunken crisp packets of his childhood, the ghosts would go on crumpling and shrinking until they disappeared in on themselves. Charity would talk about 'popping' them, like they were angry spots, but she could only *feel* them leave the living world. She could never see it happen – see what it did to them. It didn't ever look as painless and simple as 'popping'.

As this one collapsed, it seemed to shed those extra lines and shadows that had blurred its appearance before and only as it disappeared could Darryl finally see it clearly – the shade of a middle-aged man, in a plain shirt and trousers, and thick rimmed glasses. It looked so small and sad as it disintegrated, but then they always did.

Charity relaxed her arms and exhaled. 'There. Gone. Told you I could do it myself. We got any biscuits left?'

Grace stepped back into the vestry. 'Duncan's gone? Just like that?'

'Yep.'

Darryl met eyes with his mother, and then looked back at the space in the toilet where the ghost had been. Something was still wrong. The multiple shifting lines of the spirit were still etched somewhere at the back of his eyeballs.

'Do you know why he couldn't move on?' Grace asked. 'Why he was so upset?'

Charity shrugged. 'Sometimes it helps to know why, it means we can get the ghost to cooperate, but more often than not, Mum can't get a word out of them, right Mum?'

'Mm,' muttered Brenda.

'So it's better to just send them off.'

'So,' countered Grace, 'there *is* an afterlife for them to go to after all.'

'We're not sure,' replied Richard. 'But if it makes you feel better, whatever happens to them, it's likely more peaceful than wandering the earth lost and angry.'

Grace looked horrified. 'You don't know *where* you sent Duncan?'

'It's none of our business where they go afterward,' Charity told her. 'We just know that they can't stay here. They hate it here, they're always straight-up raging. I dunno what you're worried about – if he was a preacher like you, don't you assume he's gone somewhere nice?'

'Um,' said Darryl. He could still see the extra lines and shadows of the ghost. He looked at his mother again. She too was squinting at the toilet door.

'Something's still there,' said Brenda.

Charity shook her head, briskly. 'I felt it pop.'

As Darryl watched, the faint shades thickened and became more distinct. He had an upsetting sensation of double vision… no – triple vision – as they slid away from each other and became three separate shapes.

'Oh, no,' he breathed.

'Oh, what?' asked Charity.

'I *knew* that one was too big,' added Brenda.

'What's wrong?' asked Janusz.

The three shapes continued to take form. Darryl took a step away from them, instinctively. 'It brought its mates.'

CHAPTER FIVE

The Not-Richard

'Do ghosts *have* "mates"?' Janusz asked.

'This one does,' replied Darryl.

'I've just never heard of one bringing mates before.'

Grace looked around at the family of ghost-hunters. They all seemed to be in varying states of alarm and unpleasant surprise. It was not reassuring, especially coming from the professionals she's been recommended to call in to fix the problem. If you get plumbers in, the last thing you want to see is them gawping in mute horror at the absolute state of your drains.

Darryl turned to his mother. 'Three of them?' he whispered, as if double-checking.

Brenda nodded, gravely.

'Dear?' asked Richard.

'I can do three,' announced Charity, with only the slightest hint of doubt in her tone.

'One's a...' Darryl looked anxiously at Grace and then turned back to his sister. 'D-Word.'

Charity's expression didn't change. 'No problem.'

'Dear?' asked Richard again, more urgently.

'Hang on,' hissed Brenda. 'They haven't done anything yet.'

That was, obviously, the moment that the ghosts decided to do something.

Darryl and Brenda both threw themselves to the ground. The rest of the family followed suit so quickly that it must have been on instinct – and, indeed also on instinct, Grace did the same. The trestle table they'd had tea at less than half an hour ago was thrown into the air, flipped upside down and violently slammed back on to the floor. The heavy door between the vestry and the church nave started swinging wildly back and forth on its hinge and banging into the frame with a noisy force that couldn't possibly be doing the woodwork any good. The small window above the sink of the vestry's kitchenette feathered with ice and then cracked.

'Dear!' shouted Richard.

'Tell him to hold off for now, darling,' his wife called back to him. 'We can handle three of them, and they're only attacking stuff, not us.'

True, thought Grace, although it was *her* stuff that was getting broken, and *her* vestry that was now home to three ghosts instead of just one. And here they were, all lying on the floor, with the family clearly holding off on some spare resource. And she just couldn't stop thinking about how they'd just thrown Duncan out to who-knew-where, without a second thought and without anything but the barest of attempts to communicate or help him find peace. Once this was over, she was going to send a very strongly worded email to her higher-ups to determine why exactly they had recommended the Rooks to sort out her problem. She might even leave a harsh review on Trustpilot. Well. Maybe not 'harsh'. A three star review. Maybe four, because they *had* helped her tidy up, initially. Still though. There would be a reckoning.

'Right in front of you,' called Brenda, still braced in a ball on the floor.

Charity pushed herself up onto her knees and held both hands out, concentrating. 'Gotcha.'

'To your left!' shouted Darryl.

'Also your right,' added Brenda.

'Sake!' Charity exclaimed. 'I've only got one pair of hands!'

Charity continued to concentrate on the invisible force in front of her outstretched hands. Something unseen tugged at her, pulling her left arm over so that she almost lost balance.

'Ow,' she grumbled, but maintained focus. Something else unseen lifted a clump of her dark, silver-streaked hair, yanking her head to the right. 'Ow!'

'Dad?' asked Darryl.

Richard crawled a couple of feet towards his stricken daughter, watching her carefully. 'Charity? Princess? Do you need...?'

'I'm *fine*. I can do this.' Charity was pulled by the hair almost onto her feet, and thrown back down on her knees onto the thin, dirty carpet. Still, she kept her focus.

'One just let go of you,' Darryl told her.

'Yes, I know. All the better to pick them off.'

'Or it might be taking a run-up,' added Darryl.

Charity continued to focus. 'Come on... come on, you dead bugger...'

The door slammed again, a couple of times, and then the banging and shaking moved to the floor beneath it. The family ignored it, they were busy watching Charity as she gritted her jaw and concentrated. Something slapped Charity across the face. The family winced, but Charity shook it off. Grace watched the scene, but was aware that the angry patch of floor

41

had started to move, at a slow walking pace, in the direction of where Grace was defensively crouching with Janusz.

'Um?' she said, but the family weren't listening. The banging section of the floor was practically beneath her now, and a sudden cold, sick feeling crept through her. She'd felt it a couple of times before, during prior disturbances in the vestry when she hadn't been able to get outside fast enough. It was like the sensation of wet food remnants brushing past her hand while washing up, only all over. A slimy, wrong feeling that made her want to recoil and gag. Then, as suddenly as it had spread through her, it was gone again.

Charity was flung forwards, but her brother was able to catch her before she hit the floor. Her concentration didn't waver. 'Almost there…'

The floor next to Grace shook again. At Grace's side, Janusz shuddered.

'You feel that, too?' Grace asked him.

'Yes.' Janusz pulled a disgusted but resigned face. He seemed even more used to the sensation than Grace was. 'This is when the— argh!'

Janusz yelped in shock as he was hurled three feet into the air, where he hung and bounced for a moment, as if being given the bumps by invisible hands.

'Janusz!' Darryl let go of Charity, who fell forwards onto the floor.

'Dammit!' she shouted.

But the rest of the family were no longer paying attention to her. Darryl was already on his feet, ready to sprint the few paces to where Janusz hung helplessly, when his feet were yanked backwards, causing him to fall heavily.

Brenda hauled Charity back up again. Charity's nose was bleeding. Brenda glanced across at Richard, and Grace spotted an odd expression on Brenda's face. It was a silent communication between a wife and a husband – something unspoken and so personal that for a moment, Grace felt like she was intruding for even seeing it – that she should look away. She turned her attention to Darryl who was dragging himself towards Janusz. She had to help. She'd be close enough to grab Janusz if she only stood up. She tried to do so, but a great, frightening weight pushed her down again, as if delivered by big, grasping, violent hands.

'Darryl?' called Janusz, worried and pained. 'Richard? I think—'

'Leave my kids **alone.**' Richard took a step forward. There was something odd about the soft-spoken little man's tone, his voice at the end of his demand had thickened into something far more menacing. There was a low growl behind it that almost didn't register to Grace's sense of hearing. It was more that she was able to feel it, like a deep, throbbing bass thrumming through the ground from a nearby amplifier.

Janusz lowered a little, but wasn't fully deposited back onto the safety of the carpet. Darryl lurched towards him again, but again was hurled to the floor. The maelstrom of invisible violence in the room turned its focus on to Richard. Plastic cups and saucers flew at him, bouncing off his head with sad little plasticky 'dinks'. Richard, unperturbed, took another step forward, and didn't seem as small any more, or as soft. The throbbing bass of him radiated out in waves. Grace could taste something mineral and bitter in the back of her mouth with every pulse. It felt somehow worse than the sick, wet sensation of the ghost. She desperately wanted to tell Richard to stop whatever it was he was doing, but she found that she couldn't speak. There was too much of Richard, all of a sudden, and yet it wasn't Richard at all, it was something else, something that was all wrong for the sweet-faced older man that it inhabited, and the wrongness of it all took her breath away. She watched, in silent terror, as the image of Richard shifted, and became something else altogether.

Grace has no good way of describing it to herself, so I'm going to take a moment to try. Sorry about stopping the action like this, it won't take long, but you know those optical illusions where you see a duck until you change your focus and then you see a rabbit? Or magic eye pictures where it's a 2D pattern of colourful beach balls but then you cross your eyes a bit and the beach balls go all fuzzy and suddenly you can clearly see this 3D dolphin that was there the whole time? Think of it like that. Only, instead of a dolphin, it's the sort of cryptid creature that would make a middle-aged priest think she's going to be sick.

Grace felt like she was going to be sick. The form of Richard the sixty-something gentleman with the emphasis on the 'gentle' – was still there, but it had shifted somehow and become a fuzzy background to the thing that now took another angry step towards the stricken Janusz.

It had one head, one torso and four limbs, and was roughly man-sized, but that was where its similarity to a human being ended. Its many eyes were filled with a darkness that seemed to suck the light into them, like little black holes. Its claws had a sharpness that looked like they could cleave through space itself, rip protons from electrons and crush them underfoot to make some strange new element. It opened its mouth, and its teeth evoked a fundamental, prehistoric fear. Every shred of her jangled at this thing. It was ancient. It was terrible. It should not be in this place. Not in this church. Not on this earth. Not in this universe.

'**Leave,**' said the thing, '**the kids alone!**'

The family were reacting to the creature with something akin to relief – even Janusz. How? Couldn't they see it? Couldn't they feel their DNA urgently telling them to clamber up the nearest primeval tree and screech? Either they couldn't tell it was there, or they were somehow used to it.

Grace finally found her voice, buried deep within her fear. 'What *is* that?'

'He's here to help,' was Brenda's only answer.

Charity wiped the blood from her nose and held her hands out again. 'Told you the priest would freak out.'

'I'm not freaking out!' She was totally freaking out, and regretting calling the family in the first place. What harm was an occasional supernatural commotion in the vestry, in the grand scheme of things? It wasn't like she had a congregation to scare off. It wasn't like St Catherine's was the only place in Coldbay with bad vibes – far from it. She could have lived with plastic cups and the toilet seat getting flung about from time to time, couldn't she? And now there were three more ghosts and a… a *something*, and these strangers did not seem on top of the problem at all, and—

'Argh!' Janusz was yanked by the arm. He flew suddenly, violently, by a foot or so before Darryl managed to scrabble up from the floor and grab him by the ankle. Darryl tried to hold his husband steady, but something unseen was trying to pull the two men apart.

'Help!'

Out of instinct, Grace knelt up as well and grabbed Janusz's other ankle.

Blimey.

Something very strong was trying to drag Janusz in the opposite direction, towards the heavy wooden vestry door.

Janusz struggled, still suspended in mid-air, with gritted teeth. Being pulled in different directions by his husband, a priest and an unseen horror was causing him understandable discomfort.

'**Leave him alone!**'

The thing that used to be Richard leapt at Janusz, taking up too much space as it did so, extending out of the background shape of Richard like a concertina. It snarled, and clawed at the air around Janusz. Grace felt Janusz jolt. The thing slashed out with its claws again. Janusz briefly wailed in pain, and then the force heaving him in the other direction suddenly went slack. Unfortunately, it did so while Darryl and Grace were still pulling at his ankles, which caused them both to fall backwards with Janusz landing heavily on both of them, legs first.

'Sorry,' mumbled Janusz, his face on the floor and his foot in Grace's face. At least it meant he was OK.

The thing, the Not-Richard, was still going, slashing at thin air and shadow, roaring and screaming with a horrific noise that sounded, to Grace's mind, like the sound of a deranged lion trying to slowly eat an elephant alive from the feet up.

Janusz pulled his shoe off Grace's forehead. 'It's OK, Murzzzz is on our side.'

'What?' managed Grace.

'Over here,' called Brenda.

Grace had sort of forgotten about Brenda and Charity in all the hubbub. She felt a bit guilty. The mother and daughter were clearly struggling. Brenda was kneeling next to Charity, keeping her upright with considerable effort. Charity's nose was still bleeding, and both hands were straining outwards. She seemed to be pushing against some invisible, impossible weight.

The Not-Richard glanced across at them, then leaped up to the ceiling, sticking to it easily by its claws. If it were a yoga class, she'd have commended the Not-Richard on its excellent

Wheel Pose, but this wasn't a yoga class and, as just mentioned, it was upside down on the ceiling. The Not-Richard also took no time to gently stretch out its abs and back, instead it skittered at speed across the ceiling, elbows and knees out at inhuman angles, and threw itself with immense force at a patch of wall right next to where Brenda was holding Charity.

'Nearly…' ground out Charity. She spat out a glob of blood as casually as a defiant thirteen-year-old would spit out a chewed up wad of gum. 'Nearly…'

The Not-Richard continued to flail and thrash against a vicious unseen enemy against the wall. Janusz squeezed Grace's hand, and only then did she realise that she was trembling.

'It's OK.' He smiled, symmetrically. 'I was scared the first time, too. And the next time, and the next, and also a little bit now.'

Charity let out a low groan and leant hard against something in front of her. There was something there – Grace could sense it, not quite seeing it, not quite feeling or smelling it, but something in between. It was a sort of fog of wrongness, contained to around the size and shape of a man. A writhing pillar of chilly malevolence. It was right there, in her vestry, right there, against Charity's outstretched hands. And then… it wasn't.

Charity gasped in relief. 'Gotcha! Two down! Murzzzz, you got the next one?'

The Not-Richard – Grace supposed she ought to start referring to it as 'Murzzzz', since the rest of the family was – looked up from its battle with the other angry patch of fog. There were still shades of Richard about its expression, even now. It opened its terrible mouth, and spoke in its terrible voice.

'**Hang on, Princess.**'

'Murzzzz, watch out,' cried Darryl, 'the other one's—'

There was a new clatter. The kettle unplugged itself and flew at Murzzzz, twirling out a Catherine Wheel of still-warm water as it spun base over spout. The door banged again, and Janusz's laptop, left abandoned near the doorway, rose up as the next hard projectile to be hurled.

Janusz's eyes widened in true horror. He honestly looked more frightened about his laptop than he had about being manhandled by a malevolent spirit.

'No!' He leaped to grab the computer.

'Janusz,' warned Darryl.

Janusz managed to clutch hold of the levitating laptop. He wrapped his arms around it desperately. 'Not my laptop!'

'You can get another laptop!'

'I haven't backed up my files in a week, we are in such trouble if I lose them!'

'Janusz, will you—'

Janusz was hoisted up again – by the ankles this time – and this time, neither Darryl nor Grace were able to grab him before he was wrenched away, at speed, through the open door to the church. Murzzzz, still wrestling with the angry patch of mist, spotted what was going on and howled horribly.

'Janusz!' Darryl was first on his feet, sprinting towards the door, which slammed shut in his face. Grace got up and tried to help him prise it open – but it was jammed fast. Brenda and Charity quickly joined them, scrabbling and yanking at the door, which remained shut tight. From the nave beyond the door there was the clatter of candlesticks being knocked onto the floor, and the heavy scrape of wooden pews dragging along the stone floor, punctuated by the cries of Janusz as he struggled.

'Janusz,' screamed Brenda with a despair that would make anyone think the young man was her own husband rather than her son's. 'Not Janusz!'

There was an unsettling scurry of blurred flesh, and suddenly Murzzzz was right by Grace's side. Whatever Murzzzz was, it was even more unsettling close up. It pushed them all aside with an extraordinary strength, sunk its claws into the wood and pulled the whole door straight off its hinges as easily as if it were made of wet paper.

Darryl ran through the splintered hole where the door used to be. 'Leave him alone! You want to pick on someone, pick on me, instead!'

'Yes, pick on him instead,' cried Brenda.

As Charity and Murzzzz pushed past them both into the nave, Grace gave Brenda a small frown.

'What?' Brenda asked. 'Just backing up his argument.'

Grace knew there was no time for a disagreement. Janusz was screaming. Darryl was screaming. Charity was screaming. Murzzzz was making that horrible 'lion torturing an elephant' noise. She ran after the others, past a pillar that had been obscuring her view of the south window.

Then Grace saw what they were all screaming about. She stopped in her tracks and did something utterly unoriginal, given the circumstances.

She screamed.

CHAPTER SIX

The South Window

St Catherine's church was a cold, grey, damp, sad little building, for all the singing of Hosanna to the King of Kings and the Lord of the Dance that Grace did alone amongst the echoing stone, in the hope of someone joining her. It did have bursts of bright beauty in amongst the hard darkness of it though – the bright 'hands around the world' tapestry that Grace had made herself, the fair trade card display that she'd really hoped would have made at least one sale by now, but looked pretty anyway… and best of all, the stained glass windows. The grand east window, behind the altar, was a glorious explosion of colour, but she was also very fond of the smaller windows in the north and south transepts, both depicting biblical pastoral scenes. There was a nice symmetry to them, all bright green rolling hills and azure skies – neither of which were generally to be seen anywhere in Coldbay but for those two precious windows. In each scene, figures in cream and beige robes watched placidly over grazing sheep and goats. It always seemed so peaceful to her; the shepherd and goatherd's faces were so kind. Sometimes she'd look at one for so long that she'd wonder what it would be like just to slip away into one, to be one of those kind-faced farmers, to have a flock that actually wanted to come to her, to feel a warm breeze on her neck and rippling, lush grass on her sandalled feet. It was an idle fantasy, of course, but Grace had always thought it seemed like it would be nice to be in one of those windows.

Idle fantasies, she thought to herself now, were stupid.

The Rook family were bundled together in the south transept, shouting, screaming and grasping hold of Janusz – pulling him by his outstretched arms. Grace forced herself out of her shocked torpor and hurried over to help them. Janusz was still crying out for help, hanging upside down, held by some impossibly strong and unseen force. Amazingly, things had managed to get worse.

Janusz's legs were in the window. They hadn't smashed the glass or gone through it in any way – that, Grace would be able to handle. His legs were *in* the window. Her peaceful first century pastoral scene now had a pair of legs in the foreground, in a pattern of colourful tessellated glass, held together with fine lines of lead. They would have looked for all the world as if they'd been carefully crafted along with the rest of the window, were it not for the glaring anachronism of blue jeans and scuffed Adidas trainers on a lovely Judean hillside, the fact that they were floating upside down and the fact that the stained glass legs stopped at the knees, where they turned into a very real human man in his thirties, hanging upside down, holding on to his husband and sister in law, and screaming for help.

The cryptid horror that she supposed she should just refer to as 'Murzzzz' since that was apparently its name, was railing, howling horribly, throwing itself at the south window and scrabbling at the smooth, cold, bright glass with its impossible claws. Grace grabbed Janusz by the elbow and tried to help the family drag him back.

'On my count, pull as hard as you can.' Darryl was sweating with effort in spite of the damp chill of the church.

But Janusz was stuck fast, Grace could feel that already.

'Won't that hurt him?' She fretted. 'We could dislocate his shoulders, or—'

'I'm getting spooked into a picture,' shrieked Janusz. 'This is worse than a broken arm!'

Murzzzz clawed at the window again, and this time its talons were able to push inside the picture the way that Janusz's legs had. Now, the stained glass hillside had mid-range jeans, elderly trainers and a demonic pair of hands – or at least hand-like appendages, gnarled and sharp – grasping at the upside down legs. Not only that – Grace noticed that the goats and goatherds that had been standing peacefully still in the two dimensional countryside of the south window for the past two centuries had changed. They were still frozen, solid images stained and painted into a skilfully arranged mosaic of glass, as they always had been. They weren't moving – at least, Grace hadn't seen them move. But they were different now from the depictions of people and animals that Grace used to stare dreamily at. Their faces were no longer blandly gazing into the middle distance, but were turned to look at the new intrusions. Their expressions were no longer blank and peaceful, but seemed perturbed. It was as if they'd somehow noticed what was going on. This was, of course, impossible, but then so was almost every aspect of Grace's day so far, and many of the disturbances in the months leading up to this day that had driven her to contact the Rooks in the first place. Come to think about it, a lot of the tiny snippets of recent history she'd been able to find out about the community of Coldbay in general were borderline impossible and definitely distressing, so the goatherds in her window looking upset really shouldn't have hit her so hard. However, the way one might logically reason that they *should* feel about something, and how they *actually* feel about it can be very different things. It was her window! Her happy space! And something was trying to kill a perfectly nice Polish admin guy in it. Also now there were the claws of what she was pretty sure was a Demon in it. This was definitely going too far.

'One,' said Darryl, 'two—'

'Are we going on three or after three?' asked Charity, urgently.

'After. One—'

'On three would be quicker,' interrupted Brenda.

'Guys!' wailed Janusz.

'On three then,' shouted Darryl. 'Murzzzz, you got him?'

Murzzzz grunted, with a noise that sounded like several pigs being immolated at the same time.

'One two three go, I mean, one two go!'

Grace and the family pulled as hard as they could. Janusz gritted his teeth against the pain and whimpered. For a moment, it felt like Janusz was stuck fast, and then Murzzzz gave a terrible shriek of effort. There was the sound of glass being dragged against glass, and the cracking of solid lead, and Janusz's shins began to emerge from the picture.

'Yes!' cried Darryl. 'Nearly there. Come on, love.'

Janusz spat out a string of words that Grace recognised as probably Polish but didn't understand.

'I take it those are swear words?'

'Yeah,' panted Darryl, still pulling, 'I'm not translating them in front of a client.'

They gave another coordinated heave, and Janusz was painfully drawn out of the picture inch by inch until only his feet remained in the glass.

'One more should do it,' gasped Darryl. 'One, two…'

Something very cold and very strong wrapped itself around Grace's waist and hurled her from the south transept. She landed heavily on her hip, and then skidded and rolled painfully across half the width of the nave until she hit an upturned pew. She looked up in time to see both Darryl and Charity being thrown away from Janusz at the window. Charity hit a pillar back-first and slumped, winded. Darryl slammed into the side of a pew with a horrible force, but was back on his feet hurrying back to Janusz's aid almost instantly, only to be thrown again and this time further across the nave. Grace tried to get up. There were only Brenda and Murzzzz with Janusz now, and both were clearly struggling against the force that really wanted their son-in-law to be a beautiful, stained glass image of a frightened, upside down twenty-first century man.

Something inside the window moved – not a part of the stained glass as such, more a shifting shadow playing across the colours.

'No,' Brenda told the shadow, in a tone of voice that made her sound like she was chiding a boisterous dog, 'stop'. The shadow flickered and extended out of the window for just a moment, catching Brenda across the jaw and knocking her off her feet.

The focus of Murzzzz shifted suddenly, and Grace was only able to see Richard again. The claws in the stained glass disappeared, leaving Janusz's feet alone in the picture, along with three worried looking Iron Age peasants and their similarly startled goats. Richard reached down to Brenda in concern.

'Dad, no.' Darryl managed a few steps towards the window before his legs were pulled from under him again and he was dragged several feet along the floor to collide hard, head first, with the base of the font.

'I'm fine.' Brenda accepted her husband's hand to help her get back up, even as she protested that she didn't need it. 'Help Janusz.'

Janusz. There was now nobody trying to pull Janusz out of the window.

Several things happened at the same time. Charity pulled herself upright, still winded and gasping. Darryl lurched to his feet, head bleeding from where he'd hit the font, and ran screaming towards the window, tilted forwards as if going headfirst into a gale. Brenda, Richard and Grace all took a step towards Janusz.

Janusz was now just a chest, a neck, a head and one arm – the upside down image in stained glass was now far more than just the bottom half of his legs. The goatherds now stared in concern at three quarters of a young man in double denim and trainers.

Grace didn't know how she got to Janusz first. She didn't remember running. She was just… there, all of a sudden, grasping Janusz's remaining outstretched hand. It wasn't enough. He was still being dragged in. She couldn't make it stop.

Murzzzz shifted back into focus, tried unsuccessfully to push its claws into the window, then dissolved from view again, leaving Richard to shake his head.

Darryl grabbed Janusz's hand, desperately.

'Honey?'

'Zabko…' all that was left of Janusz outside of the window now was his head from the chin up and half of one arm, from the elbow. 'I'm so cold.'

'We'll get you out, OK? It'll be all right.'

'Kocham Cie.'

'Tez Cie kocham.'

Janusz's eyes glimmered wetly. 'Thank you.'

'No. We're not talking like that right now, honey.'

'Your Polish accent is so bad, it always cheers me up.' Janusz's mouth attempted a smile, even though the top half of his face had committed to some proper tears.

'Janusz, we are getting you out of there asap, right guys?'

'Don't you worry, sonny,' said Richard.

'And then I'm going to make them pay,' added Charity, hotly. 'You hear that, you bastards? You're going to wish you were dead… even deader than you already are. You'll wish you were double-dead. And then you *will* be double dead… but not in the way you wished, because…'

'Zabko, do one thing for me.' The glass was up to Janusz's lower lip.

'Anything.'

'Back up my files. And if I'm stuck here forever, the tax returns must be done by J—'

There was an almighty final heave, and Janusz's hand was ripped from Grace and Darryl's grasp. The last bits of him disappeared into the window like a terrible undercurrent dragging a drowning man under the surface of the water.

'Janusz!' Darryl put his fingertips to the glass. In the window, the upside down image of Janusz hung above the emerald hills, one hand still outstretched towards his husband, mouth still open in the middle of his tax advice. Beyond him, standing on the hill, Grace spotted a second figure that she hadn't noticed before – a malevolent shadow, lurking. It looked as smug as it was possible for a stained glass shadow to look. Whatever had dragged Janusz into her window was still there. Perhaps it had always been there. Perhaps that was where it had come from. And there was still yet another ghost in the church, wasn't there? The Rooks had found four ghosts all together and eliminated only two. There were still twice as many ghosts as Grace had originally estimated, *and* there was the ethical issue of what on earth Charity did to the spirits that she 'got rid of', *and* now there was a man trapped in her nice south window. With the urgency of trying to rescue Janusz over, the implications

56

of everything that had happened during this wretched 'house clearance' attempt began, rather swiftly, to scurry into Grace's mind. Her hands started to shake. This was wrong. This was all terrible – horrible. She'd thought it had just been one sad, scared little man who couldn't move on, but this was too much, too much.

She looked at the Rook family. A part of her told her that this was all part of her job, comforting those in need… or maybe it was part of *their* job to be on top of all this, to have another plan and put all of this mess straight. She caught Darryl's eye. He looked utterly broken. Blood ran in a thin line from his forehead, down the side of his face and over his ear. Darryl didn't even wipe it away. He slumped, his hand still pressed against the stained glass. Richard put his hand on his son's shoulder, and Grace remembered the horror of Murzzzz with a jolt. Somewhere beyond those soft, wrinkled hands were an obscene mass of curled claws.

How could she possibly make this better? How could *they* possibly make this better? She shouldn't have contacted them. *Why* had she contacted them? She should have just learned to live with the vestry ghost. Everyone else in Coldbay learned to live with their strange shadows, their eerie coincidences and their things that went bump in the night, didn't they? Or at least, they did until the freak waves and seagull attacks made living an impossibility.

She looked around the nave – the upended pews, the toppled candlesticks, the smashed vestry door, the blood on the font.

'I'm just going to…' she said, and without being able to think of a lie to excuse herself, simply left it at that and walked urgently down the aisle, out of the church and down the empty road.

CHAPTER SEVEN

The Runaway Priest

'Darryl? Son?'

Darryl ignored his father softly calling his name. It wasn't the voice he wanted to hear, right now. He kept his palm pressed against Janusz's hand, but it was just cold glass, lined with lead. The first time he'd taken Janusz's hand, years ago now, after that business with the ghost pirate, Darryl had marvelled at every sensation of it – the warmth of the other man's hands, the firmness of his grip, the elegance of his fingers, the slight tremble still present after having just been attacked by a ghost pirate. He'd known, right then. Actually, he'd probably known before then, but just by taking Janusz's hand, he'd felt at once thrilled and calmed. Cosy yet bright. The touch of Janusz's hand had been like Christmas morning.

Darryl dared to open his eyes again, and wished that he hadn't. The elegant fingers were still there, reaching out to him, frozen and lifeless in the window. Darryl looked across at Janusz's face. Janusz's perfect eyes stared back at him, wide with fear.

'It'll be all right' his dad told him. 'These little hiccups do happen in our line of business, you know that.'

'Yes, but they don't usually happen to *Janusz*,' blurted his mother. She was pacing the width of the transept with an expression that she usually reserved for when they were out of pinot grigio and the shops were shut. 'I mean, how dare they? Janusz's off limits. He just does the accounts.'

Richard left Darryl's side and went to put a hand on Brenda's shoulder. 'In fairness, dear, the ghosts weren't to know that. It isn't as if we put a sign on him saying "Accountant: do not haunt".'

'Well, maybe that would be a good idea in the future.'

'He's not your accountant,' said Darryl, quietly, 'he's my husband.'

'He's a little bit of both, son,' replied Richard, diplomatically.

'And he is trapped in a picture in a window in a sad church on a crap island!' Darryl turned to his family but kept his fingers pressed against the glass, desperately. 'Possibly forever! What sort of marriage is that going to be?'

'He won't be trapped forever.'

'Sometimes people get ghosted into a picture forever. Or decades, at least! Remember the old lady in the background of that creepy dog portrait?'

Richard sighed a little. 'Oh yes. Poor Madge. But we got her out of there.'

'After fifty years!'

'Yes well, we couldn't exactly help her when she got dragged into it in 1967 now, could we? But your sister helped Madge, and obviously she can help Janusz, can't you, princess?'

'Hmm?' Charity was leaning against a stone column, chewing her thumbnail and frowning. 'Oh. Yeah. Definitely. Sure.' She paused. 'Might take a few tries.'

'What?' replied Darryl, horrified. Considering his sister's usual bravado when it came to her skills, 'might take a few tries' displayed a stomach-twisting lack of confidence.

'Reverse clearances are really hard,' Charity told him, with a defensive huff. '*And* we've still got two active ghosts yet to deal with. I'm just saying, we probably won't be done and dusted by dinner time. Could someone rustle me up some toast or something?'

'What I'm sure your sister is trying to say,' added Richard, 'is that none of us are going anywhere, we'll stay here and get our Janusz out of there no matter how long it takes.'

'Hmm,' said Charity, eyeing up the window the way a Health and Safety officer would take in a children's play park made of asbestos, rusty wire and open manholes.

'OK?' Richard asked. He turned his attention to his unusually glassy son-in-law. 'All right, Janusz? We're all staying put till you're out of there, don't you worry.'

In the window, Janusz did look incredibly worried, which was fair enough given the circumstances. The goatherds and their animals still looked similarly perturbed which, again, fair enough – although they probably had less to get upset about.

'For now,' added Richard, 'let's all take a breath, if we can, while Charity has a little think. Maybe Reverend Grace can recommend us a good local takeaway for dinner? Everything seems a bit better with a lovely bit of fish and chips, right?' He looked around. 'Grace? Chish and fips?'

The family realised that the priest was gone.

Brenda sighed, noisily. 'Well, where's she got to? Honestly – priests. You show them actual evidence of existence after death and they run away.'

Charity shrugged. 'Forget her. She's been no help so far anyway, and she'll only get in the way now. I say, get Janusz, get rid of the last two ghosts—'

'One ghost.' Brenda pointed to the shadowy spot in the window. 'That other sod's a demon.'

Charity shrugged. 'Ugh. Typical. Well, I suppose a Demon in the window'll be the cause of all this trouble, so let's just get Janusz, blast both, get off this Hell Hole, invoice the deity-botherer later.'

Darryl turned his attention back to Janusz. While his gaze had been elsewhere, the image of Janusz in the window had moved. He was no longer floating upside down, which was something at least. He was now standing in the foreground, hugging himself worriedly while the goatherds gave him distrustful glares. The shadow in the background of the window had moved, too. It seemed further away, and it radiated a mocking menace. Everything about the shadow was sending a message to Darryl's second sight, and that message was 'Ner ner, you can't get me'. He thought about Duncan, the small, sad dead priest, carrying the other ghosts and this Demon around inside his own spirit. As much as Charity wanted to pretend that this was par for the course when a Demon was involved, he'd certainly never seen anything like it before. He didn't know what it meant, but it really didn't feel good. He thought about Duncan's blog, about the late priest's growing unease concerning the island, how it had tipped him over the edge into ranting and raving about Hell on a barely-read newsletter, before ultimately driving him to his death, and to becoming... becoming whatever weird thing that had been, back there. Darryl was letting the sadness of the dead in. He knew that that wasn't a good idea, but sod it, he was sad enough already, what was a bit more?

He thought about just how strong the Demon in the window was. The way it and the ghosts under its control had turned on Janusz. Ghosts and demons usually just went after Darryl, Brenda and Charity during a clearance and it was usually self-defence. This time, it had felt like… spite, somehow. Like the Demon was playing – showing off. It hadn't even been scared of Murzzzz. Even demons were usually scared of Murzzzz. This was all wrong.

'No,' he said. 'We should find Grace.'

'We don't need her to get chips for us, we've got Deliveroo,' said Richard.

Darryl turned to his sister. 'This island is really wrong. We need her so that we can investigate the root of the problem.'

'The root of the problem is that demon! How can you still be wanting to make this a whole thing, Darryl? Your husband's a decorative window. Mum? Dad? Tell Darryl.'

Brenda and Richard looked at one another. A fleeting expression of doubt passed over his mother's face.

'Maybe Darryl has a point,' said Richard. 'Murzzzz feels skittish – that demon was far too bold. Something's not quite right. Perhaps we should—'

'At the very least,' interjected Brenda, 'we should find the preacher so she can pay us fifty per cent upfront, considering the trouble we've been through already. Besides, I need a drink and there's nothing in this bloody church any stronger than tea – trust me, I looked.' She glanced at her husband. 'We'll go and find an offie and a chip shop, and perhaps we'll find the reverend on the way, right?'

'Sounds like a champion plan,' said Richard. 'Charity, you don't need our help with extracting Janusz, do you?'

Charity drew herself up, proudly. 'I'll be fine. Easy pie.'

Richard smiled, warmly. 'Good-oh. Janusz, you hang on in there, sunny-Jim, we'll be back with the priest and some chips. Everyone having their usual, right?'

'Curry sauce on mine if they've got it,' called Charity.

'Veggie burgers for us,' said Darryl, quietly, his hand still on the window.

'Still carrying on with the vegetarian thing?' asked Brenda, coolly.

'Yes Mum, still carrying on with "the vegetarian thing"!'

Brenda shrugged. 'If you insist.' Richard linked arms with her and they walked together out of the open door to the church.

Charity turned her attention back to the window. She held out both hands and glared at it with a furious focus, her breath hitched, her fingers tense and trembling. Darryl felt a faint, cold crackle against the glass. He gave his sister a quick glance before turning his eyes back to the window again, and saw that his husband's image had moved again. Now Janusz was crouching, holding his hand out to Darryl, as if expecting to be pulled out to safety any moment.

Charity exhaled suddenly in an exhausted gasp, and the crackle stopped. Darryl himself let go of a breath he hadn't been aware he'd been holding. He turned again to his sister, to see her walking away.

'What are you doing?' He didn't follow her. There was no way he was leaving the window. 'Where are you going? Easy pie – you just said!'

'Yeah, I know,' replied Charity. 'I just need the toilet.'

Outside, the thin rain had turned back into a lingering mist. Damp pervaded the air, without having the conviction to actually go anywhere. It just hung around sullenly, sticking to every surface, slicking the pavement, and cloying to Brenda's skin. The night had fully asserted itself, and Brenda noticed as she walked along the street with Richard just how few of the nearby buildings had any lights on. The main sources of light were from the church behind them, and occasional street lights, haloed with a sickly glow in the mist, which cast a reflective pattern on the wet tarmac, giving it the appearance of a greasy, orange river. No cars drove past, no televisions or stereos blared as they walked by. The only sounds she was aware of were of their own breaths mixing in with the damp of the air, and their footsteps walking along the shimmering pavement. Brenda kept her guard up. She really, really didn't like this place. Annoyingly, Darryl almost certainly had a point about Coldbay. There was a lot more to it than just the church. That Duncan fellow had known it, from the state of his blog, and look where it had got him. She hadn't seen a Parasite in many a year, and Duncan's ghost had had three of them. Three! And the ancient, vicious seed in the centre was a Demon. God, she needed a drink. They came to the corner of the road and rounded it, cautiously. Brenda braced herself to see some miserable lost soul smudged in the mist, but thankfully so far there were none.

'Anything?' asked her husband.

She shook her head, briskly. 'Not yet.'

They walked on, arm in arm.

'Quiet, isn't it?' Richard added.

'Mm.' They walked on a little further. 'You do know where you're going…?'

'You Know Who does,' replied Richard, cheerfully. He tapped the side of his nose. 'He can smell a priest from a good half a mile. His kind are… interested in faith leaders.'

'I actually never knew that,' said Brenda, impressed.

'You never asked. I suppose we've never had the need to track a priest before.'

'Don't suppose he can sniff out a Wine Warehouse or something while he's at it?'

Richard laughed softly. 'Sorry, love.'

Brenda got out her phone, but found that the satnav app wasn't working. 'Bloody thing.'

'Ah!' cried Richard, merrily, 'here we go.' He broke into a light jog, which wasn't really fair because Brenda was wearing heels. She declined to break out of her brisk walking pace and allowed Richard to run ahead, around another street corner. Honestly, it wasn't even that much slower a pace, it was just more dignified.

Brenda turned the corner, and that's when she *did* break into a run.

The priest had stopped underneath a street lamp. She was looking across at Richard with a furrowed brow as he jogged towards her, calling her name. The little priest wasn't able to see it, and neither was Richard – without Murzzzz's eyes but a large, grey figure was creeping silently down the street lamp towards Grace.

It wasn't as big or as strong as the Demon that had pulled Janusz into the window, but the thing slithering down the street lamp wasn't a standard ghost. It was too big, and the wrong shape. It twisted around the street lamp like a vine, feeling out with multiple small tendrils. Besides the feelers, it had no discernible shape that could be described as anything other than 'long'... and 'eurgh'. It made Brenda think of slugs and worms, and yet it didn't quite match up with those, either. It wasn't just that this thing had clearly never been a person. This thing had never been 'alive' – not in this world. It was an intruder upon this living universe. It was a Demon, from another plane of reality. Murzzzz had told her about all of this, long ago, and Murzzzz should know.

'Richard!' She waved her arms in warning at him. 'Street light!'

Her husband looked at her, and needed no other message or explanation. Even as he turned back towards the street lamp,

Richard sank into the background and welcomed Murzzzz roaring back into focus.

'Not again,' screamed Grace, and ran.

Brenda hated running and loved her impractical shoes, but she'd be buggered if they were going to spend the whole night repeatedly tracking this priest down, so she kicked off her high heels and sprinted after the fleeing woman. She gave the street light a wide berth as Murzzzz clambered up it to grab the slithering demon. That was Murzzzz's problem now.

The wet street was freezing and painful on her feet, and she very quickly lost both of her pop socks to it, but she kept running after Grace. She may have hated running, but that didn't mean that she wasn't very good at it, after decades of hunting violent restless spirits. Grace reached a fence and dithered, for just about long enough to give Brenda the chance to grab the priest.

'Let me go,' wailed Grace. 'I didn't ask for any of this.'

'You emailed to hire us. You said you were desperate,' Brenda reminded her. 'You absolutely – literally – asked for this.'

Grace pointed a shaking finger at Murzzzz, still wrestling the slug Demon down from the lamp-post. Admittedly, it looked less like a slug now that it had opened a mouth twice as wide as its head, bearing a multitude of long, jagged teeth. 'But not that... *thing*.'

'Murzzzz is an old friend, he just does our security. As you may have noticed, we do need him rather more often than we'd like.'

'The window,' gasped Grace, 'Poor Janusz... He was just an accountant! And now he's... Now I've got an accountant haunting my window!'

'Janusz will be fine,' Brenda told her, still watching Murzzzz's fight with the creature with concern. 'Eventually. Soon, I mean. We hope.'

There was a disgusting, sucking, wet sound, like jelly going down a drain, and the slug-thing was gone. Murzzzz cricked his neck, and was Richard again.

'That scared it,' he announced, happily. 'Grace! Sorry about the fright, but we do say in the contract that clients might witness scenes of an upsetting nature.'

Grace continued to gaze at him in horror. 'You're possessed. Aren't you?'

'That's a really simplistic way of putting it, I prefer to see it as—'

'Oh Lord, you are. You're possessed. Properly possessed, not "Ooh, we're from the olden days and don't understand epilepsy" stuff, you're… that thing you turn into is a Demon, isn't it? Like *The Exorcist*…'

Richard shook his head, mildly. 'I really don't care for that film. It's such a bad representation of the whole experience. So negative.'

Still in Brenda's grip, Grace put her hands to her mouth. 'What do I do? What have I done? What have I brought to Coldbay?'

Richard gave Grace a light pat on the shoulder. 'Honestly, I think Murzzzz is the last of your problems, right now, especially considering what he just saved you from was also a Demon.'

If this was supposed to calm the priest, it only served to have the opposite effect. 'What?' she asked, shakily.

'I think we need to have a nice little chat,' continued Richard, 'lay all our cards on the table, so to speak. Maybe over fish and chips, if you know a good chippie round here?'

As usual, Brenda's husband had forgotten the most important thing. 'And booze,' said Brenda. 'Really a lot of booze. A cocktail bar, perhaps.'

'Um,' said the priest, still shaking, 'that might be a problem on Coldbay.'

Brenda smiled brightly, and tried her usual response to being told she might not be able to visit a cocktail bar. She ignored it.

'Yes,' she said, 'a cocktail bar would be perfect.'

CHAPTER EIGHT

Along the Prom, Prom Prom

Charity didn't actually need the toilet that much, it was more that she needed a few minutes to centre herself and gather her psychic strength. Obviously, she tried for a wee anyway while she was in there – might as well.

Clearances. That was her forte. Her parents told her not to use the term 'exorcisms', but she was pretty sure that was what they were, really. And Charity was the only one with the power to do the actual meat of the job. Brenda and Darryl had the sight, but nobody ever got in touch with the Rooks because they wanted to be told what their ghosts looked like. Clients contacted the Rooks because their kids were talking backwards or their cutlery kept flying at them or their walls were bleeding and they really quite wanted it to stop. That part of it was all down to her. Most of the time, she was completely fine with that. It could take a lot out of her, that was true. She tended to need to carb-load, otherwise she'd get exhausted and faint, but it was all good. All good.

This was a tricky one, though. All those ghosts in one, plus a Demon? She hadn't come up against that before. She was a bit concerned that she'd only got rid of two ghosts so far, the prospect of bringing back her brother-in-law with a ghost and a Demon still floating about didn't exactly fill her with glee.

Bringing people back – now, that was *really* hard. She'd only done it once successfully, so far, and that time she hadn't had all of the extra complications of stray ghosts or her brother freaking out about his husband. It hadn't been her lovely Janusz stuck, that time. OK, she could admit while she was by herself on the toilet, that she was freaking out a teensy bit about that, too. It wasn't usually Janusz who got hurt during sessions. Usually that sort of thing was targeted at Darryl. She was *used* to horrible stuff happening to Darryl. But this was weird, all wrong.

And, it was all on her to fix it. As per bloody usual. She pulled up her pants, did up her fly, squared her shoulders, walked out of the toilet, walked back into the toilet because she still needed to wash her hands, and then strode into the church nave. Darryl was exactly where she'd left him, his hands pressed against the bottom of the window, gazing at the image of Janusz. In the window, the glass Janusz sat miserably on the balmy green hills, his own hand extended out towards Darryl. Flanking him were two goatherds, brows furrowed, fingers pointed and mouths open as if mid-rebuke. The goats seemed pretty put out by Janusz, too.

She gathered and lit some more red candles, to show the remaining spirits that she meant business, and shoved Darryl to one side. She rested her own hands against Janusz's and concentrated on pulling him out of the window. A cold crackle ran over the glass. A good sign – the first of many she'd need to pull this off. She pictured the glass as a thin membrane, like surface tension on water, and focused her mind's eye on the idea of simply pulling Janusz out of a pool. She closed her eyes and etched the image onto the inside of her eyelids.

Fingers… fingers pushing up through the surface of the pool. It's just water, Charity. Just take his fingers and drag him up and out. Up and out, up and out, easy as that…

'Watch out…' Darryl's voice threw her concentration, but she couldn't really complain because even if he hadn't put her off, the heavy, invisible body that threw itself at her seconds later would have done that anyway.

'It's the last of the ghosts,' called Darryl, helplessly.

'Wow, thanks,' she replied, rolling away from the unseen force and ducking her face out of the way of sharp nails that scraped at her from thin air, 'wouldn't have worked that out otherwise.'

'It's another priest,' added Darryl, unhelpfully. 'Actually, I think they're all former St Catherine's priests.'

Priest or not, this ghost had messed up big time. She was already concentrating on a job. She was already juiced up with the psychic whatchamacallits. She shifted her focus swiftly and completely to the ghost that had landed on her, and squeezed at it.

She felt the pressure of the ghost, the space it took up in the living world, for only a moment, and then it vanished suddenly under her psychic will, as simple and satisfying as popping bubble wrap. Three down, one to go. She got up again, dusted down her knees and turned her focus back on to the window. The goatherds looked even more annoyed. Janusz was still crouching, his hand extended, but now the tips of his fingers were poking out of the glass.

'It's working,' cried Darryl, grasping his husband's fingertips.

Yes. Yes, it was working. Admittedly, it was only working to the extent that she'd managed to get less than one per cent of Janusz out of the window so far and now she was going to have to summon all of her strength and start again, but it was working... sort of. Slowly. She slapped Darryl's hand out of the way, laced her fingers with Janusz's, and got back to the painfully slow extraction.

She really hoped her parents would be back with chips soon, like they promised. She was famished.

'Any pub will do, really,' said Brenda. 'Somewhere neutral where we can have a sit down. Doesn't have to be fancy, as long as the staff know how to mix a decent Cosmopolitan.'

They were walking down another dark, foggy street, its quiet stillness unbroken by any passing cars, its few shop fronts shuttered, the windows of the houses dreary and unlit.

'Does everybody get early nights round here?' asked Richard. 'Haven't really seen anybody up and about and it's not even nine o'clock yet.'

'I don't go out in Coldbay much myself,' Grace admitted, 'but probably a lot of these properties are empty. Coldbay's been struggling economically for a while, especially in the winter.' She looked around the street, perturbed. 'This *is* quiet, though. I'm hoping the promenade will be a bit better. That's where The Ship is.'

Brenda frowned. 'And is that literally an abandoned ship, or...?'

'It's a pub,' Grace told her.

Brenda sighed with relief. One never could tell, with weird seaside places like this – especially somewhere that had recorded quite as many freak catastrophes as Coldbay. She already had wet feet and one of her retrieved shoes was now scuffed from when she'd kicked them off to chase the priest earlier. She was not in any mood to clamber around a wrecked boat that would likely be crawling with ghosts.

'Fun fact though, it was actually named after a wrecked ship,' Grace said. 'They built the pub on the site in the sixties.'

Brenda rolled her eyes, faintly. Right, so there would almost certainly be nautical ghosts in there. Oh well, she could probably live with that as long as she could get a G&T.

'How are you doing now?' asked Richard.

'Thirsty,' replied Brenda before realising that he'd been talking to Grace.

'All right, I suppose,' the priest replied. 'Sorry about earlier, I was just... I've had a bit of a day. I thought there was just one ghost, and all of a sudden you said there were three more and they were all over the place, and...'

'Brenda calls them Parasites, don't you dear?'

Brenda nodded briskly. A brown sign directing them to the seafront – and therefore the pub – had just emerged into view through the fog, and given her a new burst of hope. 'It happens occasionally' she said. 'A restless spirit infects a living person and drives the living host to death. Then the newly dead host can't move on and remains infected by the older spirit. It's like a ghost within a ghost. They're very powerful, and difficult to get rid of because the Parasite will split away again as soon as the host is in peril of being popped away. So it's actually perfectly understandable that it's taking us a while to clear your church. If anything, we're doing a much better job than could be expected, under the circumstances.'

Brenda decided to omit how rare Parasites were, not to mention that in the few cases she'd dealt with that involved them, there had only ever been two spirits conjoined – not three and certainly never four. Up until today, she'd assumed that to be impossible. Likely the only reason it *was* possible was that the core Parasite wasn't a spirit, but a Demon. Duncan hadn't just been a ghost within a ghost, but a Demon within a ghost within a ghost within a ghost. The amount of power and control involved in maintaining that must have been extraordinary. And a Demon that powerful was now hiding in the church window… with Janusz.

'So,' continued Grace, cautiously, 'is that what happened to you, Richard? I mean, obviously not exactly what happened. You're not dead… are you…?'

Richard laughed, warmly. 'Certainly not. Murzzzz is different. Murzzzz is… well, there was this accident, you see, long time ago, and yes things were rocky for a while but we ended up making it work. Technically yes – he's a bit Parasitey, but you can get friendly Parasites, can't you?'

'Like probiotics in those fancy yoghurts?' asked Grace.

Richard gave a little nod. 'Yes, a bit like a probiotic yoghurt. If the yoghurt was an impossibly strong ancient being from a realm beyond our mortal understanding.'

Grace looked uneasy about this. 'I suppose the Lord does work in mysterious ways.'

They got to a junction in the road, where the brown sign instructed them to turn right to reach the seafront. The right turn was into a mercifully short street. Only a few metres along, the other end of it opened out onto a promenade, and the dark, misty sea.

'Here we go,' announced Grace, turning with them onto the promenade. 'The jewel of Coldbay.'

The 'jewel' was another long, bleak stretch of tarmac and paving slabs. On one side, the sea lapped against pebbles timidly. On the other, shop fronts stood in an impenetrable, tightly terraced row; dark, locked-up and forbidding. A sign above their heads boasting of 'Ice's, Souvenier's & Sweet's' groaned unnecessarily, considering how slightly the sad little sea breeze was causing it to sway. In the distance, a handful of arcade machines flashed desperately. A little beyond that was a short pier, and in the black, foggy sky above the pier, they could see something was very wrong, very very wrong. Brenda had never seen anything quite so wrong with a sky before. She stood, agog, trying to work out exactly what it might be, except 'massive and bloody terrifying'.

'Dear?' asked Richard, noticing her expression.

'Ah,' said Grace. 'Bother.' She tried the door of a darkened building with a sign outside reading 'The Ship'. It didn't budge. 'Ship's shut too. Sorry about that.'

Brenda couldn't tear her eyes off the sky above the pier. 'Never mind the pub, right now.'

'Bloody Hell,' breathed Richard. 'This must be bad.'

Brenda shakily started walking in the direction of the pier. The mist was clouding her view, but there was definitely something above it. A large swirl, disappearing upwards into… into nothing. Like someone had pulled the plug out of the bathtub of reality and everything was very slowly draining out of it, only upside down.

'You don't see that?'

'The pier?' asked Grace. 'Do you see ghosts on it or something?'

'Dear?' asked Richard again, following Brenda. 'Dear, it's Murzzzz. He's… scared.'

Brenda stopped, and stared at Richard.

'Your Parasite thingie is scared of the pier?' asked Grace, catching up. 'But you're not?'

'Oh, no,' replied Richard, 'if Murzzzz is scared of something, then I'm absolutely terrified. I just don't know what it is we're scared of. What do you see, dearest? What's there?'

Brenda turned back to the distant pier. She could make out the pier itself slightly better now. It was a rather small, modern

75

affair, clearly built on the ashes of something much larger and grander that was now gone. Brenda could make out a charred pavilion further out to sea, jutting out alone and cut off in the black water, as sad and lost as any ghost. Perhaps once that pavilion had shone white and rang with laughter – the cherry on the cake for holidaymakers in bustles and boater hats. Now it was a burnt-out ruin, waiting for the sea to inevitably consume it. Compared to it, the stunted, squat new pier looked like an apology. They were still too far to see if there were any ghosts on the pier or the crumbling pavilion, but Brenda wasn't thinking about that. She gazed in horror at the swirling fog above the pier. She'd never seen anything like it before. It was draining into… nothingness. Not the night sky, not simply darkness, but pure nothing.

'I don't know what it is,' she admitted, 'but I hate it.'

'**Hell Hole**' said Murzzzz, using Richard's mouth, and quickly sank back down into the background.

'Hell Hole,' breathed Brenda.

'It's just a bit run-down and cold,' muttered Grace. 'It's nicer in the summer. Well. A bit nicer.'

'Duncan's blog,' said Brenda. 'He kept using that term. I thought he meant it metaphorically, because, you know, who could blame him? But no. He meant it literally.' She squeezed her husband's hand. She really hated how scared this was making her feel, and with the pub shut and everything as well. 'I think this is a Hell Hole. An actual hole to the other side. Or, other sides – there might be many other planes. That's what's so wrong with Coldbay. It's a supernatural arrivals' terminal.'

'What?' asked Grace, but nobody replied to her.

Richard's expression cycled through various different shades of horror. 'Poor old Reverend Duncan,' he said, eventually. 'He must have been on to it.'

'And so the Parasites tormented him to death,' added Brenda. 'I feel bad for popping him away now, although that's rather your doing, Grace.'

'What?' asked Grace, yet again.

'Frankly, it's a miracle *you're* still alive, considering,' Brenda told her.

'Right,' replied Grace, quietly.

'Do you have any booze at your vicarage or something?' she asked. 'At this point, I'd make do with lager.'

'Um... I have some sherry, I think? Maybe an old bottle of Baileys from last Christmas?'

'That'll do,' announced Brenda, turning on her heel and marching back, away from the pier. 'We're going to need Charity to even begin dealing with this mess.'

'And Charity will need carbs by now,' added Richard.

'I think the chip shop's shut too,' admitted Grace. 'I might have some potato waffles in my freezer?'

'And I refuse to deal with another single moment of this wretched day sober,' continued Brenda. She took a look through the darkened window of the closed pub as she passed it. A miserable, human-shaped smear drifted through the tables within. It looked faintly like a 19th century sailor. Of course, as she'd suspected, it was haunted anyway. Absolutely bloody typical.

CHAPTER NINE

A Distinct Absence of Chips

Charity collapsed, gasping, to the floor. Her limbs felt weak and shaky. Her head pounded. The usual hangover-from-Hell she always experienced when she overstretched her powers. She was desperately in need of carbs and salt. Both nostrils were streaming blood. This was why she always wore dark colours and carried a pack of tissues. She wiped at the blood. Her make-up was running too, with the sweat that was slicking her face. Usually in films when pretty ladies dabbed blood from their faces, the handkerchief didn't come away caked in foundation. What did those films know? Nothing.

'We're getting there,' Darryl told her.

She looked up, and groaned at the slow progress. Janusz was a little under halfway out – his right arm and leg protruded from the window, along with the right side of his torso. The rest of him, including all of his head, was still stuck in the glass. Behind him, the glass goatherds were even more upset than before. One of them was wielding his crook above his head in a very threatening manner.

'I'm running low on psychic juice,' she panted. 'Are you sure there's no crisps or anything in the vestry? At this stage, I'd even settle for pickled onion flavour.'

Darryl shook his head. 'I double-checked, Charity.'

'Can you triple-check?'

Janusz's free hand slapped against the window with a sense of urgency.

'Yes, Janusz, I'm getting you out as fast as I can,' Charity shouted.

His hand hit the window again, pointed off in the general direction of the vestry, clicked his fingers a couple of times and pointed again.

'You want your laptop?' asked Darryl.

The hand did a thumbs down sign.

'Your... bag?' Darryl tried.

Janusz did a thumbs up.

Darryl hurried over to the vestry.

'Janusz, did you pack crisps?'

Janusz's hand twirled a finger around, the universal charades symbol for 'keep going, you're almost there'.

'Peanuts?' asked Charity, hopefully.

A thumbs up.

Charity's eyes lit up. 'Honey roasted peanuts?'

A very bouncy thumbs up.

Darryl emerged from the vestry again, already rooting through Janusz's bag. He threw Charity a large bag of honey roasted peanuts.

'Janusz, you star.' She tore open the packet, and poured a mouthful of nuts straight from the bag, like some parched desert wanderer being handed their first carafe of water in days. 'See, this is why you're my favourite brother,' she added, spitting peanut bits, caramel and salt.

Darryl made no complaint at her statement. He'd stopped doing that, long ago. 'Oh, nice, he packed Capri-Suns, too.'

Charity munched for a moment, wiped the peanut grease and blood from her mouth, grabbed her brother-in-law's hand and foot, and tried again.

She could do it, she told herself.

Yes. She can do it.

She was strong enough.

She is strong enough. There's nothing that Charity can't do.

There was nothing that she couldn't do, she told herself, firmly. She felt the surface tension between the window and the living world diminish under her will, and with a great heave, she pulled Janusz's head and torso fully from the window.

'Janusz,' cried Darryl. 'Keep going, Charity, we're almost there.'

'If you could just shut up and let me concentrate…' muttered Charity.

'Honey, are you OK?' asked Darryl, ignoring her request.

'I'm fine,' managed Janusz. 'A little cold. And those goatherds were *mean*. I don't speak their language but they did not seem happy to see me at all.'

In the window, the goatherd with the crook had brought it down on Janusz's remaining leg.

'Zabko, could you please look up on the translate app what is Aramaic for "Kindly stop hitting me. I don't like this any more than you"? Also, did I hear Richard was getting chips?'

Darryl ran his hand down the back of Janusz's neck, lovingly. 'Yes. I ordered a veggie burger for you.' Janusz nodded approvingly.

There were footsteps and the unmistakable voices of their parents at the main door to the church. Chips! Finally!

'What took you guys so long?' asked Charity, turning.

The sight that greeted her at the door to the church was disappointing to say the least. Yes, her parents had the priest with them, but all three of them had very worried expressions and, crucially, no greasy paper packages of lovely hot chips.

'There's a problem,' Richard told them. 'A really massive problem.' He nodded at his still partially trapped son-in-law, casually. 'Oh, hi, Janusz.'

'A problem with the chips?' asked Janusz, looking downcast.

'A problem,' announced Brenda, 'with the very fabric of reality between the living world and whatever realm lies beyond.

'OK, but how did that affect the chips?' asked Charity.

'Forget about the chips,' snapped Brenda.

'"Forget about the chips"? I've done three ghosts today! Janusz has been stuck in a window all evening! We're starving!'

Grace held up a hand, timidly. 'I can pop next door to the vicarage and stick the oven on, if that's OK?'

'Wait,' said Brenda. 'Three ghosts?'

'Yeah, I did one while you were out *not* getting chips.'

'So where's the last one?' Brenda turned to her son. 'Darryl? Where did the other one go? The... D Word?'

'That's the second time one of you has said "D-Word" in here,' said Grace, with a frown. 'At this point, I think I can guess what that means.'

'OK, clever-clogs, fine,' snapped Brenda. 'There's a Demon in your church. It's probably at the centre of all the hauntings and, from the state of the ghosts, it liked to collect priests. Happy?'

'Not really,' replied Grace. '*I'm* a priest.'

Brenda turned to her son. 'Is it still in the window?'

'I haven't seen it in ages,' Darryl admitted, squinting at the window. 'It sort of faded off into the glass hills, a while ago.'

'It hasn't shown up to try to stop Charity freeing me,' added Janusz. 'Perhaps it's tired, like us…' Janusz trailed off, as Darryl's eyes widened in alarm.

'We spoke too soon,' said Janusz, 'didn't we?'

'It's coming back,' said Darryl, hurriedly. 'See, that's my main reason for using "D-Word" instead of their actual name. Those things listen.'

Charity took that as her cue to get the rest of Janusz out of the window. She grabbed his arm with both hands and pulled. He slipped out relatively easy for a few inches, and then suddenly stopped.

'O kurcze!' Janusz exclaimed.

There was a tug from inside the window. Janusz was yanked slightly backwards.

'It's got me again.'

Charity's head was throbbing, and her nose had started dribbling blood again. This really was too much. After all her hard work!

'Oh no you *don't*,' she seethed. 'You are *not* sending me back to square one!' She pushed all her frustration and pain into a little ball in her chest, and added it to her psychic strength, focusing it at the window. Blood had started to pool in her mouth, behind her gritted teeth. 'I haven't even had any dinner!'

She heaved, and felt something give way, something big. Like pulling a huge weed up right from the root. Janusz fell from the window completely, landing in a shivering heap on the church floor and… something else came out with him. Even Charity could just about see it – a writhing shadow, with four limbs. The same basic shape as Murzzzz.

'Charity,' shouted Darryl and Brenda at the same time, but Charity was exhausted. She could barely prop herself up. Her head pounded, like something with sandpaper for hands was thumping her behind the eyes. She spat out a vile mixture of phlegm and nose-blood. See, she told herself, this was what happened when she was expected to do a full day of hard psychic graft on nothing but a couple of Polish Jaffa cakes and a single bag of honey roast peanuts. This was why, when one was a ghostbuster, one's family really should take the promise of chips more seriously.

'Charity,' cried Brenda and Darryl again, their eyes following the shadow as it slunk over to where Grace was standing.

Charity tried to get up, but found that she couldn't. She was officially out of juice. The shadow was almost on Grace. Murzzzz moved fast, slipping fluidly into focus, bounding on all fours up a column, along the ceiling and down onto the shadow, all within a single second.

'**Get out**,' roared Murzzzz, wrestling the thing. '**Get out before I tear out your grzlxx!! That was our accountant, Hfhfh!! How dare you?**'

A new sound echoed around the church nave – not the voice of Murzzzz, but a new, terrible voice. Dry and ancient as a mummy's bandage. It laughed, horribly.

'**We're surprised you haven't tried to run away again, Murzzzz,**' said the voice. '**You've seen the door. Too late now. Nothing can stop— ow, get off my grzlxx!**'

Murzzzz snarled, clawing his jagged nails into the shadow. '**I *said* I'd tear it out! Begone!**'

'**Pathetic,**' sneered the brittle, primeval voice. There was another horrible laugh, and the shadow moved again, impossibly fast, out of the main church door, its laugh disappearing into the damp night. Murzzzz chased after it, watched from the door to check that it was gone, then slumped, shrank, and became Richard once more.

Well. All of that was new. Charity had never heard a Demon's voice before, besides Murzzzz's. Neither before had she heard Murzzzz refer to another Demon by its name. She assumed 'Hfhfh' was a name. From the way Murzzzz had said it, it could have been a swear word though.

Charity spat out some more blood. She was trembling and still unable to get up. The church was a mess of upended pews, toppled candlesticks, spilt wax and peanuts. Darryl was hunched next to a similarly exhausted-looking Janusz, trying to rub warmth back into his arms. The goatherds in the window still looked pretty unhappy. In the middle of the nave, Grace stood rooted to the spot, looking at where Murzzzz had only just been. The priest emitted a quiet little whine of fear before forcing herself to stop.

'Well,' said Brenda, 'that's your church cleared at least. You're welcome. Now, you said something about sherry…?'

The Clergy House was much nicer than the church and its vestry. A modest Victorian build, it stood just next door to St Catherine's. It should have had that vague chill that small detached houses often get but, compared to the church, it was warm and comforting. The big radiators in Grace's living room were already on when they got in, and Darryl sat Janusz on one end of a soft, elderly sofa in as cosy a spot as he could find, covering his husband in a colourful, rag-woven throw that Darryl suspected Grace had bought from a fair trade initiative somewhere.

'A widow in Eritrea handmade that, I think,' said Grace, vaguely, before going through to the bright kitchen.

Brenda wandered around the living room, picking up trinkets with an expression suggesting she was both silently judging everything and on the lookout for a promisingly full bottle.

'Nice place,' she conceded, 'mercifully free of ghost residue, considering. Did you never get any trouble in here?'

'Not here,' called Grace from the kitchen. 'Seems like poor Duncan only lingered at the church.'

'If it was me, I would have rather stayed here after death,' said Janusz in a quiet, shaky voice. 'The church had too many ghosts.' He thought about this. 'I mean, if *I* haunted here then there would also be a ghost in this place, but it would only be me and I could do my haunting quietly.' He looked at Darryl with the face he always made when he couldn't quite find the right English words and knew that Darryl had no chance of understanding the Polish. 'From his blog, Duncan seemed to like peace and quiet.'

'Well, that Demon had other plans,' replied Brenda, 'for him and the other ghosts... oh.' She called out to Grace. 'Are there any photos of the priests from before Duncan?'

'In my office,' called Grace from the kitchen. 'Well... I call it my office. The desk by the coat hooks.'

Brenda went to check the desk. Charity turned to her dad. 'Did Murzzzz like... know that Demon's name?'

'Yeah,' said Richard, softly. 'And he's not telling me why.'

Brenda flicked through the handful of ledger folders next to the computer and gave an 'ah-ha' of triumph. She showed Darryl a couple of old photos of previous parish priests – one from around the mid-eighties and one maybe from the sixties, perhaps a bit earlier. Darryl recognised both as the other two ghosts. He didn't feel particularly triumphant about it. Not just one life, but three, dedicated to helping their community but ending up tormented, miserable and angry, trapped in the building they'd wanted such marvellous things for but helplessly driving people away and filling it with fear.

Darryl took out his phone to look at Duncan's blog again. The sadness of it all was too much – watching a man's gradual descent, frozen in time and being too late to help. He decided to look instead at the local paper's online archive, or at least what he could see of it between all of the pop up adverts for payday loans and uPVC conservatories.

'Can Murzzzz at least tell you what that Hfhfh thing meant about the door?' added Charity, taking up a ridiculous amount of the rest of the sofa and putting her feet up on Darryl's legs.

'Ah,' replied Richard, 'yes. So we come to the crux of the problem…'

Darryl was only half listening, through the swirling thoughts of what had happened to Duncan, what might have happened to Janusz had they not freed him quickly, and how to get rid of the massive ad telling him he'd won an Audi without accidentally clicking through to an extremely dodgy website. The news archive itself was quite the litany of misery. Freak death after freak death. It seemed even worse than Grace had made it initially sound. Surprising levels of violence for such a small community. A ridiculous number of fires. Coldbay really did seem like quite the—

'Hell Hole,' came his mother's voice, cutting through the thoughts.

'Mm,' muttered Darryl in agreement, scanning the website.

'Duncan used this term also,' said Janusz. 'It's… a figure of speech, right? Meaning "crappy town"?'

'No, love.' Brenda gazed across at Janusz's confused frown. 'Well… usually, but not in this case. This time I mean it literally. It's a hole. A hole in the sky above the pier. To Hell, probably, or at least to the realms beyond, who's to say whether that's Hell or purgatory or something else, but I've seen it and I hate it.'

'What?'

'I said what I said. Where is the sherry? I was promised sherry!'

'A hole to Hell?' asked Charity. 'That's bonkers.'

'Princess, you're a ghostbuster. Your brother and I are clairvoyants and your father has a Demon inside him. We don't get to say a hole in the sky is "bonkers".'

'Fair enough,' replied Charity.

'Over the pier,' muttered Darryl. He continued to scroll through the website. A considerable number of the mysterious incidents had occurred on the pier. He clicked on one story, with a large photo of the pier in question. It didn't seem particularly ominous, at first sight. It had clearly been recently rebuilt, and strings of little lights had been hung all over the place in an attempt to cheer it up a bit. There was a tea room, a bar and a couple of little rides for young children, and… and a dark smudge, above it. Something that could possibly be mistaken for a cloud by those who didn't have Darryl's eye for all things other-worldly and terrible. He held the phone out to his mother.

'This it?'

Brenda peered at it. 'What I saw was a lot more advanced than that. When's that from?'

Darryl looked at the story. The headline read:

FURTHER PROBLEMS FOR PIER AFTER DEATH PLUNGE ACCIDENT DASHES HOPES OF FRESH START

'This is from 2017,' read Darryl. 'But there's a load of stuff here about incidents that took place earlier, ever since the pier was rebuilt and reopened in…' he trailed off, aware of what was coming next.

'Let me guess,' said his mother, '2016?'

Darryl nodded.

'It's *always* 2016!' Brenda threw her hands into the air in exasperation. 'That year was cursed!'

Janusz opened his mouth. 'Besides your wedding, Janusz, that was a ray of sunshine in the storm of shit.' Janusz closed his mouth again, satisfied with Brenda's caveat. 'I might have known 2016 would be the start of all this.'

'Actually,' said Grace, coming through from the kitchen with a plate of sandwiches, 'it might not have been the start. Um. Not that I'm going against what you say about 2016 being awful – I was sad about Alan Rickman too. But there were problems with the pier long before. If you go further back on the website, you'll see. There were several aborted attempts to fix it. Local rumour was that things had actually all started to go wrong with the fire of '99.'

Darryl searched it up and found an archived news story.

THREE DEAD IN PIER INFERNO
Manager amongst casualties; Police suspect insurance scam gone awry

'July 1999,' muttered Darryl. 'Why does that ring a bell? Hey Mum, what did we do that summer?'

'Nothing,' replied Brenda, briskly. She turned to Grace. 'Did you say there was Baileys or something?'

'Oh! Yes.' Grace put the plate of sandwiches down in front of Charity, who practically inhaled two immediately. 'And, the oven's on.'

'So, we're sticking around,' sighed Janusz.

'I think we have to, sonny,' Richard said. 'We can't just leave a Hell Hole. It'll just grow, and grow and everything will get worse, until… well, until I don't know what, but it's got Murzzzz worried.'

'But Murzzzz never worries,' said Janusz.

'I know, so it must be really bad.'

Janusz groaned, reaching for his still mercifully intact laptop. 'You know what this means?'

'I'm a little bit worried it means the gates of Hell are swinging open and all the devils are scampering over here. And we may be the only ones in any position to even try to stop it,' said Brenda.

'It means,' replied Janusz, jabbing at the keyboard, 'that I need to cancel the Aldwych booking. Possibly Swansea, too. They will not be happy.'

'You can stay here, with me,' Grace told them with a forced air of cheeriness. 'This is a three bed, and I can sleep on the sofa. And did I say, I've already popped the oven on? So it's not all bad.'

'We'll have to give them back their deposits and everything,' grumbled Janusz.

'I found croquettes in the freezer,' continued Grace, 'and those potato shapes like smiley faces, and some sausages.'

'Oh,' interjected Darryl, 'um. Do you have veggie burgers? For me and Janusz.'

'Or macaroni cheese?' added Janusz. 'We like macaroni cheese, don't we?'

'Sorry about them.' said Charity through a third sandwich. 'They're still doing the vegetarian thing'.

'Right,' sighed Grace.

'And,' said Brenda, 'I do believe you've forgotten the sherry. Again.'

CHAPTER TEN

A Little Bit Psychic

There was an almost full bottle of Baileys after all, and by the time Brenda was done with that, the rest of the family decided it would probably be better if they spent the night at the Clergy House and started the wider investigation of Coldbay in the morning. After a comfortable night, and a less comfortable queue for the one bathroom, the family headed out with Grace into the cold grey streets, towards the even colder, even greyer pier.

'There's a pub here that's haunted by a sailor,' noted Brenda casually as they turned onto the promenade. 'Do you see it, Darryl?'

Darryl glanced in through the window. 'So there is.'

'I could get rid of it, if you like?' asked Charity.

'No, love,' replied her mother, 'save your energy.' She pointed over at the pier, to where absolute darkness swirled.

This wasn't the sort of abyss that would stare back if you dared to stare into it. This was the sort of abyss that, if you tried to stare into it, would snarl 'What are *you* looking at?' in infinite otherworldly voices before slashing you across the face with the broken glass bottle of reality.

'Yikes,' said Darryl, understating the situation a bit.

'Yeah,' added Charity, 'yikes. Even I can kind of see that thing.' She turned to Richard. 'Dad, how's Murzzzz feeling about it in the cold light of day?'

'Really not great,' admitted Richard.

'The fire in '99 started a few buildings along from the new pier,' Grace told them. 'I'll take you to the spot. It's a pizza place now, or at least it is during the summer.'

'Do people not also want pizza during the winter?' asked Janusz. He looked around at the closed shops and the empty promenade. The only sounds were their own feet, the waves crashing on the pebbles and a vicious gang of seagulls. 'Is this a bit weird? It feels weird, even for off season. So quiet. Is it a British thing? Because—'

'Here we are,' announced Grace, suddenly. 'Inferno Pizza. I know – poor taste. But what are you going to do?'

Like everywhere else, Inferno Pizza was closed and locked up, although a quick burst of Murzzzz's strength dealt with the locks swiftly enough. They pushed the shutters up and went inside.

'So, this place was...' began Darryl.

'In the nineties, it was the pier manager's office,' replied Grace. 'Where the fire started.'

'Got a bit out of hand,' muttered another female voice, 'that's all.'

Darryl and Brenda looked at one another.

'Who's there?' asked Brenda.

'Who's there?' echoed the voice. It didn't sound like a voice that had been left to languish, lost and angry over centuries like so many of the dead tended to do – it sounded almost personable.

Darryl saw her first. At the back of the pizza parlour. Her bright clothes sort of melded in with the mural of dancing pizza slices on the wall. She was in her forties, wearing a trouser suit, her hair only a little unkempt and singed.

'Hello?' said Darryl, gently. 'We're looking for… um…'

He gazed at Grace, helplessly, with no idea what the name of the woman might be. Grace hurriedly consulted her phone. After an overly long, awkward pause, the priest brought up a relevant news story. The black and white photo of a businesswoman matched the image of the woman whose red shirt was seamlessly blending in with a cartoon tomato.

'Melanie Ellis?'

It was always a good sign to see that spark of recognition in a ghost at hearing their own name. It meant that they weren't too far gone yet. They still had reason. They still had a sense of self. It meant that they would be easier to deal with; easier to help. It also meant that they could be communicated with – sometimes they could impart useful information.

There was that spark in Melanie Ellis's eyes. Her expression became at once sharpened by focus and also softened by relief. She looked like someone who had been worried she was getting lost and suddenly saw a familiar marker.

'Speaking,' replied Melanie, and walked forwards. Her feet retained the memory of there being an empty floor there. When the building burned-down and she had died there had never been a pizza counter on it. She passed straight through it like it didn't exist. To Melanie, this was still a smart nineties office building. If Darryl concentrated, he could just about make out the ghost noises of a cordless phone and a fax machine.

'Darryl?' asked Charity.

Darryl's mum Brenda met eyes with her son, briefly, sharing his relief that this one at least remembered her name.

'I'm Brenda Rook, this is my son Darryl.'

Melanie held out her hand to shake, but nobody reciprocated. Obviously – it was always upsetting for everyone involved when you went through a ghost. Melanie furrowed her brow at the apparent snub.

'How are you, Melanie?' asked Brenda.

'I think...' muttered Melanie, looking down at her hand, 'I might be... dead?'

'Darryl,' said Janusz, quietly.

Darryl nodded sympathetically at Melanie. Sometimes ghosts would fly into a self-pitying rage at this, but Melanie just nodded along with him.

'Thought I might be,' Melanie continued. 'You see, I have a gift, I'm a little bit psychic...'

Brenda rolled her eyes. When one has spent one's whole life with restless spirits wailing and clawing and generally making one's life a living Hell, one might be forgiven for having absolutely no time for people who claim to be 'a little bit psychic' just because they owned a deck of tarot cards and a couple of crystals. Even if that person was currently dead themselves. Still, a dead charlatan couldn't poach clients simply by being 'more personable' and 'less drunk' and then do absolutely sod all to actually get rid of a ghost thus bringing the profession into disrepute – unlike *certain* still-living mediums she could mention... like that fraud, Aurora Tavistock. Still, the principle stood.

'Darryl,' said Charity again. 'Why are you doing that? And how? But mostly, why?'

'Why am I doing what?'

'Replying to yourself and Mum in a lady voice.'

Brenda frowned in confusion at Darryl. He wasn't doing a 'lady voice'. They were talking to Melanie as normally as they would speak to any one of the more grounded, self-aware ghosts.

'You said "Speaking",' Janusz told his husband, his handsomeness creased with concern, 'and then asked if you were dead. All in a lady voice.'

Darryl blinked at this information. 'I'm… channelling her?'

Brenda turned to Melanie. 'Say "Popocatepetl".'

'Popocatepetl,' said Melanie, dutifully.

'*You* just said Popocatepetl,' Grace told Darryl, 'in the lady voice.'

'You *must* be channelling her,' said Richard, 'well done, son, you've never managed that before.'

'Thanks,' replied Darryl, quietly.

'I want to say "Popocatepetl" too,' said Charity. 'Popocatepetl!'

'And after all those years and years of trying and failing to channel spirits,' added Richard, cheerfully. 'Didn't I say it'd come to you eventually?'

'Yes, OK, thanks Dad.'

'See?' said Melanie, brightly. 'Psychic. I must be projecting my aura, I used to practice doing that when I was alive, with my crystals.'

'Crystals,' sighed Brenda, dismissively.

'We were hoping you might be able to help us,' said Darryl, over his mother.

'I take it you're mediums too?' asked Melanie, excitedly, looking around at the group. 'And you've brought a lady vicar!' The ghost made a victory sign at Grace. 'Girl power!'

Charity snorted. 'Darryl, if you could see yourself…'

'Thanks,' replied Grace, weakly, addressing Darryl rather than the ghost at his side. 'Um. We were wondering if you could tell us about the fire…?'

'So are you like a travelling vicar, or…?'

'No, I'm at St Catherine's.'

'Oh!' Melanie blinked. 'So Reverend Duncan retired? How long have I *been* here?'

'He didn't retire. Things went... bad. We were wondering if maybe it had something to do with the fire—'

'Poor Duncan,' interrupted Melanie. 'Although you know, there was a shadow over him. I could tell, there was something up with that church. You know the priest before him died there? And the...' Melanie flickered and faded a little, her expression became clouded with a troublesome memory. 'The...'

'Was there something wrong with your office, as well, Melanie?' asked Brenda, sharply. 'Maybe there was something wrong with the pier as a whole. Is that why you took action? Why don't you tell us about the fire?'

Melanie blinked, and stared at Brenda. 'Poor you,' she said.

'What?' asked Brenda.

'You have the gift, don't you?' Melanie replied. 'Only... it's different to how people like me have it.'

'Yes, it's different.' Because she actually *had* the gift and wasn't just some chancer who used words like 'spiritual' and 'healing energies', Brenda added silently.

'It's too much,' continued Melanie. 'Much too much. I see... a little girl, scared, she doesn't know why all her imaginary friends are so noisy and angry.'

Brenda looked as if Melanie had just slapped her across the face. OK. So maybe Melanie *was* a little bit psychic. Or maybe it was a ghost thing. Maybe it was a Hell Hole proximity thing. Maybe it was a combination of the three. Whatever it was, Brenda hated it. 'You'll shut your dead mouth.'

'Dear,' said Richard, gently.

'Oh,' breathed Melanie, turning her attention to Richard. 'What's *this*?'

'**Nothing.**' replied Murzzzz, automatically, before Richard was able to slap his hand over his mouth.

'What this is,' snapped Brenda, 'is the Rook family. And if you truly are "a little bit psychic" as you claim, you will know that we are *the* number one psychic cleansers in the country, if not the world. You have a Hell Hole not two hundred yards away. It was probably started when you immolated your business and yourself more than twenty years ago. We're here to fix your mess and we need you to tell us what drove you to do it, because there are weird spirits on this bloody island, and everything is wrong. Oh, and nobody does the "girl power" thing any more, so stop embarrassing yourself and tell us what we need to know so that my daughter can move you along to somewhere that isn't a sad, boarded-up pizza shop.'

Melanie stared at Brenda, then at Charity. 'One of *those*,' she whispered, and paused, briefly. 'That's your daughter?'

'Adopted,' said Charity, automatically, 'like Harry Potter.'

'I don't know who that is,' said Melanie, 'but how… fortunate, for your parents. How did you come to be orphaned?'

'Ew, you don't ask adopted people that,' replied Charity. 'You just assume it's a tragic superhero backstory and move on. Nineties people are *rude*.'

'Your skill,' continued Melanie, 'is very useful to the Rook family, isn't it? You don't wonder where it's from?'

'I am like,' repeated Charity, in a loud, clear voice, as if trying to order ham, egg and chips in English at a Spanish Bistro, 'Harry Potter.'

'It was passed to you' said Melanie, quietly. 'Through the bloodline.'

A mention! A spark! How thrilling! And for a moment, at least two of them are thinking about me – my face. Oh, it's like warm sun

beaming through a gap in the clouds. Invigorating and comforting.
A brightness. Colour. Charity twirls her streak of silver hair around
her finger, and thinks of orphaned heroes in terms of their onward
journeys rather than what they leave behind. The moment passes. The
shaft of sunlight on my face fades. It was so beautiful, while it lasted.

'Hereditary.' Melanie nodded at Darryl. 'With you, too. You're a
little like your mum, aren't you? A bit more haphazard, though.
A sponge, soaking up bits and bobs.' She thought, then added,
brightly, 'Like a paper towel.'

'Just tell us why you set fire to yourself, you annoying
woman,' sighed Brenda.

'Bits and bobs. Why haven't you told him about the Demon?'
asked Melanie.

'We all know about Murzzzz,' Darryl replied, 'he's part of
the family.'

'Ha!' barked Melanie, and there was something wrong about
the 'ha'. Something that wasn't quite Melanie.

'Tell us about the fire,' said Brenda, her voice raised. 'Your
name is Melanie Ellis. You threw your life into your work –
no partner, no family – you put everything you had into your
business and then you just burnt it down, and didn't even
bother getting out of the way of the fire.'

'"Part of the family",' sneered Melanie.

'I think we should leave,' said Richard.

'Why?' Brenda shouted. 'Why did you do it, Melanie? Was
it a failure? This business you'd thrown everything into? Was it
this island? Did the misery of it eat you up? Were there voices,
telling you to do it? Was there a darkness, like you felt at the
church? Reverend Duncan didn't have a peaceful end, you
know, not at all, he was plagued by the spirits that infest this
place, by a Demon—'

Melanie laughed. 'Funny you should say that.'

'**We should leave,**' said Murzzzz.

'Tell us why you did it!'

'He doesn't know,' replied Melanie, staring at Darryl, 'does he?'

'None of us know why you set fire to your business,' said Brenda, 'that's why we're asking you. The papers said it was an insurance fraud gone wrong. That's right, that's your legacy – everyone assumed you were a failure and a crook – an incompetent crook at that. Now, is that the truth or did something else happen?'

Darryl couldn't tear his eyes from Melanie. She smiled back at him, not rising to his mother's barbs.

'Ask your parents,' Melanie said, 'about the birds and the bees and the Parasites.'

'What?'

'"Part of the family",' muttered the ghost, 'and for how long? And if he's always there... how many fathers do you actually have?'

Darryl turned and stared at his mum and dad. He did not care for their expressions. 'What?' he asked, again.

Melanie turned her attention back to Brenda, with a polite, business-like smile. 'I set the fire because the time to set the fire had come. I was informed as such by several outside forces.'

Brenda didn't reply. She was still staring at Darryl, opening and closing her mouth, silently. After a moment, Janusz came forward, jotting everything down in a notebook.

'"Outside forces" as in, from outside the island or outside the living world?' he queried.

'The latter,' replied Melanie, briskly. 'It was in my tarot cards, my horoscope, everything. The figure in the church window. He would whisper to me about it, when I went to see poor

Duncan. I can still hear him now. A bit of him is staying with me while I wait. Keeping me sane.'

'No,' breathed Richard.

'Besides, it was prophesied, and the sun went dark, didn't it?' She smiled at Janusz. 'You're not like the others are you, my lovely, what are you doing here?'

'I do accounts,' replied Janusz, politely. 'And I'm married to this one.' He rubbed Darryl's shoulder. Darryl was still staring incredulously at his parents.

'Aww, that's nice,' replied Melanie. She did the victory sign with her fingers again. 'Gay power.'

'What does she mean?' asked Darryl.

'Sounds like,' said Grace, 'she means there's been something malevolent on this island for more than twenty years, hiding in my church window, making people... do things, creating destruction and misery. Those poor souls.'

'What does she mean, "the birds, the bees and the Parasites"?' Darryl asked his parents. 'What does she mean about how many fathers I have? Mum? Dad?' He paused. 'M... Murzzzz...?'

'We thought...' Richard trailed off and started again. 'We felt like you might work it out for yourself, and then as you grew up and the penny never seemed to drop, we started to feel like it was a "does it even really matter?" sort of thing.'

'Does *what* really matter?' Darryl stared at his parents, aghast. 'Work what out?'

'Well,' said Richard, gently, 'you know Murzzzz has been with me since the seventies.'

Darryl nodded. 'House clearance gone wrong, back when you were young.'

'And obviously you were born a long time after that, son,' added Richard, 'and, well...'

'It's not like you were born with a tail or anything,' blurted Brenda.

'What??'

'Not that we were expecting you to be born with a tail or anything,' added Richard, hurriedly.

'Are… you telling me,' managed Darryl, by now completely ignoring the smirking ghost by his side, 'I'm not your son? That I'm… *His*?'

'Not necessarily,' replied Richard, hurriedly. 'I'm saying… we don't know for sure.'

'Fuuu…'

'We're saying, you were conceived out of love…'

'…uuu…'

'And that I was present for that…'

'…uuu…'

'But, so was he.'

'…uuucccKKKKK.'

'Because he and I do everything together, son, you know that.' Richard paused. 'I hope this isn't going to be a problem, son.'

'How could this possibly not be a problem??'

'I thought you *liked* Murzzzz.'

'Yeah, as an inbuilt security officer, not as a surprise Demon parent!'

'Well, now you've hurt his feelings, son. He didn't want me to say so but I thought it best that you knew.'

'I don't care!'

'Zabko,' said Janusz, quietly, squeezing Darryl's shoulder again.

'No "zabko". Not right now.' Darryl shook his husband's hand off.

'It changes nothing, my love,' said Janusz, undeterred. 'If it's always been, it's always been.'

'I just… I need a minute, OK?'

Darryl turned and walked out of the pizza place. He walked through the shutters that the Demon Murzzzz had ripped open with inhuman hands, and for the first time in a very long while, it bothered Darryl to think about how one of them, one of his family, had the power to do that.

'Oh no you don't,' announced Brenda, 'you're not going out on your own, not with the weather outside all Hell Holey.'

She grabbed Richard and followed Darryl out.

Grace, Janusz and Charity looked at one another for a moment. Janusz glanced down at his notes.

'I wonder what Miss Ellis meant about a prophecy.'

'We should look into that,' replied Grace. 'And what was that she said about the sun?'

'We should go after them,' said Charity at the same time, looking across at the smashed shutters. 'Not much more we can do here. Can't even get a pizza.'

'That's another thing,' said Janusz as they left. 'Why is *everything* shut? I haven't seen another person here this morning, not even delivery drivers or postmen or bin men…'

And then Melanie was left again, to drift aimlessly against pictures of cheese and pepperoni, imagining the squeal of an incoming fax or the quiet clack of a word processor.

Why had she set the fire? Had it even been *her*, really? The island. The island had needed it to happen. The figure in the window had said. And then the sun had gone dark, and she'd known it was time. The prophecy. From the East Midlands would come a great terror. It had been written. It had been preordained. It's not like she could help it. She was just attuned to the inevitability of the universe, that was just her. A little bit spiritual. A little bit psychic.

CHAPTER ELEVEN

1999 And All That

*I*n the end, Melanie Ellis wasn't actually all that psychic. Not compared to the Rooks and not compared to many others, in fact. Not compared to other ghost-hunters and Demon-hunters that had gone before. I'll leave her to drift around the sad little pizza place that used to be her whole world and let her think that she's an important piece in the puzzle. It's the least I can do for her now that she's lost everything. Now that she's dead.

But here's a little secret, from me to you – she was only ever a small cog in all of this. And it doesn't seem fair, I know. She was valid. She had a rich, full forty-something years. She was loved, she was intelligent and driven and she built up a business at a time when it was harder for a woman to do so. But life, and the universe, are not fair. I learned that, the hard way.

Yes, she really wasn't that psychic. She was very good at one thing without even having to think about it, though. And she demonstrated it not long ago. Melanie Ellis was very good at burying the lede. So when information came flooding through her from another voice, using her as a conduit as it had used so many *before her, she was able to plant the more important seed subtly, and cover it up with less important, but noisier information.*

What makes me so sure that one piece of her information was more important than the others?

Because it was about me.

Darryl sat on a bench on the empty promenade and tried to ignore how the bench was sodden wet and freezing cold, and that right behind him up in the sky above the pier was a swirling chasm to nowhere.

His father – if Richard *was* his father – sat down next to him, quietly complaining about the bench giving him a wet bum. His mother opted not to sit, rather she loomed in front of him, arms folded, her attention largely grabbed by the hole in the sky.

'I'm sure that's bigger than it was half an hour ago,' she muttered.

'So,' said Darryl, 'I might be part Demon.'

'*Might* be,' his father said, gently. 'It doesn't make any difference though, does it, at the end of the day? I mean, do you *feel* part Demon?'

'Why don't you guys ever tell me about my birth parents?' asked Charity, walking up to the drenched bench.

'Because *we're* your parents, princess,' Richard told her. 'We're parents to both of you, in every way that matters and nothing's going to change that, OK?'

'Do you know what happened to them?' asked Charity. 'I mean, if I *do* have a secret tragic backstory, maybe I should know about it.'

'For crying out loud, Charity,' said Darryl, 'your life is not a Marvel movie.'

'OK, but it kind of is. I have uncanny powers… did I inherit them, like Darryl inherited his clairvoyance and tail?'

103

'I do not have a tail!'

'He doesn't have a tail, Charity,' Janusz added. 'I've looked.'

'Ew.'

Janusz shrugged. 'You started the talking about my husband's bum.'

'That's my brother's bum!'

'Then don't talk about it.'

'Ha!' shouted Grace, at her phone.

'Pardon?'

'Melanie,' said Grace. 'She talked about a prophesy, and the sun going dark. '99!'

'I don't—' began Richard.

Grace waved her phone in his face. '1999, the year people kept thinking the world would end.'

'Y2K,' said Janusz, nodding sagely. 'My father was part of the team making sure Y2K didn't happen. Very good IT technician. Terrible father.'

'Not that,' said Grace, 'well, yes that, I'm sure people like your dad did amazing work preventing that calamity and do pass on my thanks to him…'

'We no longer speak, so.'

'Oh, I'm sorry about that.'

'Do not be.'

'OK.' Grace tried to get herself back on track. 'So it wasn't just Y2K, there was a big solar eclipse in the summer. July 1999 was when Nostradamus… well, he didn't say the world would end then as such, but he wrote about a "great terror" and some people interpreted that as the start of the end of the world, and… look, just generally people were pretty doomy in 1999, even though looking back on it there wasn't actually that much practically to be doomy about.'

'Except Y2K,' said Janusz, quietly. 'That was real.'

'Yes, but I'm speaking metaphysically.'

'Metaphysically, yes' said Brenda. 'Yes, the spirits were really on edge, that year.'

'*That's* why 1999 rings a bell,' realised Darryl. 'That was the year you got me and Charity to start working. Pulled us out of school.'

'Hell Year was that long ago?' Charity asked. 'Blimey. Time flies, right?

'"Hell Year"?' asked Grace.

'It was relentless,' replied Charity. 'Darryl had to do all his GCSEs a year late as a result. *And* he only got Cs and Ds.'

'Why would you bring that up?' breathed Darryl.

'Maybe if you'd accessed your Demon powers you could have done better at French.'

'I am not a Demon!'

'What if it sparked something?' asked Grace. 'What if there are significant years? Catalyst years?'

'2016,' muttered Brenda. 'It was cursed, I tell you. Maybe 1999 only feels less cursed in retrospect because it wasn't 2016.'

'So, the year the old pier burned down, and the year the new pier tried to open and had all those problems,' said Grace. 'What if there's been something here for ages, but... I don't know, it's been growing, and the catalyst years change it up a gear or something, give it more power?'

'The focus points,' murmured Richard.

'What was that, dear?' asked Brenda.

'Focus points,' repeated Richard. 'He says, that rings a bell.'

'Ugh,' grunted Darryl. 'I don't really want to hear from Murzzzz, right now.'

'OK, but this is the first I'm hearing about "focus points",' said Richard, only half to the others. 'If this is another... well, of course it's relevant, Murzzzz!'

'Oh good,' huffed Brenda. 'They've decided to have a row.'

Charity and Janusz both sighed, wearily.

'Do we have to find somewhere to lock them up?' Charity asked.

'Possibly.' Brenda turned to Grace. 'Do you have a cage or a padlocked cellar or something?'

Grace's eyes widened with alarm. 'Not on me. Why would I have something like that? Why would you *need* something like that?'

Brenda waved a hand at Richard, who was still muttering to himself. 'Really not fun when these two have a quarrel. It usually descends into skittering around the ceiling and screaming in backwards Latin. Nobody wants to bear witness to that. Messy business.'

'We don't need locking up!' snarled a Richard who wasn't quite completely Richard. '**We can keep this civil**… we *will* keep this civil, and you will tell me everything you know about focus points and why you chose to keep that information from us until now… We did *not* 'keep it from him', Murzzzz, we just said we wanted him to work it out… And you agreed! Well, of course he's not happy about it right now. It's come as a shock! Of *course* I stood up for you, Murzzzz, you *heard* me sticking up for you… I don't know what else you want!' Richard got up, suddenly, seemingly propelled to his feet by some powerful, unseen hand. 'Yes, well *my* bottom was getting damp too, but I was sitting there to talk to *my* son, and if you don't like it, Murzzzz, well then… well then you know what you can jolly well do about it!'

'And now it's this, again,' groaned Brenda. 'You two are not going to split up, you never do.'

'They're talking about splitting up?' Grace hugged her phone to herself. 'All I did was say 1999 was a bit doomier than usual and suddenly people are splitting up?'

'They're all talk,' snorted Brenda.

'I don't care if they *do* split up,' grumbled Darryl, quietly.

'Yeah,' added Charity, 'probably doesn't matter that much now that we've got a half Demon of our own on board—'

'IamnotaDemon!!'

Brenda closed her eyes and rubbed the bridge of her nose. 'Whatever. I mean, you all know that right in front of a Hell Hole probably isn't the best place to have loud arguments about supernatural focus points and who is and isn't a Demon? You're all adults, after all. All I know is, it's been a bastard of a day.'

Grace frowned, and checked the time on her phone. 'It's five to eleven in the morning.'

'And thus far, it has been, as I mentioned, a bastard of a day. It's certainly far too early for family histrionics in a public space.'

Janusz held up a hand. 'But, as I keep saying, it's not really public. Nobody else is here.'

'I don't care!' Brenda cried. 'I do not. Care. I am cold, and wet, and tired. And I need a drink and all the Baileys at Grace's house has gone, and the pub is shut and haunted, so what on earth am I supposed to do, eh?' She glared at the others, before turning her attention to Grace.

'Not an entirely rhetorical question there, Reverend.'

'Oh!' said Grace. 'Well, I wouldn't recommend it, given the circumstances—'

'Don't care.'

'There *is* a Tesco just down Charles Street.' Grace pointed to a wide street intersecting with the promenade at the other end. 'But since no other shops here seem to be open right now…'

'It's a Tesco,' announced Brenda, clopping in the direction of Charles Street. 'They're always open. Even at the end of the world.'

'The what?' called Grace. 'This isn't… I mean it's bad, but you don't think this is the end of the world, surely?'

'I don't know,' shouted Brenda. 'Maybe. If it is, I'm too sober by half.'

Grace watched her go, and shook her head. 'No. She can't mean that. Not the literal end of the world. The world can't end at a holiday resort in the East Midlands.'

'Actually,' said Darryl, ominously, 'she's been saying for years that when it comes, it'll come from the East Midlands.'

Janusz gave her an encouraging little smile. 'Nobody imagined it would be in a seaside town, though. Most of us assumed it would be in Derby.'

'Derby just has that vibe,' Charity agreed.

Good. Nobody was following Brenda. Good, that was good. She didn't want anyone running after her, checking to see if she was OK. That would just be embarrassing. Her children had their own problems to work out, and her husband had to work on his relationship with his inner Demon, which apparently took precedence over their forty years of marriage right now and honestly that was completely fine.

Even Grace, her new do-gooder fr— no not "friend", Brenda reminded herself; client. Her new do-gooder client wasn't following her, and that was fine. The priest wasn't here in any sort of professional capacity as emotional support now, was she? She was just a client who was tagging along doing research on her phone and occasionally offering directions and plastic cups of tea.

Brenda decided she would would nip into the Tesco and pick up a few bottles. Now, *that* was the sort of emotional support she actually needed. Something to make the terrible things she saw all the time feel less… sharp. Less present. Just another part of the softly swirling world of the intoxicated.

She turned on to Charles Street. Most of the shops were shuttered and dark, but one set of lights glowed behind posters advertising cucumbers and bread rolls and – ooh, hello, twenty per cent off selected wine and whisky. Brenda clacked towards the glowing supermarket logo. The doors slid open at her approach. Always open, she reminded herself, even at the end of the world.

It was one of those smaller branches of the supermarket that you'd get on high streets and shopping arcades. What did they call them – Extra? Metro? She didn't care. It was a sort of half-way house between a supermarket and a convenience store. The important thing was that it had a booze aisle – she could see the sign for it hanging from the ceiling, right at the back.

She picked up a basket and strode towards the back of the shop with purpose, the click of her shoes masked by the inoffensive twenty-year-old pop music drifting out of hidden speakers. She didn't stop to look at the other shoppers, or lack thereof. She didn't need to ask the shelf stacker she passed for directions, and therefore didn't notice that he wasn't actually stocking the shelves with anything, but going through the motion of putting something large and heavy on a low shelf, over and over and over again.

She focused on the aisle at the back and, with her concentration set on the bottles on the furthest aisle, the human shapes that drifted about did give the impression of staff and customers, milling aimlessly. At least, that's what she told herself when she got to the back of the shop, picked up a bottle and finally looked around herself. It could just as likely have been that her second sight had been screaming at her to get out of there, but she'd chosen to ignore it.

It really didn't matter, at that point. She was still at the back of the shop, and very surrounded by a *lot* of ghosts.

CHAPTER TWELVE
The Battle Of The Aperitifs Aisle

'OK,' murmured Brenda, quietly popping two vodka bottles and a litre of bourbon into her basket. 'You've all chosen rather a depressing place to spend eternity, but that's none of my concern now, is it?'

She tried to look past them, and took a step towards the tills. There was the sound of several people loudly exhaling at the same time. Brenda's sense of supernatural danger bristled at it. She *tried* to look past them she really did – but the wall of the dead was suddenly so thick.

'Seriously?' she asked. 'There's what, twenty of you? All haunting the same Tesco? I mean – *Tesco*?'

There was that collective exhale again. She was definitely in danger. She should almost certainly stop talking now.

'Honestly, I'm sad for you,' added Brenda.

There were actually more than twenty, she realised, finally looking properly at them. Only a few were in Tesco uniforms. A few more were in shop uniforms that she didn't quite recognise – this must have been a different shop before getting swallowed up by the supermarket giant. Many didn't look like shop workers at all. Many more weren't even former humans. There were Demonic shapes amongst them – huge slug-like creatures on top of the shelves, and things with wings hovering near the ceiling.

This wasn't just an everyday hub of human misery. There was more to it than that. This was a trap, and the bottles in her basket were the cheese. She clutched the basket handle desperately. Stupid, delicious, alcoholic bait.

There would be fire exits, somewhere. And a door to the stock warehouse, somewhere.

The wall of ghosts moved slowly towards her. She clutched tight to her basket's handle, put her head down and ran.

'She'll be fine,' Charity told Grace. 'She's always doing this. She just needs space. Space, and vodka.'

'Like a cosmonaut,' added Janusz. He attempted a bright smile, but worry lines still played around his remarkably symmetrical face.

'I'm still not entirely sure any of us should be going off alone,' said Grace.

'You went off alone only last night,' Charity reminded her.

'Exactly,' replied Grace, 'and there was this… thing. I couldn't see it, but Murzzzz fought it and your mum had to take off her shoes—'

'That was a Demon,' said Richard, quietly. 'A minor one, luckily.'

'A maggot or a fly?' asked Darryl with a sigh.

'Maggot,' replied Richard.

Darryl nodded.

'So there are Demons we can't see as well as ghosts?' Grace frowned. 'But I could see Murzzzz and that window creature. I thought…'

'Murzzzz is different,' Richard told her. 'He's been part of me for decades—'

'Still really don't want to talk about *that*, right now,' interrupted Darryl.

Richard, for once, ignored his son's interjection. 'But also, he's higher ranking, more powerful. So's that thing from your window. Murzzzz knew him, from way back. Think his name's "Huff Huff", something like…' Richard paused for a split second. '"Hfhfh", sorry. He's another high ranking one, which might explain a greater awareness of him amongst Normals. There's a whole hierarchy going on, with beings from the worlds beyond. Ghosts are different, they're just former people who got stuck, there isn't really a pecking order there, although their strength varies. They seem pretty strong here, maybe because of the Hell Hole. More Demons than usual here, too.'

'Some have wings and legs,' added Darryl. 'Some are just these maggotty things.' He frowned. 'They're disgusting. Demons are disgusting.'

'Son…'

'Don't you "son" me,' replied Darryl.

'Hey.' Janusz put his hand on Darryl's shoulder.

Darryl sighed and looked up at his husband. Some unspoken conversation took place in a mere second of eye contact between the spouses. Darryl got up off the wet bench and brushed some of the water off the back of his jeans.

'You're right, Grace. We probably shouldn't go off on our own, not here. Not even Mum.'

'Your mother needs space and independence,' replied Richard. He frowned in the direction of Charles Street. 'But perhaps we can give her space and independence while waiting just outside the shop. Just in case.'

Brenda passed through the first row of ghosts with something at least close to ease. It still felt like angry, cold spaghetti had been poured onto her, but she was able to push through it. That was where her good luck – if you could possibly call anything that happened to Brenda 'good luck' – ended. Most ghosts she could physically pass through, albeit with great discomfort. Demons were a different matter altogether – and there were Demons galore in this Tesco, for some reason. Maggots and flies, there to feed off something other than the by-now rotten sausages in the chilled aisle. The Demons slithered and swooped. Brenda saw their approach and swung her basket at them. One of the bottles of vodka slipped out as she swung. It passed through a ghost, glanced off a maggoty Demon and span, to smash on the floor.

The maggotty Demon shrieked.

Brenda swore.

Glass and mid-range vodka splintered, splashed and splattered over the supermarket floor. There were more shrieks from the Demons and an acrid, sulphurous, smoky smell in the air. Brenda swore again. She knew what she had to do. She knew what she had to do, and she hated it.

For starters, she was going to have to backtrack through that cold-spaghetti line of ghosts again. She kept her eyes on the Demons, held her breath, stepped backwards and braced herself for the inevitable sickly shudder. This was going to be awful.

'It's wrong', announced Richard and Darryl at the same time, only seconds after turning on to Charles Street.

'This is what I keep saying,' replied Janusz. He gestured around at the street. 'See? It's all closed. Why is it all closed?'

'Except for the supermarket,' noted Charity.

Richard blinked, shifted and then Murzzzz came into focus.

'It's a trap.'

Darryl turned on his heel, jabbing a finger at Murzzzz. 'No. Nope. Not you.'

'But it's a trap. Your mother—'

'Don't talk to me about my mother! We'll sort it. We don't need you.'

Murzzzz faltered. Insecurity and unease aren't expressions that one would normally expect to see on the face of a Demon, and yet there they were.

'Richard?' Murzzzz asked, and slid out of focus again.

'You heard my son,' said Richard. 'Come on, kids. We'll help your mother.'

'What do we do?' asked Grace, hanging back a little. 'What *can* we do?'

Charity took off her coat. 'How many?' she asked her brother.

Darryl glanced through the window. 'Don't know. Over a dozen.'

Charity nodded, and shoved her coat at Grace. 'You can hold this for us.'

And with that, Charity ran full pelt at the shop door, screaming 'Dieeeee!!!'

The dramatic effect of her charge was ruined rather when she had to stop and wait for the automatic doors to slide open, but once they had done so, she kept on running, resuming her battle cry as if it had never been interrupted in the first place.

Darryl also quickly slid his coat off and passed it to his husband. 'Cheers, love.'

'Be careful,' Janusz told him, accepting the duffel coat.

Janusz and Grace stood together at the entrance, holding coats, and watched Darryl and Richard run in after Charity.

'Does this happen much?' asked Grace.

'Yes,' admitted Janusz. 'But I'm glad you're here, this time. Usually I have to hold all their things by myself.'

'Dieeeee!!!' screamed Charity. She knew where her mother would be. It was quite easy to find the booze aisle at the back of the shop, even without the sound of smashing glass to guide her.

'Charity, that makes no sense,' Darryl called to her from near the entrance. 'They're mostly dead already.'

'Then die *more*!' Charity shouted around the seemingly empty shop.

'Charity?' came her mother's voice from the far end of the shop. It sounded unusually strained. 'Princess, watch out, there's—'

Something very big and very heavy knocked Charity off her feet and threw her, face first, into an aisle end display of chilled raw meat. Her landing was thankfully soft, if cold and smelly. The best before date of mid-October that she found her nose pressed against went some way to explaining the smell and the softness of the meat. One of the plastic containers popped under the pressure of the elbow she had raised automatically to protect herself when she was thrown. A stinking pink-brown liquid oozed onto her sleeve.

'You all right?' shouted Darryl as he ran over.

'Eurgh,' she replied, picking herself up.

'Ew, meat juice,' said her brother, wrinkling his nose.

'Yeah, all right Paul McCartney, I didn't land in it on purpose. Next time, I'll try to get thrown into some tofu.'

'Watch out!' He grabbed her rotten meat sleeve and dragged her aside. 'Sorry – two of them. One was about to—'

'Say no more, just point me at them.'

Darryl did so, positioning her between himself and some shelves, holding on to her shoulders for support – but still, she noted, turning her into a bit of a human shield. She was used to this stance – it was a rough and ready setup she and her brother had worked out years ago, for when there was little time to communicate verbally. Darryl had just used his second sight to plonk her directly in front of a ghost. It wasn't very dignified. Frankly it made her feel more like the inanimate trap in Ghostbusters than an actual Ghostbuster, but it was fast, and it worked. She held out her hands, concentrated, and felt a ghost pop away.

'That'll learn you not to throw innocent women into gone-off chops,' declared Charity at the departed spirit.

'That's not the one that threw you,' her brother told her. 'That was… oh no—'

He didn't get to finish, because both of them were hit by an impossibly strong, heavy force that sent them, winded, into shelves of rancid yoghurt.

'We've got to get out of the chilled aisle,' wheezed Darryl, the remains of several sour Crunch Corners dripping down his hair.

Charity hauled herself to her feet and helped her brother, who had definitely fared worse out of the collision with the curdled yoghurts, to his feet.

'Duck,' shouted Darryl. Charity did so, allowing a whole rotten poultry carcass to sail over her head, missing her by centimetres. Taking her brother's hand, they ran, in search of a less smelly aisle.

'Three in the pasta aisle,' Darryl told her.

Pasta. Not too heavy, not too sharp, not stinky. Yeah, that'd do. She turned into the pasta aisle, dragging Darryl behind her.

'One next to the spaghetti,' Darryl called. 'And one by the basmati.'

Charity loved getting to do two in one go, it felt like a superhero move. She held her hands out towards the spaghetti and felt the ghost pop out of the world of living people and dried pasta, Then she turned to the packets of basmati rice on the other side of the aisle. She held out her hands again, but something was wrong this time. She couldn't feel the essence of the ghost getting trapped and then squeezed by her power. It was the psychic equivalent missing an easy catch.

'Sorry, not basmati,' said her brother, hurriedly. 'What do I mean? The kind you use for risotto.'

'Arborio.' Charity quickly changed her stance, holding her hands out towards the shelf of risotto and pudding rice, and… yes, there it was, another ghost trapped and compressed by her power until it popped away. 'Honestly, Darryl!'

'Well, I don't know all the different rice. Janusz does most of the cooking. Third one's a Demon. Wings, the lot. Watch out.'

Darryl pulled her sharply to one side at the same time that several jars of Bolognese sauce flew off the end of the pasta shelf, in the direction of where they'd just been standing. He manhandled her again, pulling the two of them back over the smashed glass and smeared tomato as a second wave of jars crashed against the shelves.

'Just point me at it!'

'Hang on, Scrappy-Doo, we're too far away.'

He yanked her forwards, as a new onslaught of Dolmio jars made an airborne attack.

'Don't call me Scrappy-Doo!'

'You are a *bit* Scrappy-Doo.'

'Yeah, well… you're Velma.'

'You know that's a massive compliment, right?'

Her brother pulled her left and right, dodging flying glass, then suddenly grabbed her shoulders and shoved her forwards.

'There! On your twelve!'

She held out her hands and felt something huge and powerful struggle in her grasp. 'Just say "In front of you"!'

'"On your twelve" is quicker.'

Charity gritted her teeth and increased pressure on the struggling demon. It had been a while since she'd last sent a Demon back – they were strong. 'You just want to sound cool.'

'Why would I bother? The only one here is you.'

'And the Demon,' grunted Charity.

'Why would I possibly want to sound cool for a Demon that fights by flinging pasta sauce?'

She really should have just concentrated on focusing her power, but her Little Sister Instinct couldn't just leave the open goal Darryl had unwittingly left for her. She grinned, through her tightened jaw. 'You know. Since now you know you might be a…'

'Seriously, Charity!' Darryl's eyes widened. 'Not the time! You're going to—'

Charity felt the Demon begin to slip from her grasp.

'No no no no…' she fumbled to regain control.

'Just get rid of it,' Darryl shouted. 'Disgusting thing.'

Charity wrangled the invisible, flailing Demon back into her grip, and immediately increased the pressure on it to as high a level as she could manage. It made one last attempt to wriggle free from her, and then there was the sensation of reality briefly giving way. The feeling of a Demon vanishing from the living world was a subtly different one to the feeling of a ghost vanishing. With Demons it felt more like they'd been pressured into opening some unseeable door a crack and slipped through back into whatever realm had sent them.

'Got it.' She turned her head to beam at her brother. He just looked furious.

'What the Hell are you doing, talking about that stupid Murzzzz rumour in front of *them*?' he asked. 'In fact, what the Hell are you doing talking about it at *all*?'

'Still a bit tetchy about that then?'

'Charity, I found out about it like half an hour ago.'

'Gotcha – too soon.'

'No, not—'

There was another smash from the back of the shop, and a crash from the fresh veg aisle right near the entrance – clearly, their dad had not got very far having not let Murzzzz out to play. Charity took Darryl's hand. 'Let's just get to Mum.'

Brenda was alone.

Well. Not alone.

She *wished* she was alone. She was, instead, surrounded by a good dozen ghosts and Demons. She was 'alone' in that nobody was there to help her. She could hear two separate fights going on – one around pasta and world foods and one nearer the front of the shop, probably around the salads. None of that was of much help to her, at the back with the aperitifs. She reached behind her, grabbed a bottle of shop's own brand gin liqueur and, with huge regret, threw it into the undead throng. The bottle smashed in the hazy patch where one of the older looking ghost's feet would be. The sweet-smelling, alcoholic liquid passed harmlessly through the ghost but splashed against the leg of a Demon behind it. There was the hiss of fast corrosion, and the scent of fruity floral notes and lovely alcohol quickly turned to one of burning, and sulphur. The Demon screamed, reached two legs down automatically to touch the injured one, found that those legs were smoking sulphur now as well and screamed even harder.

I should probably backtrack here. You might have heard of holy water being used in Demon hunting and so on, or to defeat Vampires (Vampires aren't real, by the way, but sometimes people mistake Demons for them). Holy water is, in reality, as useful as candles, chalk markings and special herbs – in that its only real use is in making ghosts and some of the stupider Demons believe that, as a hunter, you know what you're doing. If you just chuck it at a ghost then it's not going to do any damage. However, in the nineteenth century some Demon hunters reported the extraordinary power of consecrated wine on dealing with Demons. It behaved like an acid on them, not killing them – nothing has yet been discovered in this world that can do that – but causing them enough pain and injury to make them leave the realm of the living of their own accord. Perhaps there's some sort of burns hospital in whatever dimension they come from that they want to get to, get bandaged up and given some Demonic painkillers – I don't know. But here's the thing about that finding – the Victorian Demon hunters were so dead set on making sure all the weaponry in their inventory was holy that they didn't stop to think whether it might just be the base material that created the desired effect, not whether someone had said prayers over it. Soon after the word got out, underground Demon hunters in China started experimenting using ordinary Baijiu, and discovered it performed in exactly the same way on Demons as consecrated wine. It made no difference whether it was believed to be the blood of a holy man or just something to make you lightheaded over dinner – alcohol was the active ingredient, not faith. And the stronger the alcohol, the more potent its use against demons. By the middle of the twentieth Century, most professional Demon hunters in the world would ensure they had easily smashable vials of vodka or absinthe amongst their arsenals. I say 'most', because the thing about Demon hunters is that they often have at least one clairvoyant in their group, and the thing about clairvoyants is, they're often driven to substance abuse by the things they see.

Richard Rook stopped trying to pack vodka grenades back in the eighties. If he tried using alcohol it would just mean he'd end up starting every house clearance with an empty case of Demon-repellent weaponry and a very drunk wife. To be frank, that wasn't even the biggest concern of Richard's around the alcohol issue, not by a long way. There was the worry for Brenda's health, of course, but there was also the constant care that had to be taken around Brenda to ensure Murzzzz wouldn't get burned. Sometimes just catching Brenda's breath could cause Murzzzz to choke and suddenly retreat, leaving Richard in the middle of a coughing fit.

Right now, Brenda's problem isn't that she doesn't have enough strong alcohol to hand – she definitely does – but that she truly hates seeing it go to waste like that.

Brenda grabbed another bottle. Dark rum. She could really go for some dark rum, right about now. She threw the bottle, with a wince. It hit another maggotty Demon, which squealed. Some of it managed to splash on to the already smoking Demon, which was truly having the worst luck and then decided that enough was enough. Something that looked a little like the Hell Hole above the pier, only much, much smaller, opened up by a sliver in the air. The twice-injured Demon slid through it and vanished in a puff of stinking sulphur. The tiny Hell Hole closed up again in an instant. Had Brenda blinked, she'd have missed it.

She grabbed another three bottles of rum and made a dash for it, through the space that the Demon had just vacated. Spiny appendages caught her, and a slimy, maggotty tail hit her square in the stomach, knocking her back into the bottles. She grimaced and wheezed for breath, and brought one of the bottles of rum in her hands down onto what probably passed as the maggotty Demon's head. It didn't smash.

'Sake!' she managed, still winded.

'Mum?' called Charity from a few shelves beyond. 'Hang on one more minute, we're almost there, we're at the eggs.' There was a crash, and the sound of several hundred eggs breaking, closely followed by both of her children swearing.

The maggotty Demon surged towards her again. She smashed the rum bottle on the shelf she was pinned against and waved the broken bottle in a single wide arc in front of her. The broken glass passed harmlessly through the Demon, but the remaining rum hissed horribly as it spattered out into what was likely the Demon's face.

The Demon slithered backwards into a couple of ghosts, and another tiny Hell Hole opened up just enough of a notch to allow it to retreat through. The ghosts gazed blankly at the space where the Demon had been, and then turned their attention back to Brenda.

It was mostly ghosts left now. Booze had no effect on common-garden ghosts; whatever they were made of, it was obviously something very different to Demons. That was, if they were 'made of' anything at all. Brenda still had two bottles of rum in her hands. She did the only thing she felt she could do – she cracked one of them open, and took a good, deep swig.

Darryl was now covered in sour yoghurt, rotten eggs and Coco Pops. The Coco Pops wouldn't have been so much of an issue on their own, but they had stuck to the yoghurt and eggs. He looked like a rancid Rice Krispie Cake, and he smelled absolutely terrible.

Not that the aperitifs aisle at the back of the shop smelled much better. As he and Charity ran towards the sounds of several ghosts and his cornered mother, the stink of sickly sweet alcohol mixed with sulphur managed to waft through the rotten meat, sour dairy and bad eggs that they themselves were bringing to the smell-scape.

'Mum?' he called as they rounded the corner to the drinks aisle, 'Are you— Oh… crap.'

The good news was that his mother was, so far, alive and well and from the wafts of sulphur, she'd managed to repel a number of Demons all by herself. The bad news was that there were still scores of ghosts around her – lost and angry, and by the look of the clothes of some of them, they'd been stuck in the shop for a very long time, which would make anyone dangerously pissed off. The other bad news was that his mother was half way through a bottle of dark rum. Again, fair enough given the circumstances, but it wasn't exactly helpful.

'How many?' asked his sister.

'Maybe twenty?' replied Darryl. 'Maybe more?'

'Gah,' sighed Charity. 'At least there's carbs in this Hell Shop.'

Beneath her usual Charityish attitude, Darryl could tell that his sister was tired. Altogether so far, she'd had to get rid of five ghosts and two Demons, just to get here. Her nose was already bleeding. Twenty ghosts all by herself was asking a lot.

Maybe… Maybe he'd been unreasonable, demanding that Murzzzz didn't show his face for this one. Just thinking about Murzzzz made him flash with anger again. Anger, and… and other feelings that he was still too raw to acknowledge. He only allowed himself to register the rage, for now. The anger rushed through him, drowning out the little voice that wondered if maybe they should ask for the help of their demonic bodyguard in a situation like this. No. Nope. No. His parents should have told him.

Actually, no. That wasn't it, either. Murzzzz should have stepped out of his father all together, when it came to… to *that*. A new little voice in him piped up briefly, wondering if part of what bothered him about this so much was having to think about his parents having sex. The rage quickly roared up again and silenced it. His parents. How much did he really know about them? Was Richard Rook even actually his father?

'Where's your father?' wailed Brenda, pulling the bottle briefly from her lips. 'He should be here by now.'

There was a loud crash, and a muted swear word from the direction of tinned goods, still half the shop away.

Brenda turned to her children, wide eyed in alarm. 'Don't tell me he's alone?'

'Well…' muttered Charity.

'*Alone* alone?' asked Brenda.

'I don't want to see You Know Who, right now,' muttered Darryl.

'Oh for crying out loud, you whiny child,' Brenda spat. She took another large swig of rum, and loaded another four bottles into her bag. 'Right, pop these ghosts, help me get out here and then we have to go and fetch your dad.'

'Which one?' smirked Charity. Darryl glared at her. Her expression barely changed. 'Right, right. Like you said. Too soon.'

Charity held out her hands, and Darryl physically moved her into place so that the first of the many ghosts slipped into her psychic grasp. His sister grunted with concentration and the ghost – an extremely fed-up looking woman with a bubble perm and wearing a tabard and acid-washed jeans – popped out of their plane of reality. Charity exhaled, and held out her hands for the next one. Two larger ghosts lunged towards the beer shelf, and a four pack of lager span with force into Darryl's calf. He winced, but didn't move. He shifted Charity into position so that she could trap a furious little man in a bowler hat. Bowler Hat Ghost spotted what Darryl was trying to do, and managed to float out of Charity's grasp. He screeched at them, his pale, dapper little face twisted with rage. Behind Darryl, the two bigger ghosts were still playing merry havoc with the beer shelves. A bottle of craft ale hit Darryl's fingers and Charity's shoulder, hard.

'Ow! Turn me round, I'm popping whoever's throwing beer first,' Charity demanded.

Darryl positioned her in front of one of the two ghosts that were still floating halfway between the beer shelves. She trapped that one and popped it out of existence quickly, but the other ghost retaliated with a whole box of Heineken, which mercifully missed both of their heads but slammed into Darryl's shin and landed heavily on his toes. Swearing and limping, Darryl tried to turn his sister to face the other beer-flinging ghost, but strong, cold fingers grabbed him by the throat and wrenched him away from her, throwing him into several bottles of Stella scattered across the floor. He blinked up into angry, dark little eyes of Bowler Hat Guy.

'Charity,' shouted Brenda. 'Stella display. There's a little one there, but it's strong.'

'Right.' Charity turned towards the bowler-hatted ghost and held out her hands, cursing faintly when it pushed back immediately against her psychic grip.

'Fun fact,' added Brenda, raising the bottle of rum again, 'that one looks like Stan Laurel.'

'I was thinking more the little man from the Homepride jars,' Darryl said. He tried to pick himself up but had to dodge back when the bowler hat ghost slipped out of Charity's grasp and lunged for him again.

'I don't know what that is,' replied his mother. 'Charity dear, it's got away from you.'

'Yes, Mother, I know.'

The furious little ghost scrabbled after Darryl and managed to catch him by the throat again, its freezing fingers strengthened by rage. The ghost looked Darryl in the eyes and squeezed.

'It's started choking your brother,' added Brenda, matter of factly.

'Yes, thank you.'

Charity darted forwards. Years of fighting ghosts blind had thankfully given Darryl's sister an excellent sense for guesswork when it came to pinpointing them in a pinch. She held out her hands and grabbed the bowler hat ghost's head. She concentrated, and the expression of the ghost changed suddenly from cold fury to one of surprise, sadness... even something that Darryl imagined could pass for regret. And then its little pale bowler-hatted head was gone, as were the icy strong fingers around Darryl's throat. Popped to nothing.

'You know,' panted Darryl, still lying in the bottles of Stella. 'The little man in the hat. Homepride. They do, like, pasta sauces and stuff.'

Brenda swallowed another swig. 'Oh. Well, cooking has always been more your dad's remit. Speaking of, pick yourself up, Darryl.' She looked around herself. 'We still have a lot to get through before we can help your father,' she said, before adding in a mutter, 'Wouldn't *have* to help him if it hadn't been for your whinging.'

Darryl used the shelf behind him to haul himself to his feet. His mother was right – there were still a lot of ghosts. It seemed like there were even more than there had been before, in fact.

More ghosts surged. Darryl even spotted a couple of the maggot-shaped Demons at the back. Either his mother had missed them during her aperitif-flinging assault, or... or they were reinforcements, somehow? Could ghosts send for reinforcements? He'd never known that to happen before.

'Charity?' he asked.

His sister was still catching her breath. She looked exhausted. She needed a rest and an heroic quantity of carbs. This was bad. He tried to catch his mother's gaze, but she was staring off down the aisle with a concerned expression.

This was very bad.

He was still angry. He still didn't want to see or speak to Murzzzz. But he *really* didn't want to be choked to death by ghosts in a supermarket along with his family, leaving his husband alone with a coat and a flighty priest on a haunted island either.

There was another crash, nearby.

'Richard?' called Brenda. 'Dearheart, is that you? You might want to wait outside, it's a bit crowded down our end...'

The next crash was almighty. It sounded as if an entire shelf full of heavy stock had smashed to the floor – and likely, that was in fact what had happened, because the next moment a great, powerful Demon leaped to the ceiling and skittered at speed towards them.

'Murzzzz!' cried Charity.

'Thank goodness,' breathed Brenda. 'We're saved.'

Yay, echoed Darryl to himself. They were saved. Saved by an absolute dickhead.

CHAPTER THIRTEEN

I'm Afraid We Don't Serve Spirits Here

Murzzzz dropped from the ceiling, into the thronging mass of ghosts.

Ugh, thought Darryl.

Murzzzz moved so fast that you could barely see him. He was a thrashing dervish of shadowy limbs. Ghosts dispersed at the touch of his demonic claws – some streaming down the aisles of the shop in a howling blur to get away from him; others, who were clearly confined to haunt this corner of the shop wafted meekly straight into Charity's hands, to be popped away into whatever – if anything – lay beyond.

Darryl, who had very little of practical use that he could offer to the fight at this point, chose instead to stand back, watch and contemplate gloomily about how un-seriously he was taken by this family. Less than fifteen minutes after he said he didn't want to see Murzzzz, here was Murzzzz, showing off like a dick and openly welcomed by his mother and sister.

Charity popped five ghosts, one after the other... six... seven... eight... She sank to the floor, exhausted. Her mother propped her up so that she could pop another two.

'Darryl!' called Brenda. 'Make yourself useful and fetch your sister some crisps.'

'No cheese and onion,' managed Charity, drained. 'They repeat on me.'

Darryl turned and stalked off in the direction of the crisps aisle, in as dignified a manner as he could, considering he'd just had his one demand ignored and was still covered in rotten dairy products. He glowered at Murzzzz as he passed. Murzzzz was too busy fighting to even glance at him.

With the fight still raging at the other end of the shop, Darryl was left in relative peace as he picked out a multipack of cheesy Wotsits, a tube of Pringles and a couple of those fancy bags of vegetable crisps for his sister. There was only one ghost hanging around in the savoury snacks aisle, and it didn't seem to want any trouble. It was just sort of... there, hanging around in a forlorn smudge. It had the shape of an old lady in a headscarf, shapeless overcoat and eighties style glasses. It raised its head and looked at him as he grabbed the crisps. It didn't wail, didn't lunge, just looked at him, docile as a dead lamb.

Darryl allowed himself to meet eyes with it. This was a mistake. Not because it then made a violent dash for him, or anything. He could probably have dealt with that.

His mother had always warned him to avoid meeting their gaze, if he could possibly help it. Especially the ones that just looked all lost and sad. It was important not to let their sadness in because it was difficult to manage. His mother had managed to build up her own mental defence against it, through years of practice and a lot of vodka, but Darryl still kept slipping up, looking too closely and spotting details that gnawed at him. The old lady's ghost had a basket. Not a real basket, a ghost one. She'd been shopping when she'd died. Possibly she'd keeled over from a heart attack, in a supermarket, surrounded by strangers. What a way to go. And now she was stuck here, in the crisps aisle. Maybe she'd had children and grandchildren. Maybe they had grown up, grown old or even died in the decades she'd spent wafting helplessly around the Monster Munch.

Damn. He was already thinking of the ghost as a 'she'.

The sadness came flooding in. This woman with her little headscarf and basket was only one of many – so many. He thought about Melanie, still conscious in death, lingering on in a shuttered pizza parlour that had once been the busy nerve centre of her now-ruined business plans. He thought about that sailor ghost wandering helplessly around a pub that had been built on the site of his gruesome death. He thought about Reverend Duncan, tormented by that Demon in the stained glass window. He thought about how even his family didn't know where Duncan's spirit and all those other ghosts went when Charity popped them away. He thought about Duncan's hopeful early blog posts, written by a man dedicating himself to his faith and the community, a man who only wanted to make a positive change, who was ultimately popped away to nothing.

His parents always said it was a kindness, that even if those spirits simply ceased to exist, at least they were no longer suffering, lost, frightened and angry. His parents always said it was necessary to pop them away. Left to linger, those ghosts would cause more chaos and even create more death. His parents' argument was certainly backed up by the behaviour of the Parasites that had driven Reverend Duncan to the end of his wits, and had tried to take his Janusz away.

The old lady continued to gaze at him, gentle and sad. She wasn't going to attack. She wasn't going to hurt anybody. She was just stuck. Darryl tried to think back to the fight he had only just walked away from – about how many of the actual ghosts had attacked them, as opposed to the Demons, and how many had just been milling around, trapped in a huddle like tightly corralled animals. There had been some that were deliberately aggressive, definitely. There were always some. Angry spirits – like the bowler hatted guy – lashing out... lashing out as you'd expect a lost, frightened, cornered animal to lash out.

Meeting eyes with ghosts was a mistake, especially in his business. Letting in the sadness opened one up to the worst weakness of all when it came to the ghost hunting game – the weakness within. Darryl felt and a pang of guilt and then hurriedly made himself think about something else – the Hell Hole, the Parasites, Hfhfh or whatever that Demon's name was. They'd pulled his husband into a stained glass window. How dare they? Not to mention all the business with Murzzz. Yes. He was doing the right thing. They needed to find what was poisoning this whole wretched island, and get rid of the lot, before it spread. Even if that meant popping every ghost away. It was for the greater good. Also, they had pulled his *husband* into a *window*. He was pretty sure that was a hate crime.

He turned his back on the little old lady with her sad little basket, and made his way back to his family, his arms laden with snacks.

'Are you sure they'll be OK in there?' In the street, Grace hugged Charity's coat to herself and looked through the supermarket's window, worriedly. Not that she could see anything of any use, unless she was more interested in deals on selected meats than in the crashes and shouts she could hear within – which she wasn't.

'You've seen what happens when us Normals wander into their space when a ghost hunt turns violent,' replied Janusz, calmly. 'We get in the way, need saving, need pulling out of windows and so on. And that happened when we thought it was only one ghost. I'm not getting under their shoes this time.'

Grace turned her attention back to Janusz. 'You're really OK with all of this, aren't you?'

There was another crash, and a horrible, unearthly howl. Janusz smiled and pointed vaguely at the shop.

'Hear that? Murzzzz turned up. They'll be fine.'

'I don't just mean the fight in there. I mean – all of it. There's a flipping hole in the sky, Janusz! Not to mention all that stuff that happened in my church, and in the pizza place… hearing Darryl speak in some ghostly voice, saying that stuff about Murzzzz and him. I mean… he's your husband.'

Janusz nodded. 'And he is upset about it. So I will be calm about it, otherwise we will both be upset. It's like a see-saw. When I am angry, he has to be the calm one.'

'I honestly can't imagine you getting upset about anything.'

'You've never seen me have to chase a six month overdue invoice and get told they had "mislaid the paperwork".'

'But what if Darryl actually is…' Grace trailed off. 'You know.'

'I knew they were a weird family when I asked Darryl on our first date. Since then, I've only grown more used to the weirdness. Besides. I spent much of yesterday as a window. I'm nobody to complain about my husband being an odd one.'

They both gazed at the impenetrably advert-covered shop window some more. The crashes and sounds of struggle within suddenly stopped.

'Whatever happened in there, I think it's over,' Janusz announced. 'I hope they pick up more biscuits while they're there – do you know if this shop has a Polish aisle?'

There was a small Polish section, Darryl noticed, so he picked up a couple of Janusz's favourites to add to the mountain of snacks in his arms as he followed the sound of his family's voices in the now otherwise eerily quiet shop.

The others met him in the central aisle. Charity was too exhausted even to snatch the crisps off him. Darryl had to open a bag and hand it to her as she stood propped up by Richard – who was, thankfully, Richard again. Murzzzz was nowhere to be seen and it was clear from Richard's expression that he was no happier about the Demon's sudden emergence to save the day than Darryl was.

'Sorry, son,' muttered his dad, sheepishly. 'I tried to stop him.'

'It's fine. Stop feeling sorry for yourselves. We needed backup,' grunted Brenda.

'He needs boundaries, dear,' muttered Richard, gently.

'He's an ancient Demon, not a teenager,' replied Charity, through a mouthful of cheese flavoured corn puffs.

'All the more reason to enforce boundaries, princess,' replied her father. 'Does anyone have any cash? I feel bad taking this stuff out of a shop and not paying. We could at least leave a couple of notes and an explainer.'

'We'd charge them more than the price of a few bottles and crisp packets for clearing all those spirits out of the shop,' Brenda replied, 'I think the massive supermarket chain comes out of this better than we do.'

Darryl wondered as he and his family left the shop – filthy, bedraggled and supporting an exhausted Charity – whether anyone had truly come out of that one well. The shop was trashed, although there really didn't seem to be anyone around who would be left to clean up. That in itself was weird. No staff. No customers. Rotten produce. Long expired sell-by date after long expired sell-by date. Judging by the state of the food, Darryl would say that the shop had been abandoned for a couple of weeks at least, but it wasn't locked up. The lights were still on and the door still slid open as if everything was fine and dandy. But nothing was fine, or even remotely approaching dandy. Yes, they'd got rid of a handful of Demons and ghosts, but to what end? He thought about the old lady lingering near the crisps again. She was still there. He hadn't bothered to ask his drained sister to use up even more energy popping that docile spirit away. He'd spared the old lady ghost, just as they often spared other mournful spirits that just stood around, lost and bothering nobody. What they were spared from, he had no idea. Spared them, so that they could drift hopelessly forever. Spared them simply on the premise that it would be an impossible task for Charity to get rid of every forlorn spirit.

Still, he supposed, at least now they had drinks and snacks.

'Zabko!' Janusz ran to greet him at the door. His husband initially went for a big bear hug, but reeled back at the last moment. 'Baby, you stink! What have you been rolling in?'

'Deserted in there,' Charity explained, her mouth full. 'All the produce's been left to rot.'

Grace frowned. 'That's not right.'

'Crisps are still fine, though,' added Charity.

'So we still haven't seen a living soul here except Grace,' noted Janusz. 'Doesn't anybody else think that's a bit— oh! You got those biscuits I like!'

'Oh. Yes.' Darryl handed them over.

Janusz hugged the biscuits to himself happily but still, Darryl noticed, didn't give *him* a hug. He really needed a shower and a change of clothes.

'I'd be more worried if there *had* been living people in there,' declared Brenda, clopping back towards the promenade. 'It was riddled with Demons. Far more than you'd ever usually find in one spot. I'm still not sure what we're dealing with here, but it's… shit.'

'Well, that's not encouraging,' said Grace, following her along with the others.

'Ha ha, Mum swore in front of a priest,' added Charity.

Darryl caught up with his mother, and saw what it was that had caused her to swear in front of a priest.

'Shit,' he echoed.

'Language!' cried his father and his husband in unison.

'You do know it's fine to swear in front of me, right?' asked Grace. 'I'm a priest. I'm not five.'

Brenda slowed to a stop at the junction of Charles Street and the promenade. She pulled out a half empty bottle of rum and took a large gulp.

Darryl wished he'd taken a bottle for himself.

The whole doomed Tesco run had taken little over half an hour. Since then, the hole in the sky had at least doubled in size. The void at the centre of it had grown in intensity. It was a special kind of dark that hurt Darryl's eyes, as if it was trying to suck even the memory of light, the very concept of light waves being a thing that a human being could see, straight out of his brain via his pupils.

The others caught up with them.

'Do you see that?' Darryl breathed.

'Probably not as well as you and Mum,' said Charity, 'but yeah.'

Even Janusz and Grace gazed up at it in horror.

'Shit,' breathed Grace.

Charity broke the spell a little by noisily crunching her way through several Pringles, but you could tell from the way she did it that she was still upset about the whole Hell Hole thing.

Grace found herself gazing along the promenade at the shuttered pizzeria again. Melanie still played on her mind, and she was getting hungry. She could really do with pizza about now. She still wasn't hungry enough to contemplate ham & pineapple yet, though, so she clearly wasn't *that* hungry.

'Murzzzz says Hell Holes feed off misery,' Richard told her, 'but it's got to be really concentrated. You get places like that, where one terrible event affects another, which affects another… a sort of cascade happens, all falling on the same place. It creates a kind of gravity well of wrongness. Does something to the fabric of reality. Usually, they're confined to a smaller space – haunted houses, that sort of thing – so they can't get too big.'

'I recognise the sensation,' admitted Brenda, over her quickly emptying bottle of rum. '1975. Rural car showroom that had been built on so-called cursed land. They'd hung witches there. Well. Not the car salesmen, but people centuries ago had hung witches there. And, they obviously weren't real witches because there's no such thing. That's how stupid they were.'

Grace took a breath to remind everyone that she'd just learned that there were Demons wandering around the high street supermarket, there was a hole to an unknown dimension above the pier and she'd recently seen a man get turned into a stained glass window. But witches weren't real? She decided to let it go and accept Brenda's word for it.

'Terrible idea trying to sell cars in a place like that,' Brenda continued. 'Brakes would fail, engines would go on fire. Two deaths and three serious injuries later, they got me in. They blamed it on the witches' curse.' Brenda snorted. 'In a way, they had a point – in the most simplistic, asinine way, that is. The sadness and anger of the women who'd been killed still lingered there and that was just one of the layers. The women were only killed because the idiots needed someone to blame for the strange things that were *already* happening. Those things were probably caused by the anger of the families who were killed in the flash flood fifty years before the witch trials. And that flood may well have been caused by the energy from the anger of the families who died during a cholera outbreak a century before that... and so on and so forth. All that tragedy happening in the same little village. It was eventually abandoned when everyone went off to work in factories, and finally turned into a soulless box for selling Austin Allegros off an A road. It took a lot of layered misery to make that sort of psychic gravity pit, and that was teensy, compared to this. Little more than a metaphysical boo-boo. Certainly not enough to tear a hole in the sky. Still took me a month to cleanse the place.'

'Yeah,' said Charity through her crisps, 'but back then you didn't have me on hand. Or Janusz. Or Darryl, I suppose.'

'Your mother hadn't even met me, at that point,' added Richard, brightly. 'A shame really, Murzzzz really likes car showrooms. I think there's something inherently demonic about them.'

'Still don't want to hear about him right now, Dad,' sighed Darryl.

'Speaking of Murzzzz,' interjected Janusz.

Darryl turned to his husband, hurt. 'What did I *just say?*'

'Murzzzz is a Demon,' Janusz countered, placidly. 'He's probably older than the Stone Age?'

Richard nodded. 'Much.'

'So how did he get about?' Asked Janusz. 'Before you? Before cars and car showrooms? It just seems to me… there's a hole in the sky and there's lots of Demons… Is the Hell Hole some sort of Demon transport terminal maybe?'

'I think that that's maybe too simplistic a…' Richard frowned, clearly consulting an unheard voice deep within. 'Actually, no, he says that's actually pretty close. The best way he can describe it is a door, that can only open when it's powered—'

'Like a sliding door?' Janusz asked. 'Like in Tesco.'

'Well, it doesn't slide and it leads to several different realms of existence instead of Tesco and instead of electricity it needs to be powered by misery but, besides that, sure.' Richard shook his head. 'But he says there is something wrong with this one. The physical point of origin is too big. It's meant to be layered all on a smallish spot, a hectare or two.'

'What the hell is a hectare?' asked Charity.

'It's about two and a half acres,' Grace told her.

'What's an acre?'

'What did they even teach you kids at school?' snapped Brenda.

'I don't know because you pulled us out to fight ghosts!'

'But this,' continued Richard, ominously, 'is the whole island. Dozens of square miles.'

'You *do* know what a square mile is, right?'

'Yes, I know what a square mile is, Mother.'

'It's too big. Something…' Richard shook his head again, worried. 'Something's going to give. It shouldn't be able to maintain that sort of size.'

'The whole island,' breathed Janusz. 'Unhappiness and anger's been layered on a whole island, all these years. Those poor people.'

Grace found herself looking at the pizzeria yet again. Melanie had deserved so much better than that. Reverend Duncan had deserved so much better. And all the other people besides. She'd been sent to care for this island, to bring it some hope, and all she'd done had been to uncover souls that it was already too late for. She was too late for so many of them. The local paper's online archive was a litany of woe, and she'd just locked herself away in a haunted church to read through it and feel sad.

Why had she done that?

Why hadn't she gone out and done something – actually *done* something?

'The Massoods,' she breathed. 'Sold up their ice cream shop due to lack of business and were moving back to the mainland when a freak wave washed their car to sea. The Grey Twins. Saved up for years to go travelling, crashed their car before they even got over the bridge. Kayak Pete – finally got a big booking for his Kayaking place just as it was about to go under and the whole party drowned, including Pete. Twenty insurance underwriters, all gone in a single team-building exercise.'

'And where *are* they all?' murmured Janusz.

'Dead, Janusz, is where they all are,' Grace replied, starting to feel a little hysterical, 'there were bodies in Boden gilets washing up for weeks.'

Darryl walked over to the promenade's railing and gazed down the wet beach. 'Oh, yeah,' he noted. 'I think I see one. His ghost, that is. Not his body. Seeing a body there would be weird.'

Grace buried her face in her hands. 'I was supposed to help. I failed. What are we supposed to do against all this misery that's already piled up all over the island?'

'We can go and pop that gilet-wearing ghost on the beach, I suppose?' asked Charity. 'I've finished my crisps.'

'He's not hurting anyone,' argued Darryl.

'Well, we've got to do *something*,' Charity replied.

'We just cleared a whole supermarket,' Darryl retorted, 'and it has only made things worse!' He gazed at his parents for their input.

Richard looked down. He had no answer to give.

Brenda exhaled. 'Darryl's right. This isn't another Allegro Showroom situation, that's for sure. It might have gone past the point of no return already. Popping ghosts and sending Demons back might just be feeding that thing even further. Who knows, maybe we're adding to the misery just with our presence. You know, with all of Darryl's moping.'

'Couldn't just leave it at "Darryl's right", could you?' sighed Darryl.

Grace noticed with a frown that Brenda had already finished the whole smallish bottle of rum. She should probably say something, she thought. But the rest of the family seemed fine with it. Should she really rock the boat, here? She was not a boat rocker. But look where not rocking the boat had got her so far. The whole island was well and truly up shit creek on her marvellously unrocked boat. She sighed, and wondered about whether that metaphor made sense, in lieu of saying anything about the emptied rum bottle.

'What if,' said Janusz, carefully, 'we rethink our habits?'

Grace gazed across at Janusz. She was the only one to do so.

'Is this that seance idea of yours again?' Brenda asked, her voice heavy with the weariness of a parent who has already said 'no' several times.

'Every single one of Janusz's ideas, that we've actually used worked,' said Darryl, quietly, with a similarly worn down tone. They had clearly already had this conversation a number of times.

'Yes – admin ideas. He's a whizz with admin.'

'Thank you, Brenda,' replied Janusz, 'but—'

'But psychically you're a Normal,' added Brenda. 'No offence, Janusz, but you should have the good business sense to leave the psychic work to the rest of us. You don't see it like we do or experience it like we do, we've been doing things this way for decades and—'

'And this time it just made things worse, as you said.' Janusz smiled, encouragingly. 'So we should try a different way. Besides, I was a window yesterday. This was not very "normal" of me.'

'He's not going to let this "window" thing go, is he?' sighed Brenda to herself. She looked at her husband who gave her a meaningful glance. Brenda groaned.

'Oh for pity's sake.'

Charity held up her hand. 'I agree with Janusz, by the way.'

'Me too,' said Grace, quickly.

'You don't really get a vote, Reverend,' Charity told her, 'but cheers anyway. So we're all agreed to support Janusz's idea, except for Darryl.'

'Obviously I support my husband's idea!'

'Yeah, but you didn't *say* so.'

'I *did*!'

What they never talk about any more is the fact that it had initially been Darryl who had floated the idea, long ago – before a ghost pirate swinging from the hips up in a spectral gibbet in the living room of a fourth floor flat had brought Janusz Rook-née-Wozniak into their lives. No matter how often Brenda would tell her teenaged son not to, young Darryl had always had a terrible habit of letting the ghosts' sadness into his mind. And, as much as she'd tell anyone who'd listen that her *way of blotting out the misery of the dead was fine and dandy, she wasn't quick to endorse the numbing effect of the bottle to her son. Far from it, in fact. She'd say that if her son took up drinking as well, there'd be less for her. Darryl actually ended up drinking rather less than the average British male of his age group, partially because of the family business and his general air of oddness lead to him having very little by way of a social life, but also because he's always found having a family member who frequently drinks herself 'to sleep' rather put him off the stuff.*

And so, with little else to distract him from it, Darryl tends to let the sadness in. He lets himself feel its wretchedness, and consider what can possibly be done to eliminate the sadness as well as – even, sometimes in his idle fantasies, instead of – eliminating the ghost. He first asked about the possibility of trying to talk to the ghosts about their sadness when he was sixteen. The idea was swiftly and decisively shot down. Not that that stopped him from entertaining the idea. When he was nineteen he tried to engage with the very sad-seeming ghost of a little girl. The ghost threw him through a French door. He had ten stitches and didn't bring the subject up again, until the night when Janusz Wozniak asked him how he got the scar on his arm. Janusz Wozniak had also once been thrown into a door, albeit by the living. Janusz Wozniak thought that the reasoning behind the idea that had led to Darryl's scar made good sense, and was charmed by the empathy he read into it. He had kissed the scar, internalised the idea and has become the guy who keeps on bringing it up. It is still usually shot down, only lately it has been shot down with consideration and soft words, because nobody ever raises their voice or makes snide snipes at Janusz. He just doesn't have the face for it.

The family followed Grace down a bland-looking, deserted street around twenty minutes' walk from the promenade.

'It's not that I ever thought it was a terrible idea as such,' said Brenda for the fourth time. 'It's just not our usual way. We tend not to have time for all of that rigmarole. We always have to be in, out, job done and on to the next booking. And it's not us who sorts out our working schedule is it – it's Janusz who does that. So in a way, all of this is simply down to us being victims of Janusz's own success.'

'That's a very kind thing to say,' smiled Janusz, without a hint of sarcasm. 'And I'm so glad that we agree that, given the grander scale this time, this is worth a try.'

'Yes,' sighed Brenda.

'There,' announced Grace, pointing.

The family looked at the pebble-dashed building.

'A dentist?' asked Charity.

'The only one on the island,' Grace told them. 'Set up in the sixties, I think, and I'm pretty sure before that it was a doctor's surgery. I reckon the waiting room's going to be the best bet for a seance – one single place where as many locals as possible have physically been, for the past hundred years or so, at least. Besides the Tesco, and—'

'And we are not going back to that Tesco,' said Brenda.

'A dentist's,' repeated Charity, with a faint shudder. 'Now, if that's not going to be a concentrated hotspot of human misery, I don't know what is.'

Grace tried the door to the building. It was locked. A faded sign declared that the dental surgery was open until six p.m. on weekdays and yet, there they were on a weekday just after two p.m. and it was very definitely shut.

'Empty, again,' murmured Janusz, peering in the window. 'Surely dentists aren't subject to tourist season.'

'Maybe the business went under?' replied Grace, quietly.

'Shall I get "You Know Who" to do the lock?' asked Richard.

Before he'd even finished talking, Darryl had picked up a loose stone from the low wall around the front of the dentists. He smashed a side window with it, reached through and opened the lock from the inside.

'No need,' said Darryl.

Charity gasped with mock horror. 'Darryl Rook, smashing windows now is it? At your big age!'

'It's actually cheaper to fix than smashing down doors like we usually do, you know.'

'Still, though. Check out my big brother the vandal. Are you as shocked as I am, Janusz? I am *shocked*.'

'It's actually quite sexy,' admitted Janusz.

'Eurgh,' cried Charity. 'You had to go and ruin it.'

Inside, the dentist's waiting area was a disconcerting mix of pristine and shabby. The floors were well-kept tile, only dirtied by a thin layer of dust that covered everything, gathering on the laminate shelving units and sleek metal chairs. A smart coffee table in the middle of the waiting room had a neat stack of celebrity magazines on it. On the top of the pile, a pair of British Reality TV stars smiled up at Charity through the dust, in as public a celebration of their wedding day as their PR team could muster – a shame because Charity's cursory knowledge of celeb culture told her that the couple in question were now going through a messy and even more public divorce. Even considering the usual old age of waiting room magazines, one managing to outdate an entire celebrity marriage – which included two kids – was pushing it. This place had been abandoned for some time.

Brenda and Darryl gave the place a good look around, and declared it mercifully free of lingering ghost dentists, which at least set Charity's mind at rest a little bit.

'So, then,' asked Brenda, 'what do we do now? How does one even go about performing a "seance"?'

Grace frowned faintly at the family. 'Wait, you've never even *attempted* a seance before?'

'Of course not, they're airy-fairy nonsense.'

'Don't say that, Mum,' muttered Darryl. 'What if a ghost hears you?'

In the end, they decided to go with much the same process as they did in the run up to the house clearance in the vestry – the same candles and chalk markings on the floor. It was, Darryl insisted, as much about appearances as anything. And, once they'd set out a circle of chairs in the middle of the markings, placed the coffee table in the centre of it all and covered it with a bit of black velvet, it did at least give off the appearance that the family probably knew what they were doing. Grace pulled up pictures of Melanie Ellis, Mr Massood, the Grey Twins and Kayak Pete on the family's phones, as well as – and after a lot of searching – at Darryl's request, a lady called Reenie Black, who had died in the Tesco back when it had been an independent grocery store, in 1987. She pulled up the grainy obituary picture of Reenie on her own phone and laid all the phones displaying their pictures of the dead on the velvet covered coffee table.

'I feel like we should have an Ouija board,' whispered Grace. 'I mean, yes they're very much a no-no, church-wise, but if we're just scene-setting for a seance…'

'They're a distraction,' announced Brenda. 'Don't need them with me and Darryl about, and ghosts think they're hilarious. Most of the time they just spell out rude words like they're the first dead person to think of it.'

'Crystal ball then?'

'We're not telling the ghosts' futures, Reverend.'

'I think, aesthetically, it does need something,' said Richard, quietly.

Charity picked up a dusty rounded glass vase, filled with crunchy grey-brown husks that had probably once been chrysanthemums and lined with the chalky residue of long-evaporated water. She dumped the desiccated flowers into a bin, upended the vase and plonked it on the table.

'Ta-dah!'

The family regarded the table thoughtfully for a moment before agreeing amongst themselves that that would probably do. They pulled up six chairs and got Grace to join them and hold hands in a circle. They sat in silence for a while.

'So, do we say something then?' asked Charity after a lengthy pause. They all looked to Janusz.

'Uh,' said Janusz, 'you guys usually chant, don't you?'

'That's for clearances,' replied Richard. 'Usually it just winds the spirits up. If we're looking to do something that involves more of a dialogue... well you're better at that sort of thing, aren't you?'

'Also, this was your idea, Janusz,' added Brenda, 'so fill your boots.'

'My boots?' Asked Janusz, confused.

'She means "go ahead",' Darryl told him with an encouraging little smile. 'I've heard you on the phone smoothing things over with problem clients, try that sort of tone. Your "work voice".'

'Like dealing with the Exeter case?' asked Janusz. 'The ones who wanted to sue after "You Know Who" broke all their china plates?'

'He did apologise for that.' mumbled Richard.

'Yeah.' Darryl's smile widened. 'Like Exeter.'

'OK.' Janusz cleared his throat. 'Hello?' he said. 'This is Janusz Rook speaking, I understand some of you are unsatisfied with the state of matters concerning your deaths? I wondered if any of you might have a moment to talk through these concerns. I hope maybe we can come to some amicable state where we are all satisfied?'

Grace concentrated down at the pictures on the phones, and tried to ignore how much Janusz's "work voice" was making Darryl blush. How did those two ever get anything done?

There was a pause, and then a thin, weak voice began to emanate from Darryl. It was just a groan at first, but after a couple of seconds, the voice found some words.

'Is that the Manager?'

CHAPTER FOURTEEN

The Seance

The voice sounded plaintive, distant and so very tired. It sounded like a little old lady who'd been patiently waiting on hold for hours due to having no other options. The sheer, heavy sadness of it squeezed at Janusz's heart.

'So Melanie speaking through Darryl wasn't a one-off then,' whispered Charity, ignoring the old voice's pleas.

'Mm,' murmured Brenda, 'looks like this is just a thing he can do now.'

'Maybe he could do it all along,' whispered Janusz, 'he just never had the chance to.'

'Excuse me? If you please?' quavered the voice, again, with a heartbreakingly timid politeness. 'Have I come through to the right person? I've been waiting so long.'

Darryl was the only family member who didn't look impressed that there was an old lady's voice coming out of him. He didn't look conscious at all, in fact. His head was slumped to one side and his eyes had rolled back. The flush in his cheeks from moments before was gone – in fact, he was now a sickly shade. He looked like he'd just spent all night having a series of one-too-many-drinks and had passed out in the back of the first early commuter bus out of town.

'Somebody said there was a manager,' continued the plaintive old lady voice coming from Darryl's mouth. 'I heard them at the shop.' It created the effect of a very upsetting ventriloquist's puppet.

Janusz gnawed his lip a little at the state of his husband. 'He's OK though, right?'

'Probably,' said Brenda, very quietly.

'Well,' added Richard, making a stab at sounding reassuring, 'this is our first seance, so. This is probably completely normal, for a seance. Maybe.'

'Hello?' whimpered the voice again. 'Is the Manager there? I'm not supposed to be here.' There was a momentary pause. 'Is this the dentist's?'

'Yes,' replied Grace.

Janusz glanced at the priest. He wasn't really sure whether you were just supposed to talk back at a seance, but the voice sounded so wretched and lost, perhaps it was best not to keep it waiting any longer.

'They've done it up since my day,' noted the voice, absently. 'I'm sorry. I don't know why I'm here. I was down the shop. I was waiting for ages. Somebody said there'd be a manager. There was a fight, I think. Terrible business. Why are we at the dentist's? I've got dentures, you see.'

'It's just a place to chat, Reenie,' replied Grace. 'You are Reenie Black, right?'

'Reenie,' breathed the voice, a wave of familiarity and relief washed into its tremulous sadness. Clearly, Reenie had not heard her own name spoken in a very long time. Maybe it had been lost to her for a while, back there.

'You said you'd been waiting,' added Janusz. 'Were you always waiting at the shop? Was there ever a light? Somewhere for you to go to, but you decided not to go? Or you got lost, or—?'

'No,' replied Reenie, 'never. I'd heard about the light, you know, before. I didn't mind the actual… I am dead, aren't I?'

'Yes,' Janusz told her. 'Sorry.'

'It's all right, duck,' said Reenie. 'I didn't mind that. Could have done with going out a bit nicer, bit quieter, at home, you know. But I'd lost my Reg in 1982, you see so I thought there'd be all light and angels and I'd see my Reg again and maybe my old mum. But they kept me waiting, and the Manager never did come so I could explain the problem. So I just… kept waiting. Always waiting, in the same blooming spot. It's the waiting I can't stand, you see. I like to keep busy, or I did, or… that was the plan. Be a busy bee. Flit about. Costa Brava.' Reenie's voice sighed, and the sadness seeped in more. It made Janusz feel as if his heart was full of stones.

'Never flitted anywhere, really,' continued Reenie. 'Never went anywhere. Reg did, in the Great War. I always said he was lucky for that. Yes, he was in the mud on the Western Front and got his foot shot off, but at least he'd travelled further than Stoke-on-Trent. I meant to – we both meant to, but there was kids and then there was old Adolf and then there was just never the money, so we carried on in Coldbay. Costa Brava.'

'You keep saying "Costa Brava",' noted Janusz.

'Don't you have a lovely accent?' asked Reenie, dreamily. 'Costa Brava. That's in Spain, that is. We saved up. We were all packed. And then there was the storm. They had to shut the bridge. Didn't open it again 'til an hour after our flight had left the airport. Our big trip. Didn't even make it to the mainland. And then, by the time we'd managed to rearrange, it was too late for my Reg. We just… stayed put. And then, I stayed put. I do like to keep busy, though. They said there'd be a manager.'

Darryl's head snapped suddenly up, then lolled against his other shoulder.

'Did someone say this is where we find the Manager?' asked a new voice – a man's, this time. 'Wait. Is this the dentist's?'

'Hello, um…' Janusz looked down at all the pictures of the dead, unsure. 'Mr Massood? Edward Grey…? Kayak Pete?'

'Kayaks!' said the voice, suddenly. 'I was going to… it was going to be fun, something to do on the island. But the island hated it. Hates fun. Punishes fun. Is the Manager here? Why is the Manager at the dentist?'

'How can an island hate fun?' asked Charity. 'How can an island hate anything? It's an island.'

'It's not allowed,' said the voice. 'Anything that might alleviate the curse isn't allowed.'

'Curse?' asked Janusz.

'Misery on misery on misery,' said the voice. 'The island wants you to die hating it. That's what I reckon anyway. Had a while to think. I need to tell the Manager—'

'The Manager?' a third voice came from Darryl, managing to cut Pete's voice off mid-sentence. It was an older man, this time. Probably Mr Massood, Janusz decided. 'The Manager's here? This is a dentist's.'

Brenda met eyes with Grace. 'They're really thrown by the whole dentist thing, aren't they?' she muttered.

Grace replied with the sort of awkward shrug that said 'Yeah, I know, it's not ideal, but there's nothing we can do about it now'.

'We didn't want any trouble,' continued the voice. 'We just wanted to leave. The island won't let us. Why won't it let me leave? I hate this place. I hate it! Are you the Manager?'

Janusz opened his mouth to reply, but before he could, the voice was replaced again.

'A dentist?' Another male voice; this one was younger. Early twenties, perhaps, and tight with panic. 'Why are you doing this? We didn't do owt wrong! Why am I in Hell?'

'You're not in Hell,' said Grace, hurriedly. 'We're here to help? Is that Edward Grey? Or John?'

'Where's John?' panicked the voice. 'We did everything together. What have you done to him? Where is he? We didn't do anything wrong! Is it because of what I said, during the car crash? I didn't really mean it. I was just angry. We only wanted a holiday. Just a little thing. We didn't do anything wrong!'

'What was it that you said?' asked Janusz, gently. 'I'm sure it's nothing to feel bad about.'

'I cursed the island,' replied the voice, frantically. 'I was angry, so I died cursing the island, but it was already so cursed, and now I'm in Hell and I can't find John and they said there'd be someone to sort things out but nobody came and I get it now, waiting forever for someone to come is part of the punishment. But we didn't do owt wrong, not really! What's one more curse?'

'The person you're waiting for,' said Richard, 'is it a manager?'

'There is no manager,' wailed the voice of Edward Grey, 'Just the island and this dentist's, do I have to spend the rest of forever in here now? Where's John?'

'We'll try to find him,' replied Janusz. 'Would that help you, Edward?'

But Edward's voice was gone again. Reenie's voice rose up briefly, asking plaintively for the Manager, and in turn was drowned out by Mr Massood, groaning, which was then drowned out by Kayak Pete's voice telling them to get off the island if they possibly could.

'It feeds off misery,' said Pete. 'Don't let it turn you into another misery meal.'

'Where's the Manager?' asked Reenie again.

'There's a hole up there,' said a new voice – slightly different to, but not dissimilar from Edward Grey's.

'John Grey?' asked Grace. 'Your brother's looking for you. Do you think you could—'

'What am I doing here now?' It was Melanie's voice. 'Haven't you people done enough without sending me to the dentist? I don't need to go to the dentist, I'm dead.'

'Melanie, are you waiting for the Manager?' Brenda asked.

Melanie jolted Darryl's head, as if trying to roll a marble of memory to the right part of the mind. 'They didn't like my business plan. Didn't like the new pier. Not right for the island. Burn it. Start from scratch. The Manager would be in touch. Is the Manager coming? Somebody opened a door, up above. It's so big now. Is the Manager coming?'

'The Hell Hole,' murmured Brenda.

'Do you think this "manager" has something to do with that?' Grace asked.

'If there even is a "manager",' added Charity. 'Maybe Edward's got a point, maybe it's just a cruel trick.' She sighed. 'Can't believe I'm saying this, but... does anyone else feel a bit bad? For always popping them? They're just really sad.'

'This is why I don't talk to them, princess,' replied Brenda.

Charity sighed again. 'Wish we could have just got in and out. It seemed like such a simple job – rock up at the church, exorcism, off for ice creams on the beach, pile into the car and on to Aldwych. But no, instead we get all this hassle. This island sucks.'

'Get off this island,' said the voice of Kayak Pete. 'While you can. *If* you can. Don't feed it. *Leave.*'

'As soon as we've finished this job,' Richard told him.

'The job can't be finished,' Melanie told them. 'Not if *they* disapprove. They won't allow it. You'll have to explain yourself to the Manager.'

'How long has that hole been there?' asked John. 'Did you make it? How long have you been here? Have you seen Edward?'

'We just spoke with him,' Janusz told him.

Charity spoke over Janusz, defensively. 'It wasn't us. The hole. We've only been here a day. And a night. Haven't we?'

'I was only at the shop for an hour,' said Reenie. 'But it went on for so long. I've been waiting so long. I only nipped out for an hour.'

'We've only been here a day and a night,' replied Janusz, nodding. Frowning. 'Except… how long was I in the window?'

His memories of the window were already so hazy. He remembered fear, and being surrounded by cold, brittle hostility. Everything had become warped, in the glass. He'd been there for no time at all and he'd been there as long as the goatherds. He'd been there for 800 years.

'Not long,' Charity told him, but she too looked unsure. She turned to Grace. 'Just a day and a night, right Reverend?'

'Reverend Duncan?' asked Kayak Pete. 'No. He's dead. Suspicious circumstances. Started going funny.'

'No,' interrupted Reenie, 'that was Reverend Dean. That was back in my day, that was. It was in the paper.'

'Reverend Dean,' breathed Grace. 'Suspicious circumstances, again. Yes. They said, when I started… when I started…'

'What is it?' Janusz frowned at Grace.

Grace gazed back at him, with the expression of someone who just remembered that they'd left the hob on back at home

154

and had also forgotten where they lived. Her voice was a horrified whisper. '*When* did I start?'

'Where's John?' the voices coming out of Darryl were now a mish mash, speaking over one another, all of them confused and desperate. 'Where's the Manager? Been waiting so long. Eddie? Only nipped out for an hour, I'm a busy bee. We did nothing wrong. Minded our own business. Just wanted to leave. It eats misery. You have to leave. Take the priest, it likes priests. They won't allow it. You need to speak to the Manager. There's a hole. You made the hole. You need to go. We want to go. The Manager—'

Darryl choked, coughed and slid off his chair, hitting his head on the coffee table before crumpling in an unconscious heap on the waiting room floor.

'Darryl!' Janusz leaped towards his husband, catching his leg painfully on the coffee table, as is the way with all coffee tables. He patted Darryl's face gently. 'You OK?'

Darryl groaned, in Darryl's own voice.

'He's OK,' announced Janusz.

'My head,' moaned Darryl. 'It really hurts. Is it bleeding?'

It was bleeding, albeit only a bit.

'He's mostly OK,' Janusz corrected himself.

'What happened?' Darryl asked, his eyes still shut. 'There were so many of them. They all sort of pushed me to the back, I couldn't hear what was going on.'

'I think we're supposed to find a manager,' said Charity. 'Darryl, we *have* only been here for a day and a night, right?'

Darryl groaned again. 'Why are you asking me that now? I just hit my head. Janusz's spreadsheets'll have all our bookings and dates and that.'

'My spreadsheets!' exclaimed Janusz, shuffling away from Darryl to fetch his laptop.

'Wait, no,' Darryl opened his eyes and propped himself up his elbows, 'I didn't mean now.' He looked blearily across at Grace. 'You all right, Reverend?'

Grace was still gazing glassily around the room, her expression a mix of horror and confusion. 'When did I come here?' she whispered. 'I don't remember. Where was I before?' She focused on the family. 'Who gave me your email?'

The family looked at each other.

'We have no way to know,' replied Janusz after a worried moment, 'it's not on the spreadsheet.'

CHAPTER FIFTEEN

Brown Sign

'We need to do this fast,' called Brenda, even though out of all of them, she was walking the slowest. 'That hole has been growing far too quickly and by the sound of things, we're making it worse.'

'We need to get the reverend out of here first,' Richard shouted back to her as they hurried along the street. 'You heard what they said about priests. And, if she can't remember how long she's been here... maybe the whole thing's feeding off her.'

'It grew after the first time we brought her near it,' added Charity. 'Dad's got a point, Mum.'

'We'll get to the car,' said Richard, 'drive her to a safe spot off the island, come back and sort all this Hell Hole business then see if we can help those ghosts.'

'I think Skegness is not far past the bridge,' Janusz told Grace, cheerfully. 'You can stay there, nice and safe, while you remember things. Can you still not remember things?'

Grace shook her head, miserably.

'You can't just leave a priest in Skegness,' shouted Brenda. 'What did she do to deserve that?'

'I don't know,' wailed Grace, 'I keep telling you, I can't remember!'

Brenda glanced over her shoulder as she walked, as fast as her shoes would allow. The hole was even bigger than before.

The hole fed off misery. And they'd just made it worse. Popping the ghosts made it worse. Talking to them and bringing to the surface all the miseries of their lives and afterlives trapped on the island made it worse. Leaving the ghosts to shuffle about like tragic shadows, waiting for a voice of authority who would never come and sort everything out as promised, would certainly make it worse. Letting the demons pour out of the Hell Hole to slither and flitter about... that didn't just make it worse. That simply could not be allowed to happen; not on her watch.

They reached the road where the church grimly squatted in its grey haze of mist. The car was still parked, neatly, politely and making no fuss at the side of the road. Brenda realised as Richard remote-unlocked the doors with a silent and demure flicker of the indicator lights that there were now six adults in their group, and it was enough of a squeeze with five.

'Afraid you kids are going to have to get friendly,' Richard announced.

'I don't mind going in the boot,' offered Grace, 'I'm small.'

'My husband,' said Janusz, with the deadly serious gallantry of a Disney Prince, 'can sit on my lap.'

'Yeah, I'm cool with that,' added Darryl.

The family bundled in.

'OK, but if we get pulled over—' began Grace.

'Who's going to pull us over?' Charity asked. 'Look at this place. You must have noticed. Nobody's here. Nobody alive, anyway. Whole island's deserted.'

'I have been trying to say this all day,' said Janusz, shuffling his thighs to achieve an approximation of comfort under the weight of one entire husband.

'No, there must be people here,' said Grace, quietly.

'You can't be serious,' snorted Brenda from the front passenger seat. 'There's *nobody* here, vicar! From the state of the supermarket, there's been nobody here for at least a month.'

Grace strapped in her seatbelt, concentrating on hearing the click. No. The island wasn't deserted, it couldn't be. She'd have noticed. Of course she'd have noticed! They were her flock! She'd have noticed before. She'd been there at least a month and it wasn't as if she'd been holed up in her church for a whole month, was it?

Was it?

How long had she been at that church?

Richard started the car, checked his mirror for any oncoming traffic on the empty road, on what was almost certainly a deserted island, signalled to let the non-existent traffic know he was about to pull out, checked his mirror again, and manoeuvred.

Think about death. Think about the uncertainty of life, with all the thrill that involves removed. Think about the dread fear of mortality, but seen only in hindsight, with nothing that can be done about it. Think about the tedium of the mundane, stretching on and on, forever. Think about absolute isolation, of being one of billions upon billions, and yet utterly lost and alone. Think about being tied to one spot or one moment, and yet left untethered. Think about how this might affect your sense of reality, and warp your sense of time. Think about how in life, every year that you experience shocks you with the speed of its passing; your personal timer towards the inevitable ticking faster and faster.

Grace thinks of all these things as Richard pulls away from her church. She tries to remember the last time she saw anyone alive, besides the Rooks.

Think about life. Think about warm touches, and laughter, and those snippets from childhood, which get fuzzier and more dreamlike the closer to toddlerhood you try to push your memory. Think about how a tune or a smell or a taste can make a memory not thought about in decades come rushing back – a peppermint kiss, skidding off a bike onto sun-heated tarmac, the advertising jingle for a now-obsolete product by a now-shuttered company. Grace knows she *should* have those.

And yet

And yet

And yet, where are they? The peppermint kisses and the hot tarmac bloody knees? It will be Christmas soon. What are her Christmas plans, besides presiding over an empty church? What are her Christmas traditions? What had she done as a girl? There should be something. *There should be something warm. Touches. Laughter. She can't find them.*

Stuck in one place, and yet untethered.

There in the back of a Ford Focus, sandwiched by the adult Rook children, Grace lets go of something she'd been clinging to – some sort of shield against the fear.

And the fear comes roaring in.

Think about life. Think about death. Think about something that isn't quite either. Grace Barry allows herself to see the island, empty of people but thrumming with an ever growing void hanging above it, neither alive nor dead, all warped and wrong. She allows

*herself to entertain the idea that perhaps she is warped and wrong,
as well.*

*Perhaps she is not the only living resident of Coldbay Island left.
Perhaps that ship has already sailed.*

'I think,' Grace whispered, 'I might be dead.'

Everyone in the car, barring the ever road-safe Richard, gazed at her.

'Nah,' said Charity dismissively, after a moment.

'But how can you be sure?'

'It's sort of our line of expertise,' Charity told her. 'It's like calling in pest control and then asking them if they're sure you're not a pigeon. We'd know.'

'But I can't remember anything,' Grace fretted. 'It's like my brain's in a fog, and I don't know how long it's been like this.'

'You heard those poor ghosts,' said Janusz, kindly, 'the island, or Hfhfh from the window or the "manager" or whoever is doing this – they like to mess with the minds of priests. You're not the first it's happened to.'

'But you'll be the last, hopefully,' added Richard. 'Once we've got you off this... Dear, could you get the satnav on your phone please? Mine won't load.'

Richard turned left as Brenda got out her phone.

'Pretty sure it was this way,' muttered Richard.

Brenda huffed. 'Typical! Stupid machine. Mine doesn't want to play either.' She jabbed at her phone. 'It was like this last night, too.'

'Boomers,' whispered Charity, battling to get her own phone out of her pocket in the crush on the back seat.

'And then this way? Maybe?' Richard went straight on at a crossroads. 'I recognise that house. Do I recognise that house? Does anyone else recognise that house?'

Charity dislodged her phone and frowned at it. 'Must be something wrong with the app, Dad.'

'It's OK, princess, I think I know where we're... wait, no, I don't remember that mini roundabout, must have got turned around somewhere.'

'Which of you's got the road atlas?' Brenda called to the back seat.

'We still have a road atlas?' asked Charity. 'What is this? The olden days?'

'It's in the seat pocket in front of Darryl,' said Richard. 'Wait, I think we're back on track. I remember that tree.'

'If I'm not dead,' fretted Grace, 'then what's wrong with me? What if we get off the island and nothing changes? Or... will I disappear or something.'

'You won't disappear.' Darryl twisted uncomfortably on Janusz's lap so that he could reach into the storage pocket for the atlas. 'You're not dead, we swear.'

'You'd think there'd be a sign for the bridge or something,' muttered Richard.

'Brown sign!' called Brenda, pointing. 'There!'

'That's more like it... wait.' Richard peered at the sign in the gloom. 'That's for the beach so this is the wrong way.' He pulled in to do a three point turn. 'You got that atlas?'

'Is my old CD Walkman down there too?' asked Charity. 'What with that being the car's time capsule of olden days stuff.'

'Got it.' Darryl pulled out an elderly road atlas book, and flicked through it for the right page.

Richard turned the car and set off again. 'It was the opposite direction to the beach, that much I know.'

'I don't think this is a good idea,' said Grace.

Darryl continued to go through the book.

'The Grey twins,' continued Grace, 'The Massoods, so many more. It wouldn't let them leave.'

Nobody replied. Darryl kept going through the book, Richard kept driving in as straight a line as possible, away from the direction of the beach.

'What if there's another freak wave or something when we're on the bridge?' asked Grace. 'The island wouldn't let them leave. If it wants to keep me here and mess with my brain… it's not going to let me leave, is it?'

'Dad?' said Darryl. 'I can't find it.'

'Janusz sonny, could you help Darryl?' asked Richard. 'You know how to read a map.'

Darryl showed his husband the book. 'See?'

'I see the problem.' Janusz's voice was slightly strained, braced against Darryl's weight. 'It's not there.'

'What?'

'Not on the map.'

'That's not right,' murmured Brenda.

'That's your problem with old road maps,' said Charity, 'they're out of date, missing out loads of places that hadn't been built yet.'

'Not whole islands, princess!'

'We're not on the map?' Grace shook her head. 'There were maps. I'm sure there were maps… weren't there?'

'It *was* on satnav, before,' said Darryl, 'but now there's no satnav.'

'It's not going to let us leave.' Grace paused, and corrected herself. 'It's not going to let *me* leave. Maybe it's not too late for you.'

'We're not abandoning a client,' said Brenda, tartly. 'We're certainly not leaving this job unfinished.'

'But…' Grace found herself staring into Brenda's eyes. There was something terrible about that woman's gaze. Terrible and determined. Grace couldn't begin to guess what multitude of horrors over the years had etched that look of determination into Brenda's face. What Grace did know was that Brenda meant it. They weren't going to leave her, not now.

'I don't know what to say,' Grace told her. Well, there was one thing she should probably say. 'Listen, Brenda…'

Richard sighed heavily, indicated and pulled over to a sensible stop.

'What is it?' asked Darryl.

Richard pointed to the road ahead. A thick, grey line of sea was smeared across the bits of the horizon that were visible through familiar looking buildings. A brown sign loomed at them through the drizzle. It was pointing them towards the beach. Ahead, the dark void swirled in the sky.

The island wasn't going to let them leave.

'Oh!' Charity was still fiddling with her phone. 'Satnav's finally loaded.' She paused. 'Ah.' She showed the others her phone. The screen was nothing but a dark swirl, a colour that went beyond merely black. The all-consuming nothing of the Hell Hole. The others checked their own phones, and found the same.

'And now we can't call for outside help,' sighed Richard.

Brenda snorted. 'As if anyone else could have helped with this anyway. Not since the Longest Night.'

Another mention. Memories, warming me, nourishing me. Charity ignores what Brenda had said about a 'Longest Night', and glowers at her phone.

'I can't even get on Instagram.'

'You don't need Instagram to fight Demons, Charity!'

Charity pulled a face at her brother. 'How else am I supposed to document the world of the paranormal?'

'Not with selfies while steak knives are flying at your head, you maniac.'

'It is a bit dangerous when you do that, princess,' said her father. 'Not to mention distracting for the rest of us.'

'It's marketing,' snapped Charity. 'Tell them. Janusz.'

'Three of our bookings last month came from Charity's social media,' said Janusz quietly, from beneath Darryl. 'But it is still quite dangerous, Charity. Maybe it's for the best that you don't this time given that our phones are all haunted now.'

Charity sighed. 'Well, I'm not spending the rest of forever sitting around a deserted island with no way off *and* a haunted phone.'

'Oh, we're not,' said Brenda. 'Because I do believe we've run out of options.'

'And if we can't get the priest to safety,' added Richard, 'then we've run out of time.'

'I'd say we were pretty much out of time already,' said Brenda, 'from the size of that thing.'

'What do you mean, "out of time"?' Grace asked.

'It would have been nice to have seen if you could remember a few more things,' sighed Brenda, turning in her seat to look at Grace. 'I'd have liked to have found out who our real clients were, at least, since it clearly wasn't your idea to book us.'

'Are we... going to die?' asked Grace. 'You're making this sound like we're all going to die.'

'I mean, we're *all* going to die *eventually*,' said Brenda. 'And a minute ago you were panicking about already being dead, so at least this is a step up from that.'

'Dear,' warned Richard.

Brenda turned around in her seat to address the squished back seat again. 'That Hell Hole is the single most terrible, fastest growing intrusion on the realm of the living that I have ever seen. And I've seen a *lot* of terrible things. Murzzzz, you're older than civilisation, anything to add?'

Richard shifted in his seat, and a shade of Murzzzz appeared. **'It's really bad**,' the Demon said, sheepishly avoiding Darryl's glare. **'It has the potential to begin… you know. Curtains. The time for the trumpet to sound.'**

The people in the car thought about this.

'*The Muppet Show*?' asked Charity.

'What?'

'*The Muppet Show* always started with curtains and a trumpet.'

Murzzzz sank back into Richard. 'I think he means the apocalypse,' Richard told them.

'The apocalypse,' breathed Grace.

'What's that got to do with trumpets, though?' asked Charity.

'It's in the bible.'

'I never saw Murzzzz as a bible reader. Wouldn't it burn him, or something?'

'Demons are generally fascinated by human faiths,' said Richard. He shot Grace an apologetic look. 'I'm afraid they think it's all… funny.'

Grace just shook her head. 'The apocalypse.'

'Only *possibly* the apocalypse,' added Charity, brightly. 'The apossiclypse.'

'Charity, stop being glib about a possible apocalypse,' said Darryl.

'What do we do?' Grace whispered. 'What can we possibly do?'

'My suggestion is that we get out of this car,' said Janusz with a muffled politeness. 'We were called here to deal with the problem. It says on our website "No spectral problem too big or too small", so this must, by logic, include an apocalypse.'

Darryl smiled and squeezed Janusz's hand. 'That's my man.'

'Also,' added Janusz, 'my legs have gone to sleep. I would really like to get out of this car.'

CHAPTER SIXTEEN

The Manager

T*hink about the end. Think about the drip drip drip of ice into an ocean – such little drips – all tucked away somewhere so you don't have to think about it until suddenly the ocean is so big that it's lapping over your feet. Think about the drip drip drip of human misery into some little cut-off community you never even heard of before – such little unhappy lives – until it rises up as a howl so big and so angry that it breaks the sky. Think about someone tasked with managerial responsibilities over that sort of chaos. Nightmare, right? No wonder they're too busy to speak to the little people, as promised. They're too busy looking at the bigger picture. They're too busy because they're trying to find ways to pull the plug on the whole messy miserable project.*

The Manager didn't 'sit' on the beanbag, as such. It had no buttocks to sit on. Also, the furniture wasn't technically a beanbag. Somewhere in the living realm, out there somewhere in timespace, there was a philosopher coming up with the concept of an ideal chair that could exist only in the ether. The philosopher was getting it wrong, as all human philosophers do. It was beyond the philosopher's ken that actually the ether contains bean bags – perfectly imperfect, a celestial model of something that looks as if it should be comfortable but is, in fact, equally awkward for anything to try to rest upon. The Manager attempted to settle its form gently upon the ethereal bean bag and found the experience just uncomfortable enough to prevent it from feeling restful. The lights in the office were a little too cold and bright, the desks either a little too low or a little too high.

The Manager pulled up all of its data around the Resolution Opportunity.

Ah. Good. Grace Barry was still operating well. A few ruffles in the reprogramme protocol, but those would be easily dealt with in a few tweaks. The produce was really doing a super job as well, in spite of the unforeseen issue. The Rooks had not been expected to try to *talk* to them, but thankfully it hadn't sapped much energy after all. Everything was slotting into place. It was looking very positive for the proposed deal – the deal that would finally get rid of that frustrating little outstanding red sticker issue. If the Manager had had a mouth, it would have sighed. There were to be no sign-offs on project termination orders without full resolution of the red sticker issues, all departments had been very clear on that. The Manager was certain that this was the last one.

The Manager could not wait to send the project termination orders through for sign-off. It was high time, frankly.

Almost there. Almost finished. One more red sticker.

It got up out of the bean bag. It took three goes to do so, as it always did with the ethereal concept of an ideal bean bag. It drifted down the staircase awkwardly to Aubergine Floor, and made its way towards Heliotrope Room, which was where they were keeping all their doors for that reality cycle. Last reality cycle, the doors had been in Lilac Room, all the way up the stairs on the Heliotrope Floor. It had taken the Manager a while to get used to the new system and now here they were, practically at the end of another reality cycle. Flipping typical, eh? Oh well. The door to Coldbay was big enough for the Manager now. It hovered nearby, and waited. It was about to be summoned. It could practically taste those sweet, sweet termination orders. Or at least it would be able to if it could eat termination orders but, as has just been mentioned, the Manager didn't have a mouth.

They got out of the car again. Richard locked it, checked that he hadn't accidentally parked in an illegal spot, and tried the door to double-check that it was locked.

Silently, they began to walk. There was nowhere to go but the void.

Really, thought Brenda, there had been nowhere to go but the void since they had found out that there *was* a void. Likely, there had been nowhere to go but the void since they'd got to the island in the first place. They just hadn't known it then.

She could feel it drawing her now, like an undercurrent tugging some poor soul away from their capsized kayak and down, the shock filling their lungs with salt water. Like the swell of a sudden wave, throwing a family from their stalled car and dragging them under the bridge, scraping heads against tarmac and twisted metal as it went. It was a stronger pull than she'd experienced before, but it wasn't unfamiliar. She'd felt fainter incarnations of it many times before; almost constantly since 2016, in fact – and certainly whenever the work took her within fifty miles of Coldbay – but, she realised now, she'd felt it even before then. The first time she'd seen Janusz, and the way Darryl was looking at him. The first time she'd looked into the eyes of her children, even when her daughter hadn't yet been her daughter. The first time she'd met Richard and, by association, the Demon hiding inside him.

She had felt love every time, but with it, that tug towards the void. Perhaps, she thought, the two were inseparable. She was overcome by a bleakness that she put down to the fact she hadn't had a drink in a couple of hours. She reached into her bag for her remaining bottle of rum.

'You drink too much.'

Brenda turned, incredulously, to the cringing priest.

'I *beg* your pardon??'

'In case we don't have much time left,' said Grace. 'I just felt it should be said. You drink a worrying amount, I have leaflets back at the church, if you need help with it.' She paused, watching Brenda's expression. 'It can't be good for you.'

'We're all trapped on a haunted island, about to face off against a massive hole in the sky and whatever lurks on the other side of it,' replied Brenda, 'and while you're right about us likely having little time left as a result of that, it's safe to say it hardly matters what I drink, or what some vicar thinks about it. If we're dead meat, then we're dead meat, sober or not.'

'But if we *do* make it…' attempted Grace.

Richard patted Grace's shoulder and gave her a shake of the head that Brenda supposed was meant to be subtle and diplomatic.

'I wouldn't, if I were you. It's not that we haven't tried…'

Richard trailed off, under Brenda's gaze. She didn't like to be reminded of her family's insipid, annoying, tone deaf attempts to 'talk about her drinking'. They were unacceptable memories. At least the priest lecturing her on it felt like less of a betrayal. Priests were *supposed* to be overbearing scolds.

'If we make it off the island alive,' said Grace, quickly, 'can I at least give you a leaflet?'

The tug towards the void was impossibly strong now. How long had it been picking at her? Longer than she'd known Richard? Maybe from the first dead person she'd seen – all those 'invisible friends' that had terrified her from before she could even put the fear into words. Maybe the void had been pulling at her since then.

She intended to do something about it. She wasn't going to just take this lying down. She was going to damn well make a stand. Hopefully it would give the others more time. Hopefully it would give the world more time. It would probably be the end for her, though. She wasn't going to make it off the island alive. She took a long swig of rum.

'Yeah, all right, you can give me a stupid leaflet.'

Grace's face brightened, just as Richard's expression crumpled into a picture of horror.

'Fantastic,' beamed Grace.

'Dear?' asked Richard, quietly.

'Let's just get this job finished.' Brenda continued to walk briskly in the direction of the pier. She turned her face away from her husband.

He knew. He knew that she expected she would be dead by the end of the day.

They turned a corner onto the promenade, and the void loomed large from behind a shuttered block of flats. It took another five minutes to get to the pier. The family and Grace walked in silence; whatever they had to say to one another was blotted out of their minds by the terrible, gaping nothingness hanging over them.

Brenda gestured for the rest of her family to wait at the pier entrance. Charity tried to follow her anyway, but Richard held their daughter back, a grim look on his face. Brenda walked steadily along the pier to just before the locked door of an empty tea shop. She squared her shoulders, folded her arms and turned a defiant face to the void.

This was it. This was the moment she'd been waiting for, her whole life.

'I want to speak,' she announced, 'to the Manager.'

CHAPTER SEVENTEEN

The Meeting

'Speaking,' boomed the void.

'You're the Manager?' asked Brenda. 'So, what, you're just a big Hell Hole or you're hiding behind it?'

'I'm not hiding,' replied the Manager. 'I'm just in Head Office. Also please don't refer to the door as a "Hell Hole", it's neither accurate nor helpful.'

'What should I call it then?'

'It's just a door.'

'Why are you hiding behind the door then?'

'Brenda Rook. You summoned me. Surely you have more pressing questions to ask.'

'That's another thing. Why did it have to take me coming out of my way for you to show up? I was talking to people at the dentist's. You wouldn't believe how long some of them have had to wait. They were *told* that you were on the way. But you weren't, were you? You were hiding behind your door.'

'It was not yet time to reveal myself,' replied the Manager.

'Why not?'

'You should not expect to understand the mysteries or the workings of what lies beyond…'

'How so? Demons have been coming from "what lies beyond" all my life, and I've had to deal with them…'

'OK, I get that you find those annoying, but those really aren't the remit of my department—'

'*And* I've had to deal with all those stuck dead people. Me and my family have to send them on to your mysterious "beyond" ourselves, at great personal risk – my son-in-law got turned into a window yesterday – and now you're opening up a great big hole to it in the sky and you still won't tell us about it?' Brenda scowled up at the void. '*And* you're still hiding! This is ridiculous! I demand to speak with you face to face.'

'I do not answer to demands from mortals.'

'I *beg* your pardon??' Brenda knew what her tone could do. She tried not to use it on service staff; on anyone underpaid or overworked, although she wasn't above using it to override certain legal issues, including avoiding several arrests and, one time, using it to commandeer a very haunted pleasure boat.

At the entrance to the pier, the rest of the family watched, and listened. Brenda's 'Speaking To The Manager' voice carried, even over the sound of the grey waves rushing against the shore and smashing against the pier's slime-coated pillars.

'I hope your mother isn't *too* unkind,' breathed Richard.

Janusz nodded in agreement. 'Demons have feelings too, right, Murzzzz?'

Murzzzz stayed deep within Richard, and didn't reply.

That thing behind the void wasn't a Demon. Murzzzz knew as much. It was worse than that. Through Richard's eyes, he watched the swirling abyss. Nothing was coming out of it right now, but he could tell it was already well-used. His attention shifted to the priest. She wasn't speaking, or moving. She was just… watching it. There was something about her expression that upset him. That, in itself, was wrong. Religious leaders shouldn't bother him. If anything, it was traditionally supposed to be the other way around. There was something off with this priest. He'd felt an inkling of it from the start. Whenever the priest went near the Hell Hole, a sudden spike of fear would stab through Murzzzz's thorax. It really didn't help that he also felt a stab of shame every time Darryl gave him a dirty look, since the lad had found out Murzzzz had been present during his conception. Feelings were no fun at all when one was an ancient Demon dwelling in a small, pension-age man.

Speaking of Demons…

Murzzzz could see them, skulking in corners, slithering down from rooftops, hovering in the thin rain next to murky lamp-posts and faded chip shop signs like even larger and more malevolent seagulls. Silently, Murzzzz told his human host of the lingering Demons, and Richard rested a hand of warning against Darryl's shoulder.

Darryl had already noticed them. There were so many of them. Two dozen, maybe more. Slowly, and with an attempt at nonchalance that was frankly ridiculous, considering, the Demons began approaching the pier.

Above the pier, the Manager tried again. 'It is better for all of you,' it boomed from the void, 'if I speak from my side of the door—'

'I will decide what's better for me and my family, thank you.'

'You should be warned—' came the voice.

'Show yourself now, please.'

There was a pause. 'Do not be afraid.'

'I've been seeing dead people and Demons my whole life, it's a bit late for that, sunshine.'

Something came out of the void. It was almost entirely eyes. The bits of it that weren't eyes looked like they were made out of fire, if that fire had been put together by M.C. Escher after a particularly heavy night followed up by a hearty breakfast of LSD omelettes. Interlocking rings of it managed to spin in far more than the mere three dimensions that were usually at play in the living world's space.

Janusz breathed a few choice words in his mother tongue, which Murzzzz understood anyway.

'I did just say not to be afraid,' said the Manager.

Brenda, to her credit, just kept on staring up at it, peevishly. 'Right, well now that you've deemed to grace us with your presence, perhaps you'd like to tell us what the blue blazes you're up to here? Because this whole island is a total mess, and the last I checked, you weren't supposed to open massive great doors in the sky – "Manager" or not.'

'Honestly, it's just a spot of admin, really.' The Manager vibrated in impossible frequencies as it spoke. It made Murzzzz's exoskeleton itch with anxiety. The other Demons were creeping closer down the pier. Murzzzz wanted to run, but Richard was going nowhere with this body, not without Brenda.

'Admin. Really?' Brenda remained unmoved. 'This island's been terrorised for generations.'

'Our admin takes a while,' replied the Manager. 'But we're nearly done now.'

'And then you'll leave the island alone, will you? And what about all the poor sods you left stuck here waiting?'

'Oh,' replied the Manager. 'No. No, the island's ours. Containment for the produce. And then the produce make more produce, of course. You get a few mortals who escape, naturally, but I think we managed to turn about eighty per cent into produce here, which is an excellent return. And the produce are… well. Produce. We need them for the door. I thought you lot had worked out we need them for the door. Can't do our admin without a door.'

'"Produce"?' Darryl murmured. 'It can't mean…'

'What do you mean, "produce"?' Brenda demanded.

'Ghosts,' said the Manager, plainly. 'Spirits, souls… thoughts, emotions… curses. They're all good. Technically, Head Office doesn't stipulate, but the Demon Department find negative emotions are best for them to work with, and they get to call the shots on this one, I'm afraid. Not my decision. Take it up with them.'

'"Produce"?' repeated Brenda.

'Yeah.'

'You killed everyone on this island?'

'As I said, about eighty per cent and again – not me directly.'

'And you call dead people "produce"? That's utterly heartless.'

'Well,' reasoned the Manager, 'we don't have hearts. What we do have is a grand, Bigger Picture perspective, and the energy derived from mortal souls – emotions, thoughts – call them what you will. You would not believe the sheer quantity we have to organise and manage. Most of them make it to one of our client departments no problem – unless we're deliberately concentrating them for admin purposes, of course – and then we've got people like you and your Deliverer to deal with the stragglers that get lost. It had been a pretty good system up to now.' The Manager paused, emitting a positive glow. 'So I would like to take a moment to thank you folks for your good work, actually.'

Murzzzz wanted to go. Richard's feet wouldn't move. The Demon could feel his host's mind racing with questions and concerns and – in spite of himself – a faint shade of pride at being thanked for the family's work so far.

'You're welcome,' called Charity, coldly.

'Interesting Deliverer recruitment technique, might I add,' continued the Manager. 'Just taking one out of its dead parent's arms without a by-your-leave.'

Now, Murzzzz felt the panic rise in Richard. About time, too.

'What?' asked Charity.

'One might even call it utterly heartless,' added the Manager. 'Of course, I'm sure if it had been the other way round, the family of Deliverers would have just as easily taken your infant Finder from your dying arms to make up a functional Find-And-Deliver team for us, but obviously you ensured that it didn't end up that way. Didn't you, Murzzzz?'

Oh, no.

Murzzzz took over from Richard just in time to duck away from a winged Demon as it dive-bombed. He could feel a slug Demon lurching after him from behind. He sprang up, claws out, and slashed at another flying Demon in mid-air. The first Demon lashed out with heavy pincers and struck Murzzzz at the same time, sending him crashing into the side of the abandoned pizzeria. He clung briefly to the wall of the building, getting his bearings. There were around thirty Demons. A small handful were still approaching the entrance to the pier, but most of them were swarming him. He took a quick glance at his famil— at *Richard's* family. The expressions on Darryl and Janusz's faces – Murzzzz used to delight in that sort of distressed confusion. Now it made him feel sick, which was in itself a sensation that Demons shouldn't by rights understand, since they weren't created with stomachs. The horror on Brenda's face was worse still. And then there was his princess— no. Richard's princess.

'What did you do?' shouted Charity. 'Murzzzz? Dad! What did Murzzzz do?'

Think about death. Think about dying, the terror of knowing that it's imminent. A great wave, rushing towards you, knowing it's about to hit. Knowing that, whatever is beyond it, the only thing you know for certain is that there is never ever any coming back from it. Knowing you've felt the pleasure of eating your favourite food for the last time. You've scratched your last itch. You've savoured your last kiss. You will never feel another cathartic hit from a really good laugh. You don't even have time for a bloody good cry about it.

You'll never see the baby in your arms grow up.

The baby in your arms. Think about the terror swelling. What will become of the baby in your arms? How could this have happened? Where is your husband? Where are your friends? They're supposed to be helping. You're supposed to be a team! The Rooks to find the spirits, the Xus to deliver them to the world beyond. Where are they? Death is crashing in fast and your baby is still in your arms. The fear. The fear. Your friends know what that fear is like – they have to, ghost-hunting with a little boy in tow like that. Where are they? Why aren't they helping you?

You see your husband, but it's all wrong. He's all wrong. He's already dead. You saw him die, you remember now. Just before the shards of glass flew at you. No time to say goodbye. Your husband, the love of your life. Just… gone. Just a body. It was moments ago, and yet a lifetime ago at the same time. You've only been dying for a few seconds, but it feels like a hundred years.

The baby.

She's alive. You protected her from the glass with your body. Yes. She's alive. But for how long?

Beyond the body of your husband, you see a Demon. He has the saddest expression you could imagine a Demon wearing. Only a few years ago, you would never have imagined a Demon with any sort of sad expression at all. This is the Demon you made a pact with – the Demon you promised could shelter within the body of your friend in return for his protection.

He should have protected you. He should have protected your husband. He should have protected your daughter. You made a deal!

You manage to breathe his name. It comes out sounding like a curse. His name is *a curse. He's a Demon, after all. Why didn't he protect you?*

You look into his sad, terrible, eternal eyes and you understand. He didn't protect you because he'd prioritised saving the skin he was in, and the woman and child that came with Richard Rook. He'd been selfish.

*The Demon speaks. **'I'm sorry, Constance. You'd have done the same.'***

Perhaps you would – for your *husband, for* your *child. You see in the Demon's eyes that he thinks it's genuinely the same. He sees Brenda and the boy as if they're* his *wife and son. The deluded pillock. You'd feel sorry for him, if you weren't currently filled with fear, and anger, and disgust at his betrayal.*

The wave fully hits, and pulls you from this life. You can no longer feel the baby in your arms.

'Constance!' Brenda finds your body a moment too late. She's bleeding. The boy with her is sobbing. He gazes at you – not at your body – at you. Brenda could make eye contact if she wanted to, but she doesn't.

'Oh no.' She gently lifts your baby from the dead sack of meat that used to be you. 'I'm so sorry.'

The Rooks find; the Xus deliver. And there go the Rooks, with their own little Xu. Your special girl. Your princess. Not yours any more. The rage and fear have left you in death. They've all turned into sadness. It's the heaviest sadness you've ever known. It descends on you like a sudden fog, so that you can barely focus, not even on the piercing, wet eyes of the little boy staring up at you in horror.

A thought about the boy and his family spikes your foggy consciousness. You whisper it to him.

'It should have been you.'

You don't mean it maliciously, it comes to you through the fog of sadness, not rage. It's just a fact, to you. The Demon promised to protect you, and he let you down. You wish the Demon had saved you and your husband, and let this boy's parents die. You can barely see the boy now, the fog is so thick.

It should have been them.

You can't find your husband. The fog takes you… somewhere. You can see them, still. The Demon who let you down, the friends who took your daughter and your place, the daughter who should have been yours. You can always see them, but it's just so removed. You start talking to yourself about everything that they do, if just to keep your mind in some sort of order, if just to remind yourself of them.

No. Not you. Me. That's me. This is me.

And I followed them here.

And I'm watching them now.

And the Manager knows I'm here.

I have a name, my name is Constance Xu, and I was killed by a Demon attack when I was twenty-seven. I had a husband and a daughter called Charity and I can't find my husband but that is my daughter. That is my daughter. She's older now than I will ever be and she's my *daughter so I'm telling her story, and the story of the friends who took her away from me.*

They should have died, instead of my husband and me.

Maybe they're going to die now. I don't particularly want them to. I don't particularly want them not *to. Although, as long as Charity lives... Honestly? I don't care anymore. I'm not being a dick about it, I swear, it's just what the sadness does to you.*

I'm sure they'll understand. Once they're dead.

And, oh – hello. The boy is looking at me. Not a boy now. A man. He's looking at me. A thrill, at being noticed! But I'm not part of this story, not anymore.

'I know her,' breathed Darryl, gazing at a spot not far from the void. 'That sad woman. How do I know her?'

'Is now the time?' asked Janusz.

Janusz couldn't see this apparently recognisable 'her' that his husband could see. He could, however, see the void, and the Manager, which was very upsetting. The Manager hurt his eyes. Even when he tried to turn his face away from it, the pain burned through his head and spiked right through to his eyes anyway.

There was something else that was bothering Janusz. He could actually *see* some of the Demons, creeping up on them. He'd always been able to see the difference between Murzzzz and Richard, but that was Murzzzz for you – anybody could see Murzzzz once he was the one in control of the body they shared. But now, he could see shapes, like giant slugs and bloated flies. They were just faint patches – like the after-image when you look at a brightly coloured picture and then blink away – but he could see them, or at least his brain was telling his eyes that they *should* be able to see them. Maybe it was the proximity to the void. Or, maybe being dragged into that window had done something to him.

These things – the void, the Manager, the visibility of the Demons and Darryl's sudden distraction – weren't by any means the total sum of what was bothering Janusz. He still hadn't had the chance to talk properly about the seance, or Darryl's previously unknown ability to be used as a mouthpiece for the dead. As Darryl's life partner, Janusz was pretty sure that they should have an in-depth discussion about what that meant for Darryl going forward and what precautions they could take to keep him from getting permanently possessed – no offence to Richard and Murzzzz. He was also very worried by what the Manager was saying – and not just with regards to Charity. Janusz was starting to get the feeling that the family running over-schedule and missing the Aldwych booking might not matter now. That was how worried he was. He wasn't even that bothered about his spreadsheets any more.

'I know what you're doing,' called Brenda. 'Trying to distract us, with your Demons and your dredging up of the past.'

'They're not my Demons,' replied the Manager. 'And it's your past. You made it, and you carry it with you.'

'Mum!' Charity shouted. 'What did Murzzzz *do*?'

Brenda turned to Charity. As she did so, her eyes glanced, ever so briefly, over the face of a ghost, watching them from afar.

Hello, Brenda, old friend.

'It's more about what he *didn't* do,' Brenda told her. 'And, I suppose, what your father and I didn't do. We'll discuss it later.'

'You mean, when you've let Grace give you a pamphlet?' Charity asked.

Brenda didn't reply to that. She turned back to the Manager.

'Call them off,' she demanded. 'All of them.' She pulled a face as, behind her, Murzzzz launched himself off a wall and tackled two approaching Demons. 'Murzzzz, you're being very off-putting right now.'

'Not my remit to call off the Demons or the dead,' replied the Manager.

'What *is* your remit then?'

'Admin,' replied the Manager, cheerfully. 'Balancing the books so that we can finally push ahead with full project termination.'

And there it was. Brenda had always sort of known that it was coming. Still, she wanted to hear it from the horse's mouth – or at least, the terrifying eye-and-fire-creature's audible vibrations, since it definitely wasn't a horse, and didn't seem to have a mouth.

'And by that, you mean...'

'You might call it the apocalypse, Armageddon, the end of the world, when the curtain falls, when the trumpets sound.'

'Charity was right,' said Brenda. 'Those last two do sound like they're from the *Muppets*.'

'That doesn't matter any more,' replied the Manager. 'Whatever "*Muppets*" are, doesn't matter. It's done. Finito. And before you start, it's nothing personal, we're simply reacting to developments in the project. You mortals have irreversibly broken your own world, and you need a functional world to live on because, well, you're mortal. In Head Office we rather saw that as the project's way of telling us it was coming to a natural end. It just makes good sense to pull the plug now and put us all out of our misery. Everything will end. There'll be no more suffering. No more death. No more...'

'No more *Muppets*. Darryl will be glad of that at least. He was always scared of them, weren't you, Darryl?'

'Huh?' asked Darryl, still distracted by the ghost.

Oh, Darryl. I've always been here watching. No point getting bothered by me now, it's much too late to be of any use.

'You are being very glib about project termination,' said the Manager. 'I understand. It's a human thing. A defence mechanism. Can't be helped.'

'I'm being glib because I saw this coming. Let me guess – you started work on this in earnest in 2016?'

'That *is* when we started fully actioning this operation,' replied the Manager in impressed tones. 'Well done!'

'I *knew* it!' cried Brenda, victoriously. She turned and jabbed a finger at her family. '*Told* you that year was cursed. Murzzzz, stop faffing about and get those Demons, would you? There's about twenty of them in striking distance.'

Murzzzz leaped away from one Demon as it swiped. He flipped himself around in mid-air, changed trajectory and landed, claws out, on top of a slug-like Demon slithering perilously close to Grace.

'Darryl! Get your brain in gear and help your sister pop a few of those!' Brenda turned back to the Manager. 'But mostly, I'm being glib because you've already built a massive hole in the sky out of centuries of concentrated human suffering, but you still haven't ended the world, which means that, for some reason, you can't do it yet.'

The Manager glowed with a slightly higher intensity. Considering it was already glowing very intensely to begin with, this was unnecessary. 'Busted,' it admitted.

'And whatever the reason is, it needs our help to fix it, which is why you brought us here, trapped us and aggravated us instead of just killing us.'

'Also true. Though you were great at getting the produce good and agitated – really helped us finish growing the door.'

'It's not just about the door though, is it? Because we're still here.'

'Yes.'

'So, then. Whatever it is you need our help with to end the world, we simply won't do it.' Brenda folded her arms. 'Kill us if you want – don't care. You're not getting your merry way with us.'

A strange, deeply unsettling sound emanated from the Manager. It sounded like thunder being played backwards.

'Ew, is it laughing at us?' called Charity.

'You've already done it,' replied the Manager. 'See, we just had one outstanding issue with the department that coordinates Demons and so on. Can't end the living world when one of their lot is still in it.'

Behind Brenda, Murzzzz landed on a slug Demon, claws out, and then sprang immediately up from it again, as if the Demon were a large, viscous trampoline. He contorted what would, in a human, be his spine, flipped and grabbed onto the underside of an overhanging street lamp for a split second before launching himself off it in the direction of a flying Demon; his jaw gaping wide like a snake about to take on a wildebeest, his fangs wet with black slime. At the edge of the thronging Demons, a figure lurked; large and shadowy and many-limbed. It darted in and out of the grubby windows of the abandoned buildings along the promenade, relishing in the distress and the violence. Hfhfh was having fun, and he hadn't even started yet.

Brenda took a step backwards, away from the Manager.

'No,' she said, quietly.

'It's only fair,' replied the Manager. 'He doesn't belong with you.'

Janusz grabbed Darryl's arm, urgently. 'It's a trap!'

'What?' asked Darryl.

'They want Murzzzz,' breathed Grace. 'All of this was about capturing Murzzzz.'

*

On the pier, Brenda took another step away. 'He's family.'

There was another backwards-thunder rumble. 'No, he really isn't. He's been causing you nothing but trouble. We are doing you a favour.'

Brenda turned, and started running back down the pier towards her family. 'Murzzzz!' She screamed. 'Get out of there! Darryl! Charity! Help him!'

Murzzzz looked across at Brenda, momentarily distracted. Five large Demons leaped at him from the rooftops on the other side of the promenade. He was swarmed in an instant.

Darryl started running towards the melee. 'Charity, come on, you can pop them.'

Charity took a few steps, but faltered. 'And then what?'

'We'll think of something.'

'Will we? If this is a trap then we're already trapped.'

Brenda grabbed Charity's hand as she ran past, dragging her daughter along. 'Princess, I know you and your brother are upset with Murzzzz, but if they get him out of your father they are literally going to end the world.'

'Mum, we've already lost!' Charity pulled Brenda's hand off her. 'We can't get off the island, and that Hell Hole can just send more Demons. There aren't enough carbs in the world for me to be able to stop this.'

Brenda stared at her. 'I never thought I'd see *you* be the first to give up.'

'And I never thought I'd see *you* not understand a hopeless situation.'

Another hand grabbed Charity, from behind. She turned her head to see Grace, clutching her shoulder. The priest's expression was odd, and she held on to Charity with a surprisingly tight grip for such a small woman. Charity thought about traps, and bait. She thought about how convenient it was for the Manager's plans that Grace apparently couldn't remember anything about her life beyond the island, and couldn't even say for sure how she got hold of the Rooks' details.

'You can get off the island,' whispered Grace. There was something about the priest's gaze that... hurt. 'You can't close the door yourself, but you can make them do it. You *need* to make them do it.'

'Oh, well if it's as simple as just making an apocalyptic eyeball creature close a massive sky portal that we've just been making worse since getting here—' began Charity.

'You can do it, Charity. I know how we can do it, but I need *you*, specifically.'

Charity shrugged Grace's hand off her shoulder, but maintained eye contact. The priest still looked painfully intense, and utterly serious. She clearly meant it. Charity was the one person who stood a chance of averting the apocalypse. Charity had always had a feeling that that might be the case, but it was a different matter hearing it said with such conviction by someone else – let alone a 'someone else' who mysteriously seemed to know exactly how the apocalypse might go about being averted.

'You're not really a priest,' said Brenda, quietly, 'are you?'

'Honestly,' replied Grace, 'at this point, your guess is as good as mine.'

On the promenade, Darryl was thrown from his feet by a Demon. Murzzzz was still struggling to fight his way out of a huge Demon pile-on.

'And I don't think now's the time to think about it,' added Grace. 'Maybe later. When I give you the pamphlet and you tell Charity what Murzzzz did when she was little.'

Charity nodded, seriously. Oof. If they *did* manage to save the world and get off the island, it was going to be a long, awkward drive home.

CHAPTER EIGHTEEN

The Spawn

'Zabko!' Janusz helped Darryl get upright.

'I'm OK,' groaned Darryl. 'Just a scrape. I've had worse. I was thrown in rotten dairy just earlier today.'

'Yes,' said Janusz. 'You still smell.'

'OK, thanks, love.'

'In fact, the smell is getting worse, not better.'

Steady on his feet again, Darryl regarded the huge Demon fight going on along the promenade. Murzzzz was just about discernible amidst the throng of flashing wet fangs and claws. Murzzzz was still managing to fight back, but it was clear that he was tiring fast. As angry as Darryl still was with the Demon possessing his father, he still needed to help.

'Where's Charity?' Darryl looked around. 'I can't really do anything without Charity. Charity??'

He spotted her in an intense looking huddle with his mum and the priest.

'Charity!'

Charity glanced across at him and waved a dismissive hand. 'Soz Darryl,' she shouted, 'do what you can without me, I've got Chosen One shit to do.'

Darryl exhaled, hard. Great. This 'Chosen One' nonsense, again.

'Help Murzzzz or whatever,' added Charity, 'this job doesn't need you.'

In the huddle, Grace muttered something to Charity that Darryl couldn't hear. Charity slumped in exaggerated disappointment and shouted to him again.

'Actually scratch that, we *do* need you after all. Toddle on over.'

Darryl gave the increasingly exhausted Murzzzz another worried glance and hurried with Janusz over to Charity and the others. 'What is it?'

'OK,' said Grace, 'you remember how good you were at that seance?'

Darryl had been barely aware of the seance at the dentist's, his memories of it were no better than those of a swiftly fading dream. From what little he did remember, the whole thing had been frankly unpleasant. Still, he did like being called good at something.

'Uh huh?'

'We need you to do that again, but on a massive scale.'

Oh, no.

'OK.'

On the promenade, there was a terrible shriek. Darryl looked across and his stomach lurched. Murzzzz was starting to lose the fight. A huge Demon had grabbed his head and was tugging it backwards while another Demon wrenched his arms in the opposite direction, almost folding Murzzzz's neck against his back. As Murzzzz howled, his image blurred. Darryl could see faint lines of Richard's face, moving separately to Murzzzz's but also screaming in pain. They were pulling Murzzzz out of Richard. The Demon yanking Murzzzz by the head spotted Darryl looking and leered. It was Hfhfh – the Demon that had captured Janusz in the window.

Darryl turned back to the others. 'Are you sure this is the best use of our time?'

'We're going to make the Manager close the door,' said Grace. 'Everyone, hold hands.'

'Don't we need stuff?' Janusz asked. 'Candles and crystals, and—'

'It'll be fine.' Grace sounded more certain than Darryl had ever heard before. An intense urgency had grabbed the little priest. 'They'll come. We're promising them something they've been waiting for all their deaths.'

There was another howl from Murzzzz. Darryl took Grace and Janusz's hands, hurriedly.

'Thank you, Grace Barry,' rumbled the Manager. 'A prayer for the end. What a touching way to finish the project.'

'The door doesn't just go to Head Office,' explained Grace in a quick whisper. 'It's a way between many different departments – the living world, the place where the Demons come from, Head Office… Waste.'

'Waste?' asked Darryl.

'Where the dead go once the other departments are done with them or don't want them. It's probably where Charity "pops" them to, automatically, but since we're so close to the door—'

'Grace reckons I can direct them to a different department if I concentrate,' interrupted Charity.

'This island still has thousands of dead people trapped on it,' added Grace. 'We can redirect them all, through the door.'

'I still don't understand,' Janusz admitted.

'You will,' Grace told him, closing her eyes. 'Concentrate.'

'We don't have any velvet,' protested Darryl, 'we haven't even chalked any shapes on the floor!'

'We don't need them.'

'Who's going to summon thousands of ghosts without even velvet or chalk shapes?'

'Grace Barry?' asked the Manager, its voice a lot less smug all of a sudden.

Grace opened her eyes again. There was something about them that made Darryl's face hurt. 'I am.'

'Grace Barry!' cried the Manager, its voice like the clanging of a million tower bells.

Darryl's eyes rolled back into his head and his body went slack. Janusz broke the chain of hands and caught his husband, holding him in an approximately upright position.

'Is the Manager here?' It was Melanie's voice.

'Yep,' replied Charity, with a forced brightness. 'In Head Office.'

'Can you transfer me?'

'I'm going to try my best, Melanie.'

She held out her hands, and Melanie was gone. Darryl still lolled against Janusz. He spoke in another voice, and then another and another, all asking the same thing. All asking to see the Manager. Charity held her hands out towards Darryl and frowned with concentration. Every time a voice left Darryl, another one or two took its place.

'Grace Barry!' bellowed the Manager, with a voice like an infinite number of trumpets.

Charity was starting to sweat. She was going to save the world. All of it. Even the *Muppets*.

*

On the promenade, the Demons peeled away from Murzzzz, leaving him panting like a wounded animal, his head, neck and shoulders smudged with the shapes and shadows of an unconscious Richard. Exhausted, Murzzzz whined, and painfully pushed his head back into Richard instead of leaving them half-ripped out of each other. He struggled to get to his feet, wondering why the other Demons had suddenly abandoned their attack. He saw them – all of them – rushing towards his family.

'Grace Barry, this is your final warning,' roared the Manager, its voice like a tsunami bearing down on a terrified beachfront town.

Hfhfh leaped. Murzzzz leaped, too, claws out to intercept it before Hfhfh reached his family. But Murzzzz was exhausted from the fight, and still not fully in sync with Richard's body after being wrenched half-out of it. He tried to extend himself in space, to concertina time, anything to reach them before Hfhfh hit, but nothing worked. He was going to miss, and Hfhfh was going to hurt his wife and kids…

No. Not *his* wife and kids. He had to stop thinking of them like that. Brenda had given up so much, too much, to accommodate the fact that Murzzzz lived inside her husband. Charity was only with the Rooks because he'd let the Xus down and orphaned the girl. And Darryl was not his son. He was just a boy he had watched from birth to now – the likely moment of his death. Murzzzz had seen so many mortals live their whole lives in what felt like a single breath to him. He'd become far too attached, and had brought this family nothing but trouble. Darryl was an ordinary mortal man with a few limited psychic abilities. And Darryl now hated Murzzzz. He was not Murzzzz's son but that didn't stop Murzzzz's thorax from painfully clenching at the knowledge that he had failed to protect the family, after they'd given him safe harbour for so long. He'd let yet another mortal family down. They were all going to die.

Hfhfh struck, lashing out with terrible claws. Suddenly, its hand was caught in mid-air, by something that wasn't quite a Demon's hand, and not quite a human's hand.

Darryl's eyes were still rolled back, but he was no longer sagging against his husband. His husband was on the ground, winded. Darryl was stretched taut, his back arched, his neck extended, his arms out and his fingernails clawed and sharp. To a human, Murzzzz was sure that Darryl would look frightening like this. To a Demon, he looked… kind of cute. His face was frozen in a snarl – like a little domestic cat displaying a warning – his wide-open mouth displayed itty-bitty adorable fangs. He was standing impossibly on pointe, resting his entire body weight on the tips of his big toes.

Murzzzz skidded to the ground as the whole family gaped at Darryl.

Oh. So Darryl was part Demon then.

Looked like he *was* Murzzzz's son, after all.

'Darryl!' Brenda and Charity screamed his name at the same time as each other, shocked.

Janusz didn't say anything at all. He couldn't. He just stared at his husband. To Janusz's knowledge, Darryl had never done *this* before, and judging from Brenda's reaction this was new to her, too. Janusz wished he could go back to a few seconds ago when he only had his husband getting used as a vocal vessel for the dead to worry about.

Darryl launched himself at Hfhfh, springing from the tips of his toes. Janusz couldn't help but worry about what this was going to do to his husband's feet – or at least, his shoes. Murzzzz landed close by. He made a move towards helping Darryl, but Darryl already had the Demon pinned to the ground, and more Demons were swiftly closing in. Murzzzz let Darryl continue with his one-on-one fight, and instead turned to keep the other Demons at bay.

Janusz was aware that Darryl wasn't a fighter. Janusz knew how to throw a punch – he'd grown up pretty much having to – but Darryl was much more of a 'run away or at least allow himself to be sheltered behind his bigger husband' type whenever things got rough with non-paranormal aggressors. Janusz never minded – in fact, he usually took a certain amount of pride in being able to act as a protector for the man he loved. But Darryl was faring much better in this fight against the Demon than Janusz would have imagined. Janusz… didn't like it. The snarling fangs, the slashing claws, the unfamiliar ways in which Darryl's body moved and contorted itself. As used as Janusz had become to Murzzzz, and as much as he had accepted that being a Rook meant facing the impossible and uncanny every day, this was a bit too much for him. He knew he'd have to learn to live with this new development – with every new development that had come up on this island… that was, if they ever made it off the island – but for now, as he watched in shocked silence, he allowed himself to *not* like this. This… thing… was not his Darryl.

'Darryl,' shouted Brenda again, more composed, this time. 'Pack it in. We need you in the circle, let Murzzzz deal with that monster.'

Darryl… or whatever beast it was controlling Darryl… continued to slash at the Demon with his claws. 'Not this one,' growled Darryl. His voice was warped. Still recognisably Darryl, but it sounded more like a recording played backwards, through a sock. 'This one's mine.'

Janusz finally found his voice again. 'Listen to your mother,' he called.

Darryl clawed at the Demon's head. 'Tried to hurt my family. My husband!'

'Wait, is that the Demon from the church?' asked Charity.

'Darryl, seriously,' Brenda shouted. 'That doesn't matter right now.'

'Don't touch my husband,' Darryl shrieked. 'Not ever!'

In spite of himself, a part deep inside of Janusz melted. Yes, maybe this *was* his Darryl still, after all.

As Darryl was railing at the Demon, Hfhfh rumbled, horribly. It went from lying prone underneath Darryl to upright in a single, fast movement, lifting itself up easily in a straight line, its feet on the ground forming a pivot. Even in part-Demon form, Darryl's expression was one of shock. Strong, shadowy claws grabbed Darryl and held him prone. Darryl attempted another swipe at Hfhfh's head, but missed – his arms too short, by over a foot, to reach the Demon. A fresh wave of worry rushed over Janusz. Hfhfh had simply been toying with Darryl. It was too big, and too strong for him to fight it.

'**So, Murzzzz,**' said Hfhfh with his voice like ancient, musty paper, '**you did spawn after all.**'

On the tarmac of the promenade, Murzzzz allowed himself to get distracted from his battle against the other Demons for just a moment. He glanced across at Hfhfh, holding Darryl at arm's length. He couldn't get close to Darryl, he was surrounded and too exhausted to make a decisive pushback. He had no choice but to wearily return to his fight and at least maintain the temporary stalemate keeping most of the Demons away from the family.

'You know that's *very* against the rules,' continued Hfhfh. 'Especially so late in the project. Yet another charge for us to throw at you when you return to the department. I really am *so* glad that Head Office helped us to gather evidence of your flagrant code violations, it's all going to come in very handy.'

'You're welcome,' boomed the Manager. 'We're always happy to collaborate with the departments, especially on red sticker issues. Speaking of, if you could detain or eliminate that little transgression of your employee's, that would really help us to terminate the project as soon as your red sticker problem is resolved.'

Eliminate. Terminate. Janusz's husband. His family. His whole world. Even his asshole dad. No. No. Nie!

Janusz did something that surprised even himself. He turned away from the fight, away from the Rooks, and he ran.

CHAPTER NINETEEN

Match of the Day

Charity knew she was the Chosen One. She was supposed to stop the end of the world – the priest with the scary eyes had said so, and she'd been doing so well at it. So why did she feel so useless now? She couldn't send the dead to Head Office without her stupid brother as a conduit, and now he was a stupid Demon, or at least half a Demon, and that Demon from the church – Hfhfh or whatever its name was – had him captive and Murzzzz was completely overwhelmed and that stupid swirly thing up in the sky with all the eyeballs was sounding smug about it again and Janusz was actually *running away* of all things and – sod it all, was she the Chosen One or not??

'**I'm sure that just this spawn's head will be proof enough for the disciplinary committee,**' announced Hfhfh. '**You can do with the rest of him as you please.**'

Charity made a dash for Hfhfh, her hands outstretched, concentrating on popping him back to whichever realm or 'department' he'd crawled from.

Hfhfh laughed a terrible, cracked laugh, that made the inside of Charity's ears feel like they needed moisturiser. It threw the first thing it had to hand at Charity – that thing, unfortunately for Charity, was Darryl. Her projectile of a brother had no chance to stop or slow himself before he was launched into her, sending both of them skidding painfully across the tarmac.

'**Charity Xu,**' called Hfhfh as she and Darryl tried to untangle themselves from each other and get back up again, '**the Deliverer herself. Why are you helping** *them*? **After everything they did to you? To your parents? Your real parents, I mean. The ones we killed.**'

Well, that at least made it pretty clear that Hfhfh was just goading her. Nobody ever went about genuinely appealing to somebody's sense of loyalty by bragging that they killed that person's birth parents. In a way, she was glad that Hfhfh wasn't trying to use reason on her, it gave her fewer distractions. Charity got back onto her feet. Her brother – or at least, the part-Demon that she was pretty sure was still her brother – rose back onto his tiptoes and roared a roar that certainly wasn't human, but that was also, Charity had to admit, quite cute.

Hfhfh raced towards them both. Darryl leaped, tackling its legs. Charity planted both feet heavily, held out her hands, concentrated and pushed. Crap, it was strong. She'd already sent a good dozen or so spirits to Head Office and was starting to feel the need for a carb-load before this latest setback. Her head was pounding and one nostril was trickling blood, but she could do it. Yes. She was The Chosen One. She was. She...

Hfhfh wrenched Darryl off itself, threw him several feet into the air, caught him by the leg and slammed him, head-first, onto the ground, like a toddler with an unloved toy. The violence of it caught Charity off-guard. Hfhfh rushed forwards again, going straight for Charity and still dragging Darryl by the leg.

'No,' Brenda screamed. 'My babies! Murzzzz!'

Murzzzz still couldn't get away from his own fight with the Demons. He still couldn't help. Charity dodged away from the Demon's claws just in time, but was knocked off her feet by Darryl, who was now helplessly being wielded as a club.

This time, Charity hit her head hard as she fell. She could hear her mother desperately asking the priest what could be done to protect 'her babies', although she could also hear a very faint, off-key, tinkly rendition of some half-remembered jaunty tune, so it was safe for her to assume that she had a concussion. She found that the main thought filling her aching, clouded mind at that moment wasn't preventing the end of the world or worrying about what had happened to her birth parents – mostly, she really wanted to stop Hfhfh from hitting her with her own brother. It was getting super annoying.

'**That's enough of your nonsense, Deliverer,**' said Hfhfh. '**However, I shan't kill you, as long as Murzzzz complies.**'

'That eyeball thing said we were all going to die anyway,' mumbled Charity, thickly. The music seemed to be getting louder. She recognised it now. It was the theme tune from *Match of the Day*. Good grief, what had that bash to the head done to her?

'**True,**' replied Hfhfh. '**But that way, there'll be a dignity to your end. You'll go out along with everyone else in this wretched project, and you'll have the time to make your peace. How about it, Murzzzz?**'

Murzzzz just kept on fighting, grunting wearily with every swipe.

'**Come on, Murzzzz. It's over.**'

In the Demon's claws, Darryl shrieked, bent himself at the torso – exhibiting a core strength he had never, to Charity's knowledge, been remotely capable of before – and scrabbled desperately at his leg, trying to pry Hfhfh off him.

'**Oh, yes,**' added Hfhfh. '**The spawn. Let's get the head off this fellow, shall we?**'

The music was definitely louder, and there was a deep roar behind it now.

Hfhfh held Darryl up and Darryl struggled like a cornered ferret. He sank his little fangs into the Demon's hands. Hfhfh reacted with disgruntled shock, and dropped him. Hfhfh loomed over him cradling its claw. Darryl crouched low; wild, snarling, scared. It wasn't clear whether the greenish-black ooze on Darryl's face was Hfhfh's blood, or his own blood while he was in this semi-Demonic form. Charity couldn't get up. There was the sound of running feet somewhere, that low roar and that bloody music.

Hfhfh stretched out. It had so many arms – too many arms. It was too big and its many arms were too long and this was how they were all going to die. She was going to see her brother get decapitated and then the world was going to end and they were going to die and could somebody *please* shut that music off?

There was a screech of wheels and something huge roared past her, all bright colours and off-key music and badly painted cartoon characters. A cursed rendering of Spongebob Squarepants swam across her vision, sharing a wonky smile and a strawberry sundae with an upsetting looking Bart Simpson. They spun out of view as the noisy thing performed an expert handbrake turn, knocking into the church Demon, sending it tumbling backwards towards the promenade's railings. It stopped, still playing that terrible tune, right in front of Darryl.

Darryl stared up at, what looked to Charity like, a warped image of the sassy baby from Family Guy. Something about the sight of a mangled sassy baby from Family Guy softened Darryl, and relaxed him, and made him slip back into his usual, fully human form. The baby split in two, horizontally across the middle, and a muscular arm reached out of it to grab Darryl and pull it inside its sassy baby dungarees…

It was a door, Charity realised through the painful confusion. It was the door to a van – an ice cream van. There were hands now at her shoulders, pulling her up. Her mother, she realised, and Grace.

'Get in,' screamed Janusz, still hauling his husband into the ice cream van, over the driver's seat. 'Serving hatch is open.'

And then, Charity was being dragged forwards at speed by her mother and Grace, towards an open plexiglass window covered in sun-bleached pictures of multicoloured lollies and soft serve ice creams, all presided over by a wonky Sonic the Hedgehog. She barely had time to wonder why Sonic the Hedgehog was so big before he swallowed her up into the stainless steel interior of the roaring, *Match of the Day* theme-playing van and it sped away.

Brenda patted her daughter's cheek, gently.

'Princess?'

There was something congealing in Charity's hair. Brenda wasn't sure whether it was her daughter's blood or rotten meat juice from the fight in the supermarket earlier that day. She really hoped it was rotten meat juice. Whichever it was, Charity had hit her head pretty hard. Grace offered her a bottle of water from the ice cream van's cabinet.

'It's not chilled, sorry,' said the priest. 'None of the fridges or freezers are on, which might explain the smell.' She took a quick glance at the main ice cream freezer. 'Yeah, that's just a pool of liquid Cornetto.'

''S'OK,' mumbled Charity, 'I smell, too. Darryl smells worse.' She frowned, forcing herself to focus. 'Darryl. Is he...'

'Urgh,' said Darryl, in the front passenger seat. He turned to face the others in the back, his face mercifully human again, but sick looking. There was a drying green-black ooze on his chin, and an exhaustion in his eyes that reminded Brenda of when he'd been a toddler. 'Today really sucks, you guys.'

'Zabko, I just want you to know right now, I love you no matter what.' Janusz didn't make eye contact with his husband as he told him this, but to be fair, he was still driving a van at speed along the promenade in an attempt to shake off several pursuing Demons. 'We all do.'

'I'm a monster,' muttered Darryl.

'No you're not,' snapped Brenda, 'you're my son. If you can manifest as a little baby part-Demon now, then you've always been able to do it, you just haven't been in a dangerous enough situation to motivate you.' Brenda sniffed. 'That's what comes from a lifetime of coddling you, I suppose.'

'Coddling?' repeated Darryl, incredulously.

Brenda shrugged. 'Or maybe the proximity to the Hell Hole set off all your latent abilities; honestly who has the time to find out right now?'

'Charity,' called Janusz, 'how's your head? Watch out, I'm going to turn.'

The women in the back braced themselves as Janusz pulled off a tight U-turn at speed, dodging a surprised-looking Demon as elegantly as one can in a noisy, colourful van.

Charity winced. 'I'll be OK. Everything's stopped swimming, at least.'

'I'll keep you away from the Demons,' Janusz told them. 'You need to finish the job. Darryl, get in the back.'

'Someone's being unusually assertive,' noted Brenda.

'Brenda, I am sick of this,' replied Janusz. 'My husband almost had his head ripped off and they're trying to kill the world. I like the world! It's not perfect but I'm not done with it yet.' Janusz's rant descended into a string of what Brenda assumed were Polish profanities.

Whatever he said, it worked. Darryl clambered, with difficulty, into the back of the speeding van.

'Are you OK to carry on?' Brenda asked Charity.

'I could do with carbs,' Charity admitted, wiping blood from her nose.

'There's ice cream cones?' offered Grace.

'The waffle ones?' asked Charity, hopefully. 'With chocolate and sprinkles?'

'A few, yes.'

Charity perked up at this news. 'Well, then. Shove a couple straight into my mouth and I can crack on with saving the world.'

The ice cream van wove at speed up and down the promenade several times, dodging every Demon that lunged at Janusz in a greasy blur. Janusz didn't see the really big one that had attacked Darryl. What had Murzzzz called it – Hfhfh? It was a nice thought that when he'd hit Hfhfh with the van, it had just given up and gone home. A nice thought, but nonsense. He located Hfhfh eventually, in the horde attacking Murzzzz. Janusz could see that Murzzzz was really struggling now. Murzzzz looked like an old analogue TV channel that hadn't been tuned right. Janusz only glimpsed him as he drove, but he could make out both Murzzzz and Richard, moving together but out of sync. Janusz turned the van again, to try to get close enough to pick up Murzzzz, but there were just so many Demons around Murzzzz now. As soon as he drove within a few dozen metres of Murzzzz, some of the Demons surrounding him whipped around and leaped onto the bonnet of the van. Janusz had to swing away suddenly to force them off. As soon as he started driving away from Murzzzz again, most of the Demons left the van alone and got back to their objective of absolutely hammering Murzzzz.

'Hurry up, you guys,' he called to the back.

Nobody in the back of the van had the chance to reply to Janusz. For starters, it was far too noisy. Not only was the slightly out of tune rendition of *Match of the Day* still cheerfully tinkling away, but the van was now host to a cacophony of voices, all asking for the Manager. Darryl was slumped like a drunk, propped up entirely by his mother, airing the complaints of fraught dead person after fraught dead person. Charity was kneeling as steadily as she could on the stainless steel floor of the haphazardly driven ice cream van, with both hands held out towards her brother and half a waffle cone shoved in her mouth. She barely had time to listen to each dead voice that surfaced before sending them on. She sent a hundred. Two hundred. Three hundred. More. How many had been stuck here over the years? She swallowed, and opened her mouth for Brenda to feed her another bit of chocolatey waffle cone. Her head was agony. Her nose streamed blood. She could do this. Those people had been waiting too long. Next to her, Grace Barry clutched Charity's shoulder with one hand, and Darryl's with the other. Something about the intensity of the priest's expression was hurting Charity's face again. If she did save the world, she felt that they should probably have a talk with Grace about the whole scary-eyes thing.

*

'Grace Barry!'

The Manager was starting to panic. This was not the plan! Head Office was filling up, with… with *waste produce*, all angry, frustrated and demanding answers from the Manager. That wasn't fair! The Manager was busy! The Manager just wanted to pull the plug on this whole mess, and now there was waste produce clogging up the Heliotrope Room and the nice Aubergine corridor with all the inspirational decals and the floating staircase with all the chrome, all the way up to Periwinkle Floor. And they were so *noisy* and *demanding* and there was still that red sticker issue. And now there was a huge problem with Grace Barry because Grace Barry was *not* supposed to be acting this way. Grace Barry herself was shaping up to be a yellow sticker problem at least. At *least*!

And the dead kept coming. At this rate, the Rooks were going to be able to empty the whole island out before the other department were able to extract Murzzzz.

If they didn't pull him out of the living realm very soon, the Manager was going to have to shut the door, with Murzzzz still on the wrong side of it. The whole Coldbay operation, gone to waste. It was all Grace Barry's fault. Sod a yellow sticker. This was getting into amber sticker territory.

Murzzzz had barely any fight left in him. Richard was hanging half out of him and he didn't even have the strength to shove them both together again. He heard the tinkling tune draw nearer again and tried desperately to scrabble towards it, only to be pulled back. There were Demons on his arms, his legs, his tail, his horns. One familiar face sneered at him, its jagged teeth like shards of ancient glass.

'**You don't give up,**' snorted Murzzzz, '**do you, Hfhfh?**'

'**I have a job to do**,' grinned Hfhfh, through glistening fangs. '*Some* **of us actually stick to our allocated duties.**'

'**What does pulling innocent mortals into windows have to do with your job allocation?**'

'**I just really like trapping produce in windows,**' explained Hfhfh, matter of factly. '**And having a bit of banter with religious types. It's always so funny to watch them realise they were wrong all along. And Grace Barry doesn't even count – she really should have known about my little hobbies. Everyone needs a pastime, and mine's a lot less of a problem than yours. You're in trouble back at the department, Murzzzz. Big trouble. The grief you've caused us.**'

'**You tormented that poor Reverend Duncan to death,**' growled Murzzzz. '**Him, and how many others before him?**'

'**And all to bring back a senior associate who decided to go rogue, invade a man and spawn, like an idiot,**' replied Hfhfh. '**This is all on you, Murzzzz. All of it.**'

'**Did you kill the Xus, as well?**'

Hfhfh split another sharp grin. '**Why? Did you want to thank whoever did it, for the gift of a free daughter?**'

So, thought Murzzzz, Hfhfh hadn't personally killed the Xus, then. Otherwise, he would be gloating about it by now. Hfhfh wrenched hard on Murzzzz's horns again, pulling Murzzzz almost entirely out of Richard.

'**It's over,**' snarled Hfhfh.

One of the Demons surrounding Murzzzz shrieked. 'The door! Head Office is closing the door!'

'It's over,' slithered another. 'Hurry!'

The lesser Demons started taking off towards the rapidly shrinking door, abandoning the promenade as quickly as a flock of seagulls would if an overloaded bin lorry were to crash into the window display at a nearby fishmonger's.

'**But we're not done,**' seethed Hfhfh. '**We still have the red sticker issue to…**' Hfhfh trailed off and cursed a curse so foul and in a language so ancient that it caused all the weeds growing within a twenty foot radius to die on the spot. Hfhfh grabbed tight onto Murzzzz's horns, wrapped its tail around Richard's waist and pulled with all its might.

Forty-odd years was a mere intake of breath, to a being as ancient as Murzzzz. He'd seen whole civilisations rise, thrive, conquer and fall, over and over – trampling all memories of the previous great cities into the mud. He had witnessed every kindness, every cruelty and every act of indifference that the living world had to offer. He'd invaded so many people, so many minds, and then… One night, a young man attempting to perform a clearance in a chapel had left his mind wide open, and Murzzzz had slithered inside so easily. He'd tried getting up to his usual old tricks, causing mayhem, driving to distraction, but he'd come across this wall of… of patience, of gentle curiosity and optimism. The young ghost-hunter had, to Murzzzz's surprise, attempted a dialogue with him. And Murzzzz, to his even greater surprise, had found himself responding. Perhaps this young ghost-hunter had caught Murzzzz in a moment of weakness, when he was feeling weary and unfulfilled, desperate for either the living realm or the Demon realm to show him something new for a change. The warmth of Richard Rook had filled a void in Murzzzz. Suddenly, Murzzzz had felt joy – Richard's joy – at the simple things in life. Sunlight on petals, the scent of summer rain, the fat, lazy purr of a woodpigeon. The tightness of the stomach and pumping of the blood on seeing a beautiful woman. The giddy thrill of discovering she was a fellow ghost-hunter. The breathless disquietude of learning that she knew about Murzzzz. Kisses. Sex. Proposal. Marriage. A pregnancy test. The anguish of loss. Another pregnancy test. The anxiety of watching her belly grow, knowing what could – again – go wrong. Holding a baby boy. Looking into his dark eyes and thinking '**Yes, this one is yours, and hers, and also mine**'. The joys of friendship with another family. The shame of letting them down. The anguish of loss, once more. Looking into another baby's dark eyes and thinking '**This one is special. This one needs to be ours too**'. All of that, in the intake of an ancient one's breath. A whole life. He didn't want to leave. Richard Rook was such a nice place to stay. Such a nice person to be. He loved Richard entirely. He didn't want to leave.

Richard was still not on the surface of consciousness, yet he wasn't as buried as he usually was when Murzzzz was in charge of the body. He knew that something was horribly wrong. He usually felt safe, when Murzzzz was in control, but now he was scared. He felt pain. Terrible pain. Like he was being torn in two. And then… the worst emptiness. A sudden loneliness, a sudden hollowness. He couldn't hear Murzzzz any more! For the first time in many decades, he couldn't hear Murzzzz. He was alone. Oh, no. He curled up into a ball, so small, so scared, so empty. Everything was gone. All the Demons, the hole in the sky. It was just him, alone on the cold, wet tarmac, and… was that an ice cream van?

'It's gone.' Brenda gazed out of the van's serving window. The hole in the sky had shrunk fast, a hastily slammed door. The sky was back – whole and dreary and already fading from Old Bra Grey to the darker Old Leggings Grey, with the early setting of the November sun, somewhere beyond the thick sheet of cloud. For the first time in a long while, Brenda welcomed the horrible dismal British sky in all its ugly glory.

The voices of the dead had suddenly fallen silent. Darryl twitched a little in her arms. She brushed his hair away from his half-closed eyes, tenderly. He was still breathing, and warm. He was just exhausted, like when he was little and the noisy spirits would wake him in the night. She would hold him, like this, until Murzzzz was able to chase them away. That was before Charity, of course.

Charity.

Oh, Brenda had a long, awkward chat ahead of her with Charity now, didn't she?

Charity was slumped forward on her elbows, gasping, exhausted and surprised, like the shock winner of a marathon.

'I did 'em all,' she huffed. 'All the ones who wanted to be transferred. Few thousand, I think.'

'Princess,' breathed Brenda, impressed.

'That wasn't even all of the dead,' Charity added. She spat out a mouthful of blood. 'I think the others might have just... wandered off.' She paused, thinking about this. 'We should give ghosts the chance to just wander off if they want. I don't want to pop people any more. Not after that stuff about "waste". They're not waste. They're just all dead and sad and scared.'

Brenda sighed. She was used to Darryl talking nonsense about letting the sadness of the dead get to them, but now Charity had started on it, too?

'I used to think that way too, princess, but—'

'But you're not me, Mum. And you're not Darryl. And it all feels different now. If that eyeball thing behind the door doesn't care, well then... something should care in its place. Even if it's just us.'

'Princess, I'm only trying to protect you.'

'I know. I get it. But we're grown-ups. I just pulled off a proper Chosen One move, and Darryl's been a sort of Russian

Doll of surprise secret powers all day. We know what we're up against. And I think you should listen to us. And yeah, for the record, I do think Darryl had it right all along about sympathising with the ghosts.'

'Uh?' grunted Darryl.

'Your sister just said that you were right all along,' called Janusz, helpfully.

'Huh,' muttered Darryl. ''S'been quite a day.'

'Truth,' agreed Charity. 'Also, Mum, you do need to tell me all about what happened to my birth parents and this whole "finder and deliverer" thing. Feels important.'

'Urgh,' replied Brenda, grumpily.

'And you said I could give you a leaflet,' added Grace.

'Urgh!' complained Brenda, turning the grump in her tone up to something that transcended mere grumpiness, and bordered upon disgusted outrage.

'And,' added Charity, 'Grace needs to explain why that eyeball was so angry with her, and also how she was able to summon all those spirits just then and why it made my face hurt.'

The priest blinked and frowned. 'Huh?'

Think about loss. Think about thousands of trapped spirits being summoned to speak to your baby girl, but not you. Think about having to remain, watching from the sidelines. Grace Barry did not call on me to be sent on to the Manager, and I certainly don't want to just "wander off". I'm here to watch Charity and to tell you her story. And her story isn't finished yet.

But for one of the Rooks at least, the story in this world is over. The Rooks are about to understand loss, too.

CHAPTER TWENTY

McEscher

'I don't see Demons any more,' said Janusz. 'Maybe just because the hole is gone?'

Brenda looked out of the window again. 'I can't see them either.'

Janusz slowed the van to a gentle stop, and opened the door. 'Hey Richard.'

Richard didn't move. He remained a tightly curled ball on the promenade.

'You OK?' Janusz asked. 'We think it's over. You and Murzzzz can rest now – you look exhausted.'

There was still no reply. Brenda got up and poked her head through the open driver's seat door.

'Up you get, dear, you'll catch your death lying there like… oh, no.'

Janusz looked at his mother in law in concern. 'What is it?'

'Murzzzz.' Brenda scrambled to squeeze out of the van. 'Richard!'

Brenda kneeled next to her husband. She gently took his hands and peeled them away from where they were covering his face. Richard was one of those men who, if he needed to have a little cry, would do it alone in the shed so as not to 'be a bother' to his nearest and dearest. Brenda had spent decades silently unsure whether this was the best way for him to go about it. But Richard was crying now. In full view of everyone. Brenda told herself that a psychiatrist might have called it a breakthrough, and then took a second to mentally punch that completely imaginary psychiatrist in the face.

'They took him,' whispered Richard. 'They won. Darling... he's gone. He was... he was half of me. They ripped me in half.'

They'd won. The breath caught in the back of Brenda's throat. She tried to imagine life without Murzzzz, and found that she simply couldn't. Something else was gnawing at her spinning mind – something more pressing and more practical than the impossibly large and intangible loss of half of her husband. The Demons had won. The red sticker issue was now resolved.

Brenda looked up from her husband – not up to the sky where the hole had been, but across to the dull grey lines where the promenade's railing gave way to the sea beyond. There was something very wrong about it. Iron railings cemented into tarmac were not, the last time she checked, supposed to ebb up and down with the waves.

'Get in the van.'

Richard grabbed her arms, tears running freely down his face. 'Brenda! He's gone!'

'I know.' Brenda turned over her shoulder to address her son-in-law. 'Janusz! Put those ridiculously toned arms to use, would you?'

'What happened to Murzzzz?' Janusz asked.

'Just help me get my husband out of here,' was Brenda's only reply.

Janusz easily prised Richard's hands off Brenda's shoulders, and manhandled him into the ice cream van.

'Drive', demanded Brenda, getting into the passenger seat. The railings beyond were looking increasingly unsteady, and the edges of the promenade were starting to wobble with them, as if in sympathy.

'Where?' asked Janusz, starting up the van again. 'We couldn't leave.'

'It's OK,' said Grace. 'The island can't stop you now. It's empty. It's lost its grip – its gravity.'

'See,' piped Charity, 'that's the sort of stuff I mean we need to talk to you about, Vicar. How do you know all that?'

Grace gazed blankly at her. 'All what?'

Charity frowned. 'Seriously?'

'We don't have time for this.' Brenda glanced nervously at the railings again. They were starting to concertina in on themselves. 'Just drive.'

Darryl gazed blearily out of the serving window. 'The street lamps look drunk.'

Janusz turned the van and started driving them away from the seafront. 'OK. OK. We'll get away from here, but I still don't know where we're supposed to go *to*.'

'Somewhere I can have a shower?' asked Charity.

'The car,' mumbled Richard.

'My church?' asked Grace. 'I need to pick up a pamphlet.'

'Oh yes, very good, a slow sightseeing tour, why not?' snapped Brenda.

'Brenda,' sighed Janusz. 'That Manager said Murzzzz was the last red sticker issue, yes? So this is why you want to get off the island right now… You're seeing things start to… I don't know, disappear, maybe?'

'It all wants to fold in on itself,' Brenda told him. 'Pretty soon you'll start seeing it too.'

'I see some of these shops are beginning to look like they were drawn by McEscher,' replied Janusz. 'But—'

'By who?' asked Grace.

'McEscher, the one who did all the crazy stairs.'

'He means "M.C. Escher",' said Darryl.

'My point is,' interrupted Janusz, 'if Murzzzz was the last red sticker issue, then it doesn't matter if we make it off the island or not. If they won, then won't it be McEsh— *Em Cee* Escher all over? Everywhere?'

Brenda thought about this, as passing roofs and telegraph poles McEschered into one another.

'Shit.'

'So,' said Darryl to his husband, 'why are you still driving?'

'Because Brenda asked me to, and I'm a good son-in-law,' replied Janusz. 'And because we did promise Grace we'd get her off this island if we could. And you and Charity stink, so maybe if we can beat the Em Cee Eschering to a hotel with a shower you can at least face the end of the world with a clean smell.'

Darryl weakly reached over to touch Janusz's hair. 'God, I love you. Even though you made it all the way to thirty-eight thinking that staircase artist was called McEscher.'

'Please don't further rub your bad smell on my hair, my love.'

Janusz turned the van again, onto a street that had decided that lying flat on the ground was for losers, and had opted instead for the sort of bumps, bends and odd angles you could expect on a waltzer.

'Sorry,' muttered Janusz, not losing any speed as he hit the bumps, causing every stomach in the van to feel as though they were being left to dangle in mid-air. He turned yet again onto a road that was even worse, but did have one extremely promising aspect to it – at the end of it, contorted and swaying dangerously, but there nonetheless, was the bridge to the mainland.

Janusz swore, suddenly.

'What is it?' asked Darryl.

'Sorry. I just looked in the rear view mirror. It's not good.'

Brenda took a look behind them, and joined in with Janusz's swearing. The beachfront of the island – promenade, pier, pizzeria, haunted pub and all – loomed above them on its side, dripping seawater, the pier jutting high into the sky, as if the entire island had been folded in the centre and was teetering at a right angle.

'Bloody Hell,' breathed Darryl. 'It's folding in on itself. We're going to get trapped in an island calzone.'

As Brenda watched, the pier in the sky wobbled and toppled downwards with an alarming speed, crashing along the, still very vertical, high street that towered over them, sending twisted metal, brick and tile raining down on to the street below. Janusz, to his merit, only yelped with alarm a little bit, then deftly wove the van around three falling chunks of masonry and a sign for a betting shop, which violently struck the road right in front of him with a force that lodged it on its side in the tarmac, like a carefully thrown dagger.

As Brenda watched, more of the promenade above began to collapse downwards.

'Might be more of an island pizza roll at this point,' she muttered.

'Could you all stop talking about food?' Charity asked. 'I'm still carb-starved, here.'

More brickwork fell in their path, but Janusz performed a tight turn around it and squeezed the van onto the bridge, which was already wobbling dangerously. Dirty seawater buffeted the van from every direction. Janusz swore again, and pressed a button, which made the *Match of the Day* tune start playing again.

'Sorry,' shouted Janusz, 'I thought it was the wipers.' He pressed another button, and the tune changed to 'Oh I Do Like To Be Beside The Seaside'.

'Stop pressing buttons,' screamed Charity. 'Just drive!'

'I can't see,' replied Janusz, in a tone of voice that very, very nearly indicated he might be losing his cool.

'It's OK,' said Darryl. 'Janusz, you tried your best, but I think it's too late. They're just going to keep rolling us up, aren't they? Until the whole living world is gone. I don't think we're going to make it to a hotel.' He sighed. 'So many people died on this bridge. Maybe it's fitting we just stop here. Another family in their car who just didn't make it off.'

'But this isn't even our car,' said Richard, softly.

'I'm not going to stop,' said Janusz, even as the bridge lurched. He grunted with effort to keep the van steady.

'Honey,' said Darryl. 'Stop. If we're going to die I want to do it holding your hand, so we're less likely to be separated. I don't want to be like those twins, or that other sad ghost by the Hell Hole.'

He saw me!

'We should all just hold hands here for the end,' continued Darryl. 'There's nobody else stuck on this bridge right now. We must have helped them all leave. It would just be us. Together.'

'We're not together,' breathed Richard. The grief in his voice ached.

'Even you, Grace Barry,' said Darryl. 'You're welcome too, if you want—'

Grace lurched forward, with a sudden ferocity. She grabbed Janusz's shoulders.

'Janusz! Get us over the bridge!'

'I am *trying*!' Janusz sped up. A falling street sign glanced off the back of the van and tumbled, spinning, into the sea.

'It's just the island,' said Grace, intensely. 'We just need to get off the island before they delete it.'

'But the red sticker—'

'There's a new red sticker issue. They can't end the world yet, we still have time'.

'A new red sticker?' Brenda asked. 'How do you know? What is it?'

Something crashed down right in front of them. It was an unassuming family car, of moderate size, a sensible, polite shade of silver, carefully checked oil and tyres, properly serviced, taxed and MOTed. It was also on its roof, smashed, mangled and covered in seawater.

'My car,' wailed Richard.

Brenda glanced behind again – the island was folded in on itself, with upside-down shops and houses bearing down on them like jagged teeth in a hungry mouth.

'Go around it,' demanded Brenda.

Janusz tried. 'I can't without seriously scraping the van and the Ford,' he said, apologetically.

'The car is dead, Janusz, do what you have to do.'

Janusz winced, and forced the van a little way past the upturned car. Metallic scrapes sounded through the van like the cries of a dying animal.

'So sorry,' Janusz told Richard, who could do nothing but watch in horror.

'Throwing our own stuff at us,' noted Charity. 'That's low.'

'At least we only left the car behind,' said Darryl, 'nothing else for them to…' It was Darryl's turn to notice something horrible behind them. 'Janusz! Go! Go! Right now!'

'But the—'

'Sod the car, sod the van! Just get us over the bridge!'

Janusz revved, and the metallic wails grew more frantic. Brenda looked up at what Darryl was seeing.

Oh, crap.

Masonry was sailing towards them at speed – a lot of it. Not just masonry – old stone bricks and pillars. Coloured glass glinted briefly amongst the flying debris. The collapsing island had uprooted the whole of St Catherine's. It was throwing an entire church at them.

With a particularly loud and anguished scrape, the van cleared the wrecked remains of their family car and sped along the bridge, its loud, out-of-tune rendition of 'Oh I Do Like To Be Beside The Seaside' still its only defence against anything that might come at them from out of the blinding torrent of seawater.

'Hurry!'

The font that Darryl had been smashed against only twenty-four hours beforehand crashed into the bridge right next to the van.

'I *am* hurrying, zabko.'

'Faster!'

An entire stained glass pastoral scene, stone frame and all, landed with an almighty cacophony in the spot of tarmac where the van had been only a half second before. As annoyed as the Bronze Age goatherds had appeared at having their countryside idyll invaded the night before, Brenda could only imagine how upset they must have looked as their centuries of quiet, glassy existence came to such a sudden, violent end on an ugly bridge in an attempt to stop a badly painted van that was loudly declaring a love of being by the seaside while simultaneously trying to escape the seaside.

'I am going as fast as I can, Brenda!'

'What's the speed limit like on this bridge?' murmured Richard.

'Seriously?' Janusz's tone of voice tipped into the realm of 'not entirely cool with this'. It could almost be described as 'miffed'. 'I love you guys but sometimes you're impossible.'

He sped up further. A large decorative marble angel landed in front of the van, somehow still balancing perfectly on its elegant white feet. Janusz screamed in shock, and pulled on the handbrake, causing the van to skid on the surface water, a full 180 degrees around the statue. Janusz threw the van into reverse and skidded away again, just in time to see the entire church spire crash down right in front of the windscreen. The steeple bell sounded out its last, mournful clang as the hastily reversing van tinkled about the lots of girls beside it would like to be beside, beside the seaside, beside the sea.

And then...

The churning of the tarmac beneath them stopped. The whipped up seawater suddenly abandoned its furious assault, and was replaced with a thin whinge of drizzle.

'We're over the bridge,' announced Janusz. He stopped the van next to a sign that told them, rather too late, to drive carefully, and that the speed limit was thirty.

'Grace was right,' said Brenda. 'Whatever they're doing to the island, it's not happening this side of the bridge.' She cleared her throat, thinking of ways she could quickly move the conversation along without having to dwell too much on the fact she'd just admitted that a priest had been right about something. 'At least, not yet.' She turned to Grace. 'What's the other "red sticker issue" then?'

'I can't remember,' said Grace.

Brenda sighed. 'How convenient.'

'No. I still can't remember *anything*,' Grace replied. 'I thought maybe if I got off the island… what if it wasn't the island that made me forget?'

Brenda watched out of the van's filthy windscreen as, on the other side of the bridge, the island continued to fold over, consuming itself. The bridge shuddered and crumbled, falling into the sea in great chunks. Whatever answers there were out there, they weren't going to get any more from Coldbay. There wasn't a Coldbay any more.

'Good Lord.' Grace got out of the van, watching the island's final throes of self-destruction, agog. The others, bar the still very sickly looking Richard, got out and joined her.

'Ever seen anything like this before?' Janusz asked Brenda.

She shook her head. Nothing on this scale. She never even imagined anything like this – not even in her grimmest idle thoughts since 2016. Bloody 2016. She still blamed that stupid year.

'Think we'll see anything like this again?'

She nodded, grimly. Outstanding red sticker issue or not, this was just the beginning. If the Managers or whatever they were calling themselves had created a door out of the layered misery of Coldbay, Brenda knew only too well that there were plenty of other places in this wretched world that were just as bleak, if not more.

'Is Dad going to be OK?' asked Charity.

'I don't know,' sighed Brenda. That was *another* thing she was going to have to deal with.

'Is…' Darryl faltered. 'Is Murzzzz going to be OK?' He glanced anxiously at Brenda. 'I mean, they just took him to his home dimension, right? So he's going to be OK? Cause don't get me wrong, I am still extremely pissed off with him, but I don't actively want the guy to get hurt or anything. He's… he's Murzzzz. He's a dick but he's family. He's going to be OK? Right?'

Brenda couldn't answer. The last of the bridge collapsed into the sea, like it was made of wet cake.

'You need to tell me what happened to my birth parents,' said Charity.

Yes, Brenda. You do.

'Maybe after you've had a shower, princess,' Brenda told her. 'It's a bit too much of a long, sad story to tell to someone who smells like a skip in a slaughterhouse.'

Delaying the inevitable won't help, Brenda.

'Delaying the inevitable won't help, Mum.'

Ha! Jinx!

'Jinx,' muttered Darryl.

'What?' asked Charity, thus breaking jinx.

'Nothing,' said Darryl.

But he knows it's not nothing. He sees me, waiting for them in the van. I'm going with them. I always have, ever since I lost everything, but something about the island fed me – made me stronger – helped me follow them closer. And now, I get to be right by their sides.

Think about life. Think about a family – spouses, parents, children… a new friend. Or, at least, they think *she's their new friend. Brenda hopes that she is. Brenda hasn't had a friend since me. I certainly hope that, if Grace is her friend after all, things go a bit better than they did the last time. This story ends with life – ugly, painful life, full of secrets and loss and regrets, full of questions left unanswered and unreliable memories. Full of growth, and change, and new chances. It ends with a family looking out at a dark sea that used to be an island, from their spot next to a road sign now warning about coastal erosion, which mere seconds ago had warned them to drive safely on a bridge that no longer exists, to an island that they will never again find any record of. The island belonged to Head Office, and so Head Office expunged it, just as they're waiting to do with the rest of the living world, as soon as they get rid of that last pesky outstanding admin issue.*

This story ends with the family knowing that it is not the end. It ends with them knowing that after some hot showers and good sleeps and very awkward talks about their feelings, there will still be the pressing issue of giant flaming eyeballs trying to use the suffering of the dead to rip holes in the sky and bring about the end of the world. There will also be the pressing issue of Murzzzz's abduction back to the Demon realm from whence he came. Brenda has a horrible feeling that the family are going to want to rescue him. She has a further horrible feeling that she's going to want to rescue him, too. She is correct about both of these things.

As the sun sets behind them unseen, a tiny sliver of light from the rising moon slips through a slight break in the clouds near the horizon, and dapples the sea water with a thin sprinkling of silver. It falls on the scraped, sodden, badly painted and barely functioning van, highlighting a glossy sheet of wet paper stuck to the van's side.

The priest – if she is, in fact, a priest – notices the paper hanging doggedly on in the moonlight, and scrapes it off the side of the van.

It's the one piece of the church to have made it off the island.

A leaflet on alcohol abuse.

You're welcome, Brenda.

The family get back into the van, and drive on – together, but all lost in their own thoughts – to find a roadside hotel with hot running water, clean sheets and no ghosts – present company excepted. They eat chain-pub food and Brenda pleasantly surprises her family by ordering a lemonade, before exasperating them all again by then ordering a bottle of house white. She agrees – definitely this time, she absolutely means it – that she'll talk to Charity properly in the morning, after they've all had a proper rest.

Maybe she does mean it this time.

She stops at the door to her hotel room, when all the others have gone in, and finally looks me in the eye.

'I'm sorry, Constance,' she says.

I nod.

'You staying around then?'

I nod.

'Well then. I'll see you tomorrow, shall I?'

Yes, Brenda. There will be a tomorrow. And you will see me.

Preview

Out of Service
(The Rooks, Book 2)

The Rooks are getting more bookings than ever. Which is no bad thing for the family business, as ghost hunting isn't the most lucrative work at the best of times.

En route for a new mission, they find there's something incredibly wrong with a motorway service station that they pass as they're wrangling with the satnav. It's empty, completely empty, except for lingering, sad ghosts. Service stations are never completely empty.

Can the Rooks close the Hell Hole that is forming in time, and keep their family together in the process? Surely, keeping the underworld from pouring into the living world shouldn't be something outsourced to a small, chaotic family business? Or is the world on its way out anyway?

COMING SOON!

Also available

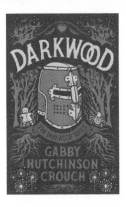

Darkwood
(Darkwood series, Book 1)

Magic is forbidden in Myrsina, along with various other abominations, such as girls doing maths.

This is bad news for Gretel Mudd, who doesn't perform magic, but does know a lot of maths. When the sinister masked Huntsmen accuse Gretel of witchcraft, she is forced to flee into the neighbouring Darkwood, where witches and monsters dwell.

There, she happens upon Buttercup, a witch who can't help turning things into gingerbread, Jack Trott, who can make plants grow at will, the White Knight with her band of dwarves and a talking spider called Trevor. These aren't the terrifying villains she's been warned about all her life. They're actually quite nice. Well… most of them.

With the Huntsmen on the warpath, Gretel must act fast to save both the Darkwood and her home village, while unravelling the rhetoric and lies that have demonised magical beings for far too long.

Take a journey into the Darkwood in this modern fairy tale that will bewitch adults and younger readers alike.

OUT NOW!

About the Author

Gabby Hutchinson Crouch (*Horrible Histories*, *Newzoids*, *The News Quiz*, *The Now Show*) has a background in satire, and with the global political climate as it is, believes that now is an important time to explore themes of authoritarianism and intolerance in comedy and fiction.

Born in Pontypool in Wales, and raised in Ilkeston, Derbyshire, Gabby moved to Canterbury at 18 to study at the University of Kent and ended up staying and having a family there.

She is the author also of the acclaimed Darkwood trilogy, a modern fairy tale series for grown-up and younger readers alike.

About The Rooks

The Rooks is a series of supernatural horror comedy adventures, about the Rook family, who run a little family business. Ghost hunting. And gracious, business has certainly picked up recently. Something's wrong. It's been getting noticeably worse since, ooh, 2016? Bad spirits are circulating...

The full series –

Wish You Weren't Here

Out of Service

Back to Business

Also by Gabby Hutchinson Crouch – the Darkwood series

Darkwood
Such Big Teeth
Glass Coffin

Acknowledgements

Thanks to Dom Lord and Abbie Headon for all their support and help. Thanks to everyone at Duckworth. Thanks to everyone who bought, read and recommended the Darkwood series, giving me the impression that I can, in fact, write books. Grace was originally going to be called Lucy until I decided that was too weird, but thanks to Lucy in particular for her support and to Sarah for the quote.

Huge thanks to Nathan, Violet and Alex, especially since this was another Partial Lockdown Book. Being locked in a house with three other people is never easy, especially when one of them is scowling at a laptop, trying to think of the right synonym.

Again, no thanks at all to my cat, Spooky, whose input consisted of occasionally screaming at me.

This one is for the families – blood relatives or not, living or dead. The full car I sometimes drive at night with children sleeping in the back still has all of its occupants. The Austin Montego I would sleep in the back of is long gone, from where I stand here in 2021, and has lost one occupant. This is to the car with Tim, Rory, Gabby and Nadine in it as much as it is to the car with Nathan, Gabby, Violet and Alex.

Note from the Publisher

To receive updates on new releases in The Rooks series – plus special offers and news of other humorous fiction series to make you smile – sign up now to the Farrago mailing list at farragobooks.com/sign-up.